W9-AEC-676

THE DAY OF THE SERPENT

Also by Cassandra Clark

The Brother Chandler mysteries

THE HOUR OF THE FOX *

The Abbess of Meaux mysteries

HANGMAN BLIND
THE RED VELVET TURNSHOE
THE LAW OF ANGELS
A PARLIAMENT OF SPIES
THE DRAGON OF HANDALE
THE BUTCHER OF AVIGNON
THE SCANDAL OF THE SKULLS
THE ALCHEMIST OF NETLEY ABBEY
MURDER AT MEAUX
MURDER AT WHITBY ABBEY *
MURDER AT BEAULIEU ABBEY *

* *available from Severn House*

THE DAY OF THE SERPENT

Cassandra Clark

SEVERN
HOUSE

First world edition published in Great Britain and the USA in 2021
by Severn House, an imprint of Canongate Books Ltd,
14 High Street, Edinburgh EH1 1TE.

Trade paperback edition first published in Great Britain and the USA in 2022
by Severn House, an imprint of Canongate Books Ltd.

severnhouse.com

British Library Cataloguing-in-Publication Data
A CIP catalogue record for this title is available from the British Library.

ISBN-13: 978-0-7278-9090-0 (cased)
ISBN-13: 978-1-78029-822-1 (trade paper)
ISBN-13: 978-1-4483-0560-5 (e-book)

All Severn House titles are printed on acid-free paper.

Typeset by Palimpsest Book Production Ltd.,
Falkirk, Stirlingshire, Scotland.
Printed and bound in Great Britain by
TJ Books, Padstow, Cornwall.

PROLOGUE

Woodsmoke slanted over the thatched roofs of a dozen cottages in a clearing on the edge of manorial lands a little south of Knaresborough.

Summer crops were almost harvested and it was going to be a good year despite the recent storms. Agnes gave a pot on the fire one last stir then went to the door of the one-room cottage and glanced out. 'John,' she called, 'are you coming in to eat or not?'

A well-set, fair-haired young fellow looked up from his task with a grin. 'Stop your nagging, woman. I'm fixing Nate's bow for him.'

'Do that after, you clod, or it'll not be worth eating!'

She went back inside and in a minute her man, grinning from ear to ear, came striding indoors. 'Where is it then, you nag?' He took her in his arms and nuzzled her neck and she turned to snap her teeth at him playfully until the action turned into a long embrace on the brink of desire.

She pushed him away. 'Not now, you lunk.' She darted a last kiss on his lips and he shut his eyes with pleasure before saying, 'I've fixed his bow. Where is the little devil?'

A voice piped from outside. 'I'm here, Pa, if it's me you mean!' A bright-eyed smaller replica of his father appeared in the doorway. He held the mended bow in his hand. 'This is grand. I'll be beating you yet, with this'n.'

'That'll be the day.' His father ruffled his son's hair then turned back to his wife. 'So come on then, missus, where's this grub you keep promising?'

'Are you missing your sisters, Nate?' his mother asked as she doled out three generous helpings of pottage into their bowls.

'Not me! Those lasses'll be driving Grandma mad with their racket.'

'Are you just saying that? You could have gone, you know.'

'I'd rather stay here with you and Dad. Towns are not for me.'

The three of them ate in silence for a while until Agnes put down her bowl and went to the door.

She stood looking out with a puzzled frown.

'What's up, lass?' John called.

'There's a stench out here and I can't place it. It's worse now than it was before.' She sniffed the air and glanced across the clearing to the other cottages and beyond them to the road that ran through the woods.

Bringing his bowl with him John came to stand beside her, ready to tease her, but after sniffing the air a look of alarm crossed his face.

She was quick to notice. 'What is it, John?'

'Something's not right. I've smelt this before. It was when the lord sent me up to Scotland with the army.' He turned to her. 'Get back inside.'

He glanced towards the other cottages. Everything looked peaceful. On an impulse he put his bowl down and ran over to one of the neighbours shouting, 'Alarm! Tom! Everybody! Army on the march!'

It was after that everything changed for ever.

ONE

January 1400.

Chandler pushed his hood back and looked up at the darkened house. He stood in the shadows for some time. Matilda must be asleep he decided when she did not appear. His meeting with his old spy-master, Knollys, had taken longer than planned and because of the curfew he had walked the long way round to the poet's house in order to avoid the Watch and their pettifogging questions.

Matilda was a young maid at the house – his contact although she did not suspect it – for a man under surveillance for his Lollard beliefs. If he battered on the door now the whole street would be roused from sleep and her reputation would be in tatters. He stood for longer than necessary until he was convinced she would not appear at her bedroom window before reluctantly turning for his lodgings in Aldgate. The scent of her skin and the touch of her long red-gold hair trailing over his body as they made love earlier taunted him with renewed longing so that he was nearly up to the gatehouse where his chambers lay before he saw he had visitors.

A cluster of armed horsemen were waiting in the moonlight. He noticed they were armed. The man on the destrier in their midst wore gold flashes on his sleeves and the basinet on his head glittered in the flames from the burning torch one of his men carried. Chandler's heart sank. Sir Thomas Swynford. What did he want, armed and at midnight?

When he was close enough, Chandler hailed him and dropped to one knee. 'My lord Swynford?' He looked up at the fellow heaped in an ungainly fashion in the saddle and wondered why Knollys had said nothing.

'I hear you gave my men short shrift earlier today?' Swynford growled.

'Were they your men, my lord?' Innocent. Still on his knees.

Swynford turned his head and bellowed, 'Get this man a horse!'

He turned back to Chandler. 'You're coming with us, brother. That's what they were trying to tell you. Get your gear, we're leaving now.'

'My lord?' Chandler slowly rose to his feet.

'You heard.'

'Are we going abroad?'

Swynford looked mystified for a moment. 'You don't need to know where we're going.'

He jerked his head towards Chandler's lodgings to suggest haste in gathering his things but Chandler shrugged. 'We friars travel light, my lord. I always have with me whatever I need. There is only one thing I have to do. I must leave a message for my sacristan. Shall we be away long?'

Swynford ignored his question. His men were equally close-mouthed. Chandler was aware of the excellence of their arms and armour and did not press the point. Resistance was not an option. He went swiftly into his chantry across the street and left a message for his sacristan to give to his housekeeper and another, even more enigmatic one, for Matilda, putting it where she might see it, and by the time he was back outside a horse had been brought and the men were moving off.

Chandler had been sold into the House of Lancaster as an orphan. It had never troubled him until last summer when Henry Bolingbroke, King Richard's cousin, had invaded England and now ruled in his stead. Thomas Swynford, stepbrother to the usurper king, was Chandler's liege lord.

As they rode out of the City gates he briefly regretted that he had complied with Swynford's unmannerly request – but how could he have objected without paying a higher price than the matter seemed to warrant? Henry of Lancaster was his paymaster so it followed that he owed him service – and with no idea where they were going he rode headlong into the night with the rest of them.

2

They made only one stop early in their journey. It was at Windsor Castle.

The new king, after celebrating his first Christmas as King

Henry IV, was still in residence for the Twelve Days with his four young sons beside him. It was all revelry and triumph in the Great Hall, his men drinking themselves to the floor in celebration of their own valour in deposing King Richard and of their lord's audacious theft of the crown. An endless stream of food was brought in, suitable for such victors. Chandler ate morosely in a corner, avoiding meat and anything that looked less than monastic, and tried to make sense of things.

It was while he was trying to work out where they were going and why the secrecy, that Henry swayed to his feet at the top table. He held a gold goblet in one hand and was no doubt aware of his archbishop's grip on his brocaded sleeve on the other. In a voice loud enough to cut through the rabble of music and the roar of a hundred fighting men in song, he declaimed, 'Hear this! Thomas, my lord Archbishop Arundel, is right as ever!' The sound of revelry faded. 'He is right to warn me of enemies . . . so take heed and warn anyone who wavers: if there is a rising in the country against me, I vow that my cousin, the one-time King Richard II, shall be the first to suffer!'

Cheers reached the rafters. A toast to the new regime followed. And followed again until long after the men had forgotten what they were cheering about.

3

Next day, after leaving Windsor, they reached the Great North Road and continued without a break for many long hours except to change horses until the landscape became harsher and there was snow on the uplands. It was then he guessed they might be nearing journey's end. He still had no idea where they were heading but he was beginning to guess they might find someone special when they reached their destination.

At the time when King Richard was removed from the throne there was a brief show trial in Westminster Hall when he had not even been allowed to put in an appearance in case his quick wit and persuasive tongue caused trouble. Imprisoned in the Tower for a short time, eventually his whereabouts became a mystery. Where is the king, people who cared about such things asked themselves. Nobody knew.

To Chandler's way of thinking Swynford's secrecy now could mean only one thing. They were on king's business.

Once the holy anointed king of England, Richard had been relegated to the status of a mere knight, Sir Richard of Bordeaux. Chandler did not know what the new self-crowned king intended to do with his royal guest. Alive, he would always be a danger to the usurper. No matter how strongly Richard claimed that he was willing to give up his rights, his supporters would never accept the legality of Henry's seizure of the crown.

They rode on through the night. It gave him plenty of time to think.

The present situation started for him after he led his small congregation in prayers for lady mass one morning before the traders on Cheapside had put their wares on display. Afterwards, returning to his lodgings within the walls at Aldgate, he found himself unexpectedly involved in a spat about swords with some men-at-arms.

Their captain, a burly, bearded fellow, well armed in casque and mail, had spurred his horse right up to Chandler, who was on foot as usual and wearing only his pale friar's robes with a woollen cloak slung over them, and greeted him in a menacing tone, saying, 'We want to talk to you, *brother*.'

Chandler, disliking the man's manner, and foolishly forgetful that he was outnumbered by men in full armour, had ignored him and walked on. A couple of men dismounted and stepped in front him, drawing their swords and smiling. The upshot was that Chandler, poorly armed under his robes, had even so won a couple of weapons for which he felt he had no use, and the men had been driven off. Forgetting all about this incident he had gone about his business of tending the souls of his congregation throughout the rest of the day.

Later, long after curfew, the chickens, as it were, had come home to roost. Now here he was in some godforsaken northern county for no apparent reason other than the whim of Sir Thomas Swynford. He knew there was more to it and he had plenty of time to think about it, half asleep on the war horse that had been requisitioned for him, but there was nothing to go on except speculation.

The inescapable fact was that along with the sneers about the defeated king the shroud of secrecy over his actual whereabouts was impenetrable. His first spell of imprisonment in the Tower of London had entailed the cessation of Chandler's own work there, interrogating suspected enemies of the realm for the Lancastrians, and everyone not directly involved in Henry's power grab had been cleared out. The Tower swarmed with Lancaster military that autumn and Richard's apparent and hardly credible cheerfulness at having the crown taken from him had been announced from there.

Then suddenly nobody knew anything. Where was the king? Was he still alive? Chandler prayed so. He remembered his courage at Smithfield when he was only fourteen and no more than a gleaming and golden child, beloved of everyone except the Lancastrian war faction.

Chandler himself was fourteen then, just ending his training in arms under Gaunt's war captains and on the verge of making the choice of a more spiritual life in the service of his saint. He had watched agape as the armed rebels lined up on the killing ground of Smithfield to outface the boy-king while Wat Tyler laid forth their just demands for an end to bonded labour.

He had even seen how a massacre had been averted by the king's reckless courage in leading the rebels away from Smithfield when Tyler was stabbed in cold blood by one of Mayor Waltham's knights. 'Follow me! I am your captain and your king!' Richard had shouted. And they had followed him. He could have led them to the ends of the earth and down into hell itself in those days.

Chandler, half asleep as they covered the endless miles now, had time to recall the rumours that Richard was imprisoned in Leeds Castle. Not far from London, it was Kentish territory.

Chandler had been sceptical when he first heard this. Henry's desire to rid himself of his inconvenient royal cousin had become more urgent recently but the last place to keep a king you wanted rid of was Leeds with all those Kentish men around with their long memories of the Great Revolt.

He remembered how for many years afterwards it was considered a marvel that Richard had offered the bonded men freedom from slavery. The great landowners, feudal Norman overlords like the Lancasters and Arundels, were in uproar. They were appalled at the prospect of losing their free labour force. When Richard even had pledges written out to guarantee their freedom and handed them to every bondsman who asked, they could do only one thing. They forced him to rescind these manumissions on the order of the Royal Council.

Headed by John of Gaunt, evil old Lancaster himself, he had made the young king look a fool, a puppet, a breaker of promises, nothing but a light child with no power of his own.

That and his courage at Smithfield in averting a massacre was a memory that lived on in the minds of those, like Chandler, who had witnessed it.

So not Kent then, judged Chandler. Somewhere safer than Kent had been found. Too many friends willing to risk their lives for him in Kent.

Then Swynford and his men turned up at his door.

And now they were riding north.

4

Dawn light was filtering over the hillside by the time they came within sight of a vast many-towered castle with double walls and a long incline leading up to the drawbridge. Chandler understood it as journey's end. It was Pontefract Castle.

Gaunt's massive stronghold was in the Lancastrian heartland. It was the key to the North and to possession of the throne of England.

Henry, his son and heir, had been able to raise an invading army here from the vast numbers of northerners owing him military service at knight's fee.

He could demand their allegiance as his right, his inheritance. They were his vassals. His war fodder. He could demand anything. He could demand their lives.

So it was, the moment Chandler saw the immense castle looming on its crag and made impregnable by Gaunt's rebuilding in the previous two decades, he understood that Pontefract had been their destination all along. And he knew who they would find.

5

The raftered Great Hall was set with dozens of long trestles. It was swarming with men-at-arms. Logs blazed in the wall hearth. Sweating servants struggled in with endless platters of food, forced to weave a path between Swynford's knights, vassals of no particular fame, and their esquires, their varlets, pages, messengers and the general riffraff of a busy and important garrison. It equalled Windsor in its certainty of the right to a new ascendancy. The turmoil was augmented by packs of hunting dogs roaming in the mesh for scraps.

Chandler, travel-stained, stiff from too much riding, climbed onto the end of a bench at one of the trestles adjacent to the dais and reached for some bread while he tried to work out what use Swynford had in mind for him.

A trestle-table full of bowmen and assorted men-at-arms sat alongside, eating like men new to food, ravenously, suspiciously, testing the array of delicacies, the pies and pasties and other concoctions laid before them and passing on their judgements to their comrades in strong local accents. They ignored Chandler. *A friar. What could they have to say to him that couldn't be turned against them?*

He was sufficiently taunted by his present speculations about Swynford's plans to keep it that way.

On the dais, Swynford plied his captains with wine and was as spry as ever. He was tough, give him that, thought Chandler. He looked no worse after their hard ride and bleak dawn arrival than any man sitting at ease in his solar. Squat and ungainly, it was impossible to believe his mother was *la belle Katherine*, Gaunt's long-time mistress, mother-in-law of the king now the proprieties of marriage had been observed.

Still suspicious about the task planned for him he became aware that a little varlet was tugging at his sleeve. The lad had a message. Sir Thomas asked that Brother Chandler would have the courtesy to join him in the yard at once.

Chandler lifted his head in time to see Swynford sweeping out with his entourage.

He grunted when Chandler appeared moments later and jerked his head before marching towards the Great Tower. It was one of ten or so, built at different times, the two latest, the King and Queen Towers, being only recently finished under the now-dead John of Gaunt's instructions. To an accompaniment of steel boots striking stone and the rattle of arms they ascended the steps to the top.

Two alert guards saluted Swynford and his men and eyed the friar with indifference. After exchanging a few words and rattling some keys in the locks they conducted Swynford into a small, dark prison cell in the roof of the tower with his bodyguards crowding in after him.

From the shadows a figure rose from the stone flags, barefoot and wearing nothing but a thin linen garment to his knees. The prisoner's hair was shoulder-length, unbrushed, but of a dark, springing gold that was familiar from the days of his regality.

When he rose to his full height he towered over Swynford. Even in these dire circumstances the gaunt beauty of his face was unmistakable to anyone who had chanced to see him even once.

Swynford blustered forward, aware no doubt of the iniquity of what he was being ordered to do by his stepbrother, keeping a king imprisoned, and despite the red and gold attire, was conscious that the safety of the realm – of the new king – and of himself – was his alone.

A few sharp questions were delivered – restiveness from the guards – blades casually displayed – cold glances to match cold steel – while Chandler tried to distance himself from the embodiment of threat they gave off. It was as rancid as the smell of sweat.

The visitors inspected the prison, noting one narrow aperture hacked between the stone slabs of the prison wall when it was built. It allowed a glimpse down into the space between the inner and outer defences, into what the bowmen called 'the killing field', a wide area where no one could hide from the bolts of their crossbows. The weak light that trickled through this slit was the only illumination, apart from the prisoner himself.

In any crowd, in whatever state, thought Chandler, Richard would still be recognized as royal. It was true what they said. His enemies could take his crown, his lands, his life, but he would remain England's true king.

After making their presence felt, Swynford's men were abruptly trooped back down the spiral steps in a thunder of boots to emerge into the bailey's winter light.

Swynford waited until Chandler, blinking, stooped beneath the lintel and straightened. 'Well, brother?'

'My lord?' Chandler's lips scarcely moved. There was no way out. His mind ran and raced and was continually blocked. He lifted his head. What did Swynford want of him?

'Remember you mentioned bladderwrack to me at Windsor when I asked you what might put a man off his food?'

'I do, my lord.'

The gormandizing at Windsor came back in a memory of swinish greed.

'And you no doubt remember the courtier standing by who had a better solution?'

The courtier in question, adorned in Lancaster's colours, smilingly told them he would demonstrate the remedy he knew.

'It's this.' Pursing his lips he aimed a gob of spit into a nearby dish resting on a gold platter.

Even Swynford had looked sick.

Now he said, 'I think we can dispense with your bladderwrack, brother, don't you? Sometimes the simplest solutions are the best.'

'And you want of me—?' Chandler asked.

'To keep an eye on him. Serve his vittels. See if it loosens his tongue. Find out if he has any supporters left and who they are.'

'Am I to stay at the tower or venture into the kitchens?'

Swynford scowled at his abrupt tone and lack of deference. 'Stay. Somebody will bring it to the door.'

Such was his first morning within the bastion of Lancastrian power when his purpose here became clear.

6

There was a popular prophecy going the rounds called the Prophecy of the Six Kings. When he went into the Great Hall later the men at his trestle were discussing it with every appearance of believing in it. They were the same trio of hard-drinking longbow-men as before and he listened as they started to argue about the prophecy – the lamb would be defeated by the Mold-warp was what concerned them most. The lamb was generally accepted as representing King Richard II and the Mold-warp a usurper who would bring the realm to ruin. They gave surreptitious glances at Chandler to assess what he, a Lancastrian interrogator and a friar, thought of it.

Will, a barrel-chested, strong-boned Welshman, was their natural leader, followed by a fellow called Fulke who wore a small beard of a reddish, Saxon hue and had the sharp eyes of his craft. Next to him was a well-set, fair-haired fellow younger than the other two and given to long silences, known as Underwood.

Looking askance at his grey robes one of them eventually said, 'So you're here to attend Dickon in his prison cell, are you?' When Chandler nodded he said, 'Them Lancastrians must trust you.'

'I hope they do,' replied Chandler holding the man's glance until he turned away. He watched him adjust the leather wrist guard he wore.

It turned out that they were mercenaries, not the usual garrison men, and had joined the army for pay per diem. They were given to ribald northern banter, causing them to thump the table with big fists, their roars of laughter shaking to the rafters.

7

The climb to the prison chamber rendered the pottage, the slop, the swill, he was forced to offer, offensive even to a starving man, and he presented it with a deep apology the first time.

The prisoner, rising from his corner, waved his apology aside. 'Better than nothing.'

'I am not sure it is, majesty.'

The guard who had decided to lean on the wall just inside the chamber to listen in, watched in a derisory manner but without comment.

Lowering his voice Chandler said, 'I suggest you eat round this,' he pointed with one finger where a translucent glob caught the light.

The king peered at it. 'I trust you.' He laughed without humour. 'That is my fate, my downfall. I always trust. I am the easiest man to betray. A wicked child could fool me if he smiled on me.'

'I do not seek to fool you, lord, merely to help in any way I may.'

They were eye to eye. Despite the gloom the king gave a small exclamation of surprise. 'Don't I know you, brother?' He narrowed his eyes and leaned forward. 'I never forget a face . . . Forgive me, your name escapes me for the moment—'

'We met at Eltham some time ago. I was young and reckless enough to try to warn you of a plot—'

'Yes, it comes back for some reason. Robert was alive in those days—'

'The earl of Oxford paid me well and because of him the plot came to nothing and—'

'And, I'm told, you were even then in the pay of Lancaster?'

'As then, so now.'

'And you suggest I trust you?'

'As you did before.'

'I would not want a man like you on my side.'

'Those most trusted are often the least trustworthy.'

He grimaced. 'So I have learned to my cost.' He paced a couple of yards across his prison and back. 'So you're suggesting we should trust the untrustworthy?'

'It depends on their love of truth for their soul's sake. If it's truth you want.'

He gave a bark of laughter. 'As the poet Langland would suggest with his Lady Meed. Maybe we should listen more often to the poets?' His smile left his face. 'Master Chaucer happens to be a droll fellow but I hope he has enough sense of danger to keep his Lollard beliefs to himself now Arundel is in power?'

Chandler could say nothing to this. Mention of Chaucer allowed into his thoughts the memory of Matilda, her spread hair, her trusting surrender . . .

Richard took the wooden bowl from Chandler and went to sit on the embrasure, not eating, staring down into the mess, glancing up, then back at what he held. After a moment he carefully placed the bowl on the stone ledge beside him.

'So tell me, what led you to this?' He spread his arms to include the prison chamber, the castle within its double-crenellated walls, the town, the county, the realm and all that lay beyond.

'Destiny, my lord. We were born under the same ill-fated star. Hence we are both prisoners here.' Chandler indicated the chamber with a tilt of one hand. 'I am prisoner here,' he tapped the side of his head, 'and am therefore doubly a prisoner, as are you because of your anointing and your crown.'

'How did destiny arrange it so for you?'

'I was given to a trusted friar when my father made an orphan of me and was then again orphaned when the kind old friar himself died. His last gift was to ensure that I was taken into the Lancaster household, thinking Gaunt would provide better than the streets of London. I found, instead, a cage.'

'And this?' He indicated Chandler's robes, the red saint's emblem sewn onto it.

'A choice I made shortly after Smithfield. Your courage then disarmed me—'

'As a child, then?'

'As were we both? Choices perhaps we might stand by despite the force of destiny? It was clear, I could either become an esquire to one of Lancaster's knights and pursue a life of violence or follow the example of an uncle who died in a state of grace as a follower of a saint in Castile—'

'The emblem is not one I recognize.'

'Saint Serapion.'

'The martyr? I understand. He gave himself to the Saracen as ransom for a kidnapped Christian. His followers are enjoined to give their own lives to save others.'

'Quite so.'

8

Chandler followed Swynford's orders for several more days with little happening to suggest that his inevitable suspicion was justified.

His hood, as befitted a friar of some foreign and possibly dangerous cult, was worn half over his eyes, shading them. That way he avoided questions and made his way about the castle as if invisible. No one seemed to know anything. A febrile atmosphere filled the place. Something was brewing. But what? He could not sleep.

Every day when the sun was at its milky zenith he trudged up the steps with the contaminated food for the prisoner.

This duty fitted in with attendance at the Holy Hours in St Clement's, the chapel built against the wall of the gatehouse. It was also the first port of call for visitors and was the first to receive news from outside. Otherwise he was left to his own devices.

9

The rains lasted for three days and nights, striking the pounded earth with dagger-points, turning the bailey to mud. For most of the day at this dark time of year the torches were kept alight in their iron brackets and smoked like the black fumes of hell against the lime-washed walls of the keep.

Epiphany had been and gone but not long afterwards three knights attired in the red and gold of the king showed up. They were well armed. Their faces gleamed with purpose.

From the shelter of St Clement's, Chandler witnessed them sweep inside the bailey before the grinding slam of the portcullis crashed down after them. Bustle and commotion followed. Smoke coiled everywhere as a swarm of servants appeared with burning brands to take charge of their steaming horses.

Swathed in the wet folds of riding cloaks, faces concealed by strips of cloth, the men dismounted and stood, dazed and yawning, gazing round at the castle and the northern garrison with the contempt typical of royal envoys until Swynford, shrugging a cloak round his shoulders, put in an appearance. Clearly he had not been expecting them.

With all the swagger of a landless man newly appointed as Constable of the Castle by his half-brother-king, usurper or not, Swynford waded through the mire towards the newcomers. Chandler, hood pulled half over his face, watched from the lee of the wall.

He saw Swynford thump them on their backs. *All good fellows. Piers, old man, well met.* He watched them cross the yard and ascend a couple of steps into the chapel porch. Swynford had flung an arm round the shoulders of the one Chandler knew to be Piers Exton, son of a London merchant, while the other two trailed after them, throwing their weapons into the porch before they entered the chapel. Chandler detached himself from the shadows and strolled to the door.

Glimpsed through the portico the place was ablaze with candles as the sacristan bustled round. In moments the altar was gleaming with a look of perfect sanctity.

Near on vespers, Chandler thought, a good enough excuse.

When he approached the door two guards clashed their pikes in front of him. 'Not tonight, brother,' said one out of the side of his mouth.

'I see the lord constable has guests?'

'He has.'

Mildly, 'Anyone of interest?'

'Not our business.' The man's eyes flickered from side to side. Fingers drummed on his sword hilt. The other fellow stood as if carved in stone.

Chandler turned away without comment.

Three horsemen arriving with the secrecy and arrogance of Lancastrian envoys could only make things look black for Richard. He watched with a sense of foreboding as the newcomers swiftly left the chapel, buckled on their swords and followed Swynford to the Great Hall. He decided to follow to see if his fears would be confirmed.

Finding space on a bench near the dais he watched as the newcomers started to wolf down their meat as soon as it was set before them. Grease dribbled down their beards. Fingers were licked. Wine was poured and poured again. They were letting Swynford do the talking. To Chandler, the three, begrimed by travel, had the faces of assassins.

He kept his head down. Unnoticed. Muttering through a prayer. His skin inside his warm, woollen friar's robes chilled as he considered the men and their purpose. Something like a serpent began to slither down his back.

10

Throughout the next few days after their arrival nobody hinted at any possible reason for the Londoners' presence. They must, judged Chandler, have been ordered north not long after they themselves had set out. Riding hard to reach Pontefract with a message from king Henry. Pontefract was sealed from the outside. The town, where rumour might have spun its web, lay at the foot of the crag, its sleep disturbed only by the daily fears of a country on the verge of civil war.

As he watched and waited he began to notice small changes. Guards were doubled on the outer walls. A different set of men-at-arms guarded the stairwells. He saw the inner bailey cleared of loiterers; varlets and esquires were ordered back indoors. Other changes he couldn't help but notice: produce for the kitchens brought in through the narrow back-postern by porters allowed to enter only one by one; kitcheners hustled indoors to attend their duties instead of gossiping outside between chores; stable lads and dog boys confined to their yards; the falconers ordered to stay in the mews. He slowly discovered that the newly arrived crossbow-men on the wall-walk and the armed guards posted in every doorway in the inner bailey had orders to kill.

Chandler was aghast at the prospect of what was about to happen. The horror of the End Days, as the Prophecy called them, seemed about to unfold.

* * *

Standing outside the chapel of St Clement's he was considering how impregnable the Great Tower was when a rider came hurtling into the yard shouting for the Constable as stable lads converged on his horse.

Chandler's glance travelled to where, entering the tower through the single door, Swynford turned back. The messenger fell to his knees and offered a sealed document from his bag bearing the arms of the King of England. Swynford read it. Stuffed it inside his jacket, dismissed the messenger, turned back towards the tower and shouldered his way inside, his personal bodyguards close on his heels as usual.

A few moments later he came down again and paced across the yard towards the Great Hall where his guests were presumably enjoying the hospitality of the castle kitchens.

Despite the haste of this messenger from Westminster the three envoys gave no sign of their purpose. They congregated on the dais, lolling at ease as if waiting for something else, while, every day, feasting continued. Swynford kept his men happy with jugglers, acrobats and a minstrel, a white-faced buffoon with coarse jokes, double-entendres and obscene prancing. Drink was supplied in abundance, ale barrels were emptied and more rolled in.

To Chandler it remained an unending confusion of capons, geese, pork, bacon, hares, turbot, saffron, almond milk, numbles of deer, and everything braised, boiled, seethed, and made into every form the cooks could devise with the additions of all the spices and art at their command, a constant stream to fill the bellies of the garrison and keep them obedient.

Used to monastic fare by choice he picked among the bones and the flesh that fell from them and searched for something that had not involved killing some living creature to keep men in strength. His neighbours, the bowmen, continued to tuck in, their empty dishes stacked on the trestle, the scrapings enough to feed a peasant family for a week.

Meanwhile the royal envoys gorged on everything with relish and drank and ate and licked their fingers and joked and one of them sang well enough to put the minstrel to shame but to Chandler they still had the faces of assassins.

Fulke held up the wine jug with a questioning glance and Chandler pushed his flagon forward and watched him refill it and pass the pitcher down the trestle to the other end, emptying as it went. If the king could have been invited into the hall, he was thinking, he would have had enough to fill another book of recipes like the one he commissioned from his master cooks. Instead he had to make do with what Chandler brought him.

Haunted by the king's privations as much as by the example of his saint, Serapion, in his Castilian prison, he felt he owed it to them both to eat frugally as a sign of respect. He was driven by a sort of resigned necessity as he thought of what was offered in the present mean-spirited manner, the contaminated fare he was obliged to take up. The waiting. The unnatural sense that something evil was looming nearer.

What were they waiting for? The garrison was too besotted on meat and ale to speculate. No rumours suggested any reason but that which to Chandler was obvious and inevitable.

11

By adopting an air of spiritual vagueness he found a way of beguiling the tower guards into allowing a morsel of cheese and some wastel to be smuggled in, along with the regular bowl of pottage made from kitchen scraps and spittle.

'If I had the power I would make you a duke,' the king muttered, stuffing the cheese into his mouth. 'Forgive my ill-mannered guzzling. I hope for your sake they did not notice?'

The guard, bored, remained outside the door these days. After all, there was nowhere either of them could go and if they tried to escape they would be cut down as soon as they reached the next landing.

'I will try wine in my water bottle next time.' Chandler indicated the leather flask at his waist.

'Is it drinkable, Swynford's wine? I doubt it!' He gave a half-hearted chuckle. 'The fellow's a swine used to swinish things. Swine-ford. Swine by name, all that. But anything would be welcome. Take care and don't arouse suspicion. A knife might do some good? What do you think?'

'I could get one. But there's a well-armed guard at the door as you've seen.' He glanced across the chamber and lowered his voice but the losel was still lounging outside. 'At every landing there's another guard and at the bottom where the door leads into the bailey there are usually two or sometimes three.'

'A knife will do me no good then.'

'The bailey itself is an inner yard surrounded by walls where guards patrol in twos along the battlements. Beyond that is the outer yard, defended by towers and a gatehouse. Then comes the barbican, a corridor between high walls, itself defended by further towers at the entrance. Next to be traversed is a drawbridge over the moat. The whole place is overlooked by a crenellated outer wall patrolled, again, by guards, crossbow-men. The entire edifice is built on the summit of a crag. Gaunt made sure he and his son would be physically invincible.'

'Is there a well on this crag?'

'A large one within its own protected walls, sixty feet deep.'

'No escape then. I am cast down.'

'I come not as a bringer of despair.'

'Of course not. You remind me there are miracles. I shall transform myself into a bird. What do you say? A hawk or maybe an eagle for preference? When the time comes I shall soar to heaven on wings of gold.'

12

There was a subtle change of atmosphere when he entered the hall later. Swynford, if he had any orders, however, was keeping them to himself. The longbow-men seemed to know no more than Chandler but when Underwood happened to catch his eye while giving his usual morose assessment of his friar's robes this time he leaned across the table.

'Forgive my comrades, brother. They're longing to be down at Kingston though I tell them they too would have doubtless finished up face down in the Thames with their own arrows in their backs.'

'What? Is there news?' Chandler exclaimed.

'There certainly is – a rebellion no less!'

Chandler went cold. 'What have you heard?'

'A handful of earls with their ten-thousand-strong army. So the story goes – I tell them that's if you count the camp followers and then it reduces to no more than a handful all told.'

'Bitter odds. When did this happen?'

'We got it from one of the horse lads earlier.' He lowered his voice. 'They say there was a battle near Windsor where some thought to waylay Henry at the Epiphany joust, murder him and his four whelps, and reinstate King Richard on his throne. We understand Henry's army is in pursuit. Who knows which way it will go?' He turned back to his comrades.

Chandler bit into a tartlet of some spiced beans and considered things.

The fellow was incautious in such a hotbed of Lancastrian passion to name the new king with such lack of respect. Henry, indeed! As if he was no more than a regular man-at-arms. And talking openly of Richard as king? Irony would not save him if Swynford decided to drag him in for questioning. He hoped he himself would not have to oblige. Such free talk had already been censured down in London, hence his increasing work at the Tower before he was dragged north.

Chandler glanced at Underwood again. He was describing an event concerning one arrow and its apparent devastation of an entire vill '. . . as well as the demise of a filthy losel who deserved everything he got.'

To shouts of disbelief that even a well-placed arrow could wreak such havoc he added that it was a fire-arrow shot into the thatch. His boast instantly called forth similar triumphs. In the eyes of the brotherhood of bowmen, the soldiery who wielded axes were despised as little more than brutes. Only the longbow-men, trained from childhood at the butts, their skill feared throughout France, were worthy of the name warrior.

They made life simple. Find your target. Hit it. Collect your pay.

They were still arguing about the longbow-men holding the bridge at Kingston, or was it Maidstone? – there was some argument about that – when he got up to leave.

The gist of the latest rumour was that one of the rebels, the earl of Surrey, Tom Holand, had heroically held the bridge against Henry for the best part of a day until the rest of the rebellious earls had made good their escape into the west. When he and his handful of longbow-men tried to follow they had been captured and now awaited punishment in Oxford.

Bolingbroke's vow at Windsor rang in his ears.

His next thought was that it could be a set-up by Henry, an excuse to get rid of his cousin with apparent justification. Next he wondered who were the other earls involved in this folly. There had been no shifting glances at the mention of anyone at Windsor. Was it known if they were for Richard or against? For Henry, or against? Anyone in Richard's menye would know the inevitable result of an uprising. Henry's vow, such as it ever was, would have been broadcast everywhere.

13

Still no orders came. News from the south was kept out. The rebellion was scarcely mentioned in hall next morning. The only hint of something brewing was a rise in the volume of conversation, but even so it amounted to arguments concerning ale and arms and little else.

He went up as usual to see the prisoner.

He came across his cell when he heard Chandler greet the guard. 'There were comets in the sky the year of our birth, did you know that, brother?'

Chandler replied, 'Think not that the stars have power to determine our fate, majesty. We hold our destiny in our own hands, by God's grace.'

'Last year comets brought prophecies of the death of kings, of rebellion, civil strife, of pestilence and famine, did they not?'

His expression bleak, he went to stand before the slit with its near view over the killing field and the more distant sight of hills and sky beyond the walls.

'When do these events not occur, majesty? It's in the nature of our life on earth to endure such calamities . . . We must trust in God's good grace.'

'Seek not to comfort me, brother, nor to compromise your honesty. I'm braced for what happens next. To meet my beloved Anne, and my mother and father, and my dear little brother, Edward, and dear Robert and Simon and all the glorious pantheon of the dead, all my brave friends and allies, done to death so vindictively by the barons of this benighted realm – I welcome meeting my friends again with all my heart.'

He turned to give Chandler a piercing glance. 'So, this rebellion?'

He uttered the word Chandler had been afraid to speak. 'Tell me which brave fools have sealed my fate.'

'Brave fools?'

'It is my death warrant. Do they know that? The guard was happy to tell me they had been routed.'

'There will be more news. It cannot all be bad.'

'Bad for me or bad for Henry? Certainly bad for my dear nephew, Tom. Held at Oxford, I'm told? Henry and his puppet-master, Arundel, will not spare him. He is already a dead man as am I.'

'He lives and the rest remain free as far as we know. You might believe the best will happen yet.'

'You say so? After this? Has that serpent sent you to play devil's advocate?'

'Ordinary folk – forgive me, my lord – some blame you for seeming to take into your own hand your cousin's inheritance when his father the duke of Lancaster died.'

'Why? I did not parcel it out as I had a right to do with the property of a man guilty of treason and in exile!'

'They do not know that. They know nothing of the plot hatched against you. They merely see you as keeping his lands for yourself and maybe doling them out piecemeal as gifts to some favoured few.'

'I wish I had thought to do so! I left his lands intact in the keeping of the duke of Aumale, dear cousin Edward. I might have used Henry's lands to buy more loyalty!'

'Bought loyalty is often not worth the having.'

'True. Those dear friends of mine who were executed without trial after the Merciless Parliament before I came of age did not expect to be bought. Nor would I have whored them by trying to set a price on their loyalty. Such cruelty. Such malice. It broke my heart.'

He moved towards the window as if seeking escape then turned to Chandler. 'Hear this, brother, my litany of the loyal. These names I commend to heaven to be honoured in your prayers: my beloved old tutor and guardian Simon Burley, murdered by these fiends, my dear Robert de Vere, earl of Oxford, my chancellor Michael de la Pole, my chief justiciar, Robert Tresillian, Alexander Neville, Archbishop of York, now dying in exile, my keeper of the signet, Richard Medford, and other clerks such as young William Serle, many courtiers and those esquires who showed me loyalty, too numerous to mention . . . all close in my heart. I bless them . . . and now these other precious few . . .'

14

It was not good news he took up next day. The rebellion had foundered on betrayal by the duke of Aumale.

'Again!' Richard exclaimed when he was told. 'He betrays me again? Edward? My cousin Edward? I made him duke of Aumale! I made him Constable of England! What more did he want?' Tears in his eyes. 'And his sister, Constance? Did she betray me too?'

'She rode with the rebels and is now secured in the abbey at Reading.'

'A prisoner?'

'So we hear.'

'And more?'

'Her husband, the lord Despenser, has escaped to his castle in Wales.'

'God preserve him.'

15

Next day the bowl of pottage was ignored.

Richard was in a rage.

Without greeting, he said, 'Remind them all, brother, when you come to give your own account of this, that I never beheaded anyone. Traitors I gave leave to live elsewhere. The judges tried Richard, earl of Arundel and found him guilty of treason and gave a lawful verdict. Which others do they accuse me of executing?'

'None that I know of, my lord.'

'I should have thought myself a lesser man and king no longer, to take such barbarous measures against any living being than to execute a man without fair trial!'

He was pacing back and forth and turning angrily at every sixth or seventh step between the walls.

'Did Henry allow me to defend myself before parliament when he accused me of invented crimes? No. He knew he had no evidence against me. So he had me imprisoned to silence me. Is that the action of a just and reasonable man?'

He paced another length before asking, 'Does he not know – my benighted cousin Henry – that he is not the measure of all things? He is not God to kill, to punish, to execute as he chooses! Kingship does not give him leave to act without due process of law. Are we animals to tear and rend each other as it suits us?'

Another length, another turn.

'This so-called king even had himself anointed with fake holy oil to outdo my own true anointing – as if that would make his heinous betrayal acceptable! Imagine, going to such lengths to justify his theft of my crown! His vicious reign will bring this country to ruin! Let him live in hell!'

It was clear Swynford had been here already this morning.

He continued. 'Even his pretend coronation was held on my Saint's day as a deliberate insult to the regality of the crown. How vindictive is that! He knew full well what he was doing – but by insulting me he insults England! The dolt! Anointed? They must have set the servants to hunt out some long-forgotten ampulla in a cupboard and filled it with pig fat. He always stank, my dear cousin Henry. Such a red-faced, sweaty man. Does he imagine his followers are really taken in? Cannot he see their smiles behind their hands? Robert had a cruel tongue, mocking the sad lump, I give you that. But is that a reason to hate me so much?'

He stared at Chandler as if he might have an answer, forcing him to murmur, 'For some men it might be sufficient to hate you if they saw you standing in the way of their ambition – and if they knew in their heart they were the lesser man and the less beloved. In such a case their hatred might be unbounded.'

'Yes, witless as he is, ambition runs in his blood. His problem is he is such a sotwit he needs somebody to tell him what to do. First there was his strong-minded governess, Mistress Swynford, then her lover, his benighted father, old Gaunt, and now Thomas Arundel, plotting how he might become pope! Pope! At least Arundel knows what's what. Sharp, that one. Watch him rise! He is now the ruler of England. Jerking the strings of his mannikin.' He added on a different note, 'Poor Robert. Brought down by a boar? Never. They murdered him as surely as they murdered William Rufus. Robert was never rash when hunting. They killed him, even though he was in exile and could do no harm. Likewise poor Mowbray.

Naively confessing to being a witness to Henry's plotting? Believe it was the plague if you will. He was poisoned in Venice. It was nothing to do with the plague as they claim. Henry fears to leave me with allies, such is his fear of my kingship. And now my poor, loyal Holand and his friends . . .' He turned away to hide sudden tears.

Chandler pondered the subtlety of Arundel's planning. He too had no doubt that it was the self-appointed archbishop who was behind the latest news. It was to his advantage to encourage rebellion. Not only would it lure Henry's enemies into his sights, it would be his excuse to rid himself of his arch enemy, Richard. All so ominously clear. And yet the three envoys still showed no hint of their own purpose here.

Swynford must have exulted in the malice of rumour-mongering and given a gloating account of Henry's victory over Thomas Holand in the hope of demoralizing his prisoner. Instead it had the opposite effect.

Richard clenched his fists. 'They fear not the wrath of God. But their actions will sweep them to damnation. The truth will be told. Lies must never prevail!'

16

The Great Hall was turning rowdy again. A simmering excitement arose as more news of the rebellion came in. The atmosphere of violence spread throughout the castle, increasing as night fell. Torchlight made grotesque shadows leap across the walls. Much ale was drunk, speech, such as it was, had begun to slur. Raucous chanting, harsh and ugly, deafened the ears. Smiling at it, the men on the dais continued their conversation behind their hands.

As Chandler climbed from the bench he noticed one of the garrison men at a nearby trestle kick a dog scavenging under his feet. It was a young deer-hound following its elders' example. When it continued to push its muzzle through the mesh the fellow kicked out again with more force, metal boot thumping into the hound's side. It retaliated at once, grabbing the man around the leg and hanging on.

He lumbered to his feet, kicking out and swearing, 'Cur! Whore-dog! Be gone!'

When the hound refused to let go, true to its nature, the fellow raised his eating-knife and plunged it into the dog's eye. Its howl silenced everyone. The man withdrew the knife and lurching a little attempted to plunge the blade into the animal again but it slumped onto its side, whimpering, pawing helplessly at the blood streaming down its muzzle.

Underwood, sitting next to Chandler, sprang to his feet and had his hands round the man's throat before anyone else could move.

Those who saw what had happened backed off to give them space for a brawl but Underwood drew his fist and planted it soundly into the drunk's face before he could move. He keeled over, bringing flagons of ale crashing to the floor. Men scattered. Swearing loudly, he struggled to his feet about to raise his knife against the bowman when a couple of his drinking companions pulled him back, shouting, 'Enough, Jed! Enough!'

Servants hurried over.

While the men-at-arms dealt with their own the serving men put their hands underneath the hound to lift him and a dog boy glared balefully at the knife-man as they struggled to raise the creature to its feet.

'Done for,' someone observed, flagon halfway to his lips. 'Waste of a good deer-hound. That vicious bastard needs doing over.'

Without saying more Chandler rose to his feet as the drunk shook off his captors but before he could weigh in to restrain him several more pike-men were there before him.

Chandler did not want to get involved but the hound's plight forced him to examine it to see if anything could be done.

The dog boy, hands covered in blood, was in tears. 'He's a brave creature. It's not right.' He glared up at the perpetrator but the fellow was too drunk to notice and was already reaching for his flagon.

Chandler tried to reassure the lad. 'I believe he might be saved, although his hunting days may be over.'

'Life is better than death, brother.'

'Then help me take him somewhere quiet where we may see what we can do.'

Several willing helpers heaved the dead weight of the hound to a storeroom off the kitchen corridor and laid him carefully on his side. Water was brought. The wounds were cleaned.

'You see, things are never as bad as they first seem,' Chandler assured the tender-hearted young fellow who had hurried to the rescue. 'God does not intend him to leave us yet but someone will need to stay with him all night when I've fixed him up.'

'I will.'

'Then let me see what I can do.' He searched in his scrip to find something to stem the bleeding. 'I'll also give him a little something to send him to sleep.'

'He's called Math after the king's hound,' the boy told him. 'One of the best. We were hoping to see him in his prime. There would have been none to outshine him.'

'It's his eye,' Chandler murmured. He did what he could to save it but after the blood was washed away he saw that it was too far gone. 'Never mind,' he told him. 'Some good animals because they're so good learn how to compensate for their wounds and live happy and useful lives.'

'I'll sit by him and pray all night,' the lad vowed.

'Get someone to sit with you in case you fall asleep. There now, Math, old fellow.' He sat back on his heels and let the hound lick his fingers although he hardly had the strength to open his jaws. Chandler rose to his feet. 'I'll come back around prime to see how he's doing.'

17

Thinking about the hound pup later as he drifted off to a raucous lullaby audible from the Great Hall, Chandler returned to the plight of the king and his own helplessness. Anything might happen now the military was on the boil.

He shuffled about in his bed-straw for most of the night, thinking about the king, the rebellion, the hound, himself, his role here, and a certain distant girl letting down her golden hair in a darkened house. He heard the regular change of guard along the battlements, to the hoot of an owl, the toll of a bell and the gradual empty fall into silence of the entire castle.

18

Prime was welcome. As soon as he heard the bell from St Clement's, cracked and ill-found, he crawled forth, shook the straw from his garments and went outside.

Nobody was about much. It was too early. It was scarcely light. He took a wedge of warm bread and a piece of pie from the tray of a bleary-eyed servant as he passed through the hall and ate the bread as he walked down the kitchen corridor to the store-chamber.

The dog boy, tousled, snoring with his mouth sagging, opened his eyes the moment Chandler entered. His hands were deep in the fur of the hound. Another lad was sleeping soundly close by.

'All well?' Chandler whispered, not to wake him. He could see by the light in the hound's one eye that life had reaffirmed itself.

'He's restless but who wouldn't be,' the dog boy frowned. 'A wound like that. Poor, brave creature.'

Chandler crouched down. 'Math? How are you this morning, old fellow?'

The animal made a feeble attempt to lick Chandler's hand.

'I have a duty to attend,' he told the lad. 'Let me give you this cure for him to have with his meat. Can you give it to him?'

The lad looked scornful for a moment. Then he grinned. 'I can and I will, brother. Trust me. We'll have him running around like a pup soon as ever.'

'I don't doubt it. You've been most attentive and he's showing true valour.'

Slightly heartened at the lad's goodness, Chandler went outside and crossed the yard to the tower door.

19

When he made his ascent he found him sitting on the floor in a corner. His piss pot was full and stinking, the straw around it wet. The hem of his linen garment was rank with dried shit. A bruise had appeared on his left cheek. They were showing even less respect than ever. Something more must have happened last night to make them feel safe enough to get away with such contempt.

When Chandler appeared he scarcely raised his head at the wedge of pie he held out. He regarded it listlessly for a moment before reaching out a hand.

'Not to disregard your gift nor belittle the danger you run by bringing it, brother, but I can hardly—' He sighed. 'My gratitude, nevertheless.' He took it and put it to one side on the floor.

After a while he raised his head again. He looked beyond Chandler and spoke as if to himself. 'It was when I made that foolish mistake of believing what Northumberland told me at Conwy . . . Can you believe he and Arundel swore on the Holy Sacrament that Harry meant well and only wanted what he thought was his? . . . I did not see it as a blatant lie to prise me from Conwy . . . outright blasphemy to swear on the Sacrament. "No," they lied, "your dear cousin Harry does not wish to deprive you of your crown. No, the very thought!" they lied. "He certainly has no intention of keeping you a prisoner, he wishes only for your good health and safety—"' He gave a resigned laugh. 'I believed them! When I rode forth with only dear Montagu and the French fellow, Creton, and some others attending me I was in good hope that we could be friends again. But then, rounding a cliff, what did I see? I saw Northumberland's army spread out across the plain in full array and I knew . . . I knew then I was a dead man.' He looked up. 'I have been suffering my death throes ever since, brother—' He gave a resigned smile. 'And I am still not dead.'

Chandler crouched beside him. Nothing to say. He untied the water bottle from his belt and urged him to drink.

Lifting his head he said to Chandler, 'Christ had only one Judas. I have many. All my true friends have been taken from me. Because of me they have viciously been done to death.'

'Not all are gone. And others will be drawn to the justice of your cause. You are still our anointed king. You are not hated. You have not been a tyrant driven by blood-lust. When people hear the truth they will come to your rescue.'

'You say this to me? On whose instructions?'

'On my own. On the instructions of my heart.' He paused. 'At present they believe the lies told about you but later – the truth will come out.'

'No matter, I'm impatient for my flight to heaven now – I yearn to hold my beloved Anne in my arms again – and to have all my saints and loyal allies around me. We shall dwell so until the end of time in peace and harmony. I know it. I believe it. I have confidence in God's mercy.'

20

Three of the king's horses were in the yard when he went down. They were saddled up, caparisoned in the Lancastrian colours, ready to go somewhere. The envoys, still looking like assassins, were standing about as if ready to leave. At the same time Chandler noticed a new detachment of pike-men on duty.

Swynford was crossing the bailey followed by his usual retinue of bodyguards. They were clearing everybody back indoors except for the harried stable lads attending the horses. The number of crossbow-men on the wall-walk above the yard had increased.

Chandler went to stand in the chapel doorway. He could not return to the tower at present no matter how hard he tried to make himself invisible. A dozen unfamiliar men-at-arms were patrolling warily in twos and threes, their orders clearly to keep everyone out.

He watched them staring round like yokels at the soaring towers and the massive double walls as if they had never seen anything like them before but they kept their hands on the hilts of their swords and walked with the belligerence of men who knew what a blade was for.

Swynford disappeared inside the Great Hall.

Chandler decided to take his chance and trust that the new men were as yet unfamiliar with the routine of the inner bailey and their ignorance would work to his advantage.

He strolled unhurriedly with the air of someone bent on a familiar task across the yard to the kitchens and, once inside, managed to filch a bowl, pile it with food good enough to eat and, with a nod to one of the cooks who made some remark about it being hungry work praying, he was able to carry it across the silent yard without being stopped by anyone. *A friar. Unarmed? What sort of vermin was that for captains to bother with?*

The moment he reached the tower door, however, an unfamiliar figure slammed a pike across his path. He pushed it aside and with assumed asperity said, 'It's his vittelling as usual, soldier, did they not bother to tell you?' And was allowed up with a jerk of the man's head.

When he got to the top he told the guard what was what and went in before he could object. He found Richard still standing by the window-slit staring at the distant hills.

'Take this, my lord.' Chandler held out the bowl. 'I guarantee no extras from Swynford.'

Nodding towards the new guard pacing outside he remarked, 'This is an unexpected call, brother. Is something happening?'

'We're sealed off. I doubt not that something is going on—'

'They say they wish to move me in view of the rebellion. I believe it will be to a place not in this world.' He took the bowl and began to eat at once.

'In that case I have something else for you.' Chandler drew a narrow blade from his sleeve.

Richard's head jerked up and he stepped back. 'Is this my requiescat?'

'Not from me. Hide it somewhere. Under the straw where you can get at it.'

'For a moment I thought my trust was being rewarded in its usual manner. My gratitude, brother – again!'

He smiled with a sudden flash of his brilliant and habitual charm that had brought so many to his side and after filling his mouth once more he put the bowl aside, took the knife and, with a hasty glance towards the door, inspected the blade, murmuring, 'He will never allow me to go free. He knows he will lose the crown when people understand what he is doing. He cannot afford to let me live. I am the crowned and anointed King of England. I am a Plantagenet. I am Richard II. Nothing he will do can change that. I am prepared for whatever destiny brings.' He dropped the knife into the straw in a corner of his cell and kicked it out of sight.

At that moment a different guard, a captain, if his self-confidence was anything to go by, pushed his way into the chamber and told the two men-at-arms who followed to get rid of the friar.

'I'm going.' Chandler put up his hands to show he was leaving.

When he looked over his shoulder before the door was slammed behind him Richard was standing with his back against the wall.

21

Before he was halfway down, passing the second landing and nearly at the next one, Chandler met the three envoys ascending. He flattened himself against the wall rather than be trampled under their boots. Ignoring him they hurried up, sweating, cursing, regardless, and he heard them reach the top.

The sound of the door being kicked in echoed down the column of stone and when the door smashed back on its hinges he heard a crash from within echoing and re-echoing like the roar from a bell-tower as it resounded between the walls.

Oaths followed the bellow of a man in pain and another began to shriek above it all. More shouting and the sound of things breaking added to the cacophony and, before Chandler could race back to the top, he found himself being hauled by the neck of his robe and slammed hard against the wall.

The sound of someone cursing and a slow slithering of something heavy being hauled across the floor above were almost the last things he heard until, through a blur of swirling stars when he came to, an unearthly silence broken only by someone sobbing closed in.

He was aware of an assailant looming over him and, his own fingers striving for purchase, grappling onto a hauberk, hanging on, as he heard another oath when somebody rushed past him, followed by footsteps thumping overhead. A man roared down the stairs for more muscle.

Chandler's head had been cracked against the stone-work when he was stopped in his tracks and to his surprise he found he was being punched in the face. With an effort of will he managed to drag his assailant forward, unbalancing him, then together they rolled part-way down the steps. He got a better grip on his assailant's hauberk and yanked him off his feet as they both toppled further down the stairs until Chandler suddenly let go, kicked the man's legs from under him as he tried to get up and with one hard shove pitched him backwards all the way down to the turn where he lodged awkwardly, moaning and trying to rise to his feet.

With Chandler's rough help he slid even further down to stop at the next level where he crumpled and lay still.

Already the hollow thud of men tramping up the steps from the yard reached his ears.

He stood dizzily shaking some sense into himself then, fingers slipping on the smooth stone, he began to crawl upwards to where the sounds of the fight had come from.

A figure in chain-mail much like the one his assailant had worn loomed in the doorway of the king's prison chamber. He held an axe, ready for throwing. Chandler, still on hands and knees, held his glance for a moment, looked again at the axe, was unsure whether it was blood dripping from it, and decided not to ask.

He stumbled back down the steps, negotiated the body of the motionless guard, pushed some newcomers to one side who were answering the call for more men, and aided by the momentum of his downward course, reached the outer door before they could call him to account.

Blood was flowing from his nose or was it his mouth or some other wound? He had no idea. He wiped the back of one hand across his face, noting that it came away red.

All he could think was: Henry said he would do it and now he has.

22

The yard was deserted. Faces appeared from all round where he didn't expect them. They appeared at the window slits, behind shutters, at apertures in the storehouses, in the crack between half-closed doors, anywhere where they thought they could see without being seen. Eyes everywhere. An uncanny silence prevailed.

The only ones not cringing out of sight to seek a better view were the bowmen ranged high up along the wall walk, crossbows aligned on this new killing field, maintaining a cordon of steel.

Nobody but a fool would dare venture into the yard.

Chandler felt his skin prickle as he emerged within range and, in the expectation of being shot by a bolt before he walked two paces, he strode, head down as if it would protect him, through the ringing silence towards the chapel.

It was done. It was done. How could it have been done? Had Bolingbroke no regard for his immortal soul? If the answer was no, what about the code of chivalry? Where in the annals did it say it was a right and good thing to cut down an unarmed man, a prisoner, and an anointed king?

He knelt helplessly at the altar with a mind as barren as a desert and his heart bursting with sorrow. Wrath would come later, he knew that . . . for what good it would do. For now, all he could do was try to ease the pain of grief, grinding like a knife between his ribs.

23

As he knelt before the deceiving display of Lancastrian piety on the altar, the sun alighted on the gold of the crucifix and an image floated into his mind of another kind of gold. It was the living gold of her hair, wild tresses of fire, unloosed, and her skin gleaming, her eyes green sparks, her lips eager to receive his own hot searching . . . Hastily rising to his feet he offered her name as a prayer: *Matilda.*

'Wait for me, Mattie,' he had asked her, not wanting to let her go, and she had replied, 'Now and for ever, Rodric. You know I will.'

'I'll be back after attending to a few duties at Aldgate.' It had not been a lie. He intended to return but his meeting had taken longer than expected and when he returned to the house where she lived the place was in darkness.

She had been more than incautious about the absence of her master, the poet. While he was in Calais or wherever he had secretly taken himself, she told him they would have the house to themselves for a whole night. Later he convinced himself that she would be compromised by his appearance at the house at midnight.

The running of his thoughts made a sob shake through him. Henry had done it. The faithless tyrant had done what he had set out to do. It was done. It was done. It could never be undone.

When he walked over to the chapel door and peered outside, men-at-arms were hurrying in and out of the Great Tower. Four bodies lay in the yard. It was obvious they were dead. Blood soaked into the ground from their wounds. Those who walked past them did so with averted glances and feigned full attention to their tasks as if it was business as usual.

A commotion over by the tower revealed Swynford, closely accompanied by his personal guard, coming out into the yard and looking pleased with himself.

The group were followed by the three envoys Chandler had seen going up. The one he took to be Exton's son stood next to Swynford and said something that made both men laugh. It sounded incongruous when everyone else was standing in mute horror.

Before the two of them finished speaking the horses were brought forward. The envoys wasted no time. The portcullis was already being cranked up. Before it was fully open they were spurring their mounts underneath and were off, galloping out into the barbican and down onto the road to the south, soon out of sight, mission accomplished.

Swynford and his men were waiting for something. They had fallen silent again. Some milling-about took place. Then a sign may have come from one of the guards inside the entrance because there was a sudden stiffening of attention, an attempt to align themselves without appearing to. Swynford briefly stood alone until a wave of movement carried him towards the tower.

Four men, two in front, two behind, were hefting a hurdle between them. They halted in the doorway, some problem in manoeuvring themselves through it, until, with a few heaves of their shoulders they managed to hoist their burden into a better position and proceed with it into the yard.

Swynford stepped forward. Somebody had thrown a cloak over what lay on the hurdle and now he tweaked it to one side, gave a small nod, and the bearers proceeded, slightly out of step, and entered the yawning dark of the Great Hall.

It was the signal for the secret watchers to come tumbling into view. Crossing themselves they swarmed after them. Swynford gathered his bodyguards and followed.

Giving everyone time to clear the yard Chandler went over to the open door of the tower.

24

A lone guard was sitting on a barrel just inside the doorway. He glanced up without interest when a friar appeared. Chandler indicated the stairs but didn't say anything and the fellow turned his head to gaze outside.

When he reached the upper chamber he hesitated before stepping through the open door. It would be too soon for anything to have been cleared away. He braced himself and stepped over the threshold.

It was as it had been left a few moments ago. A lot of blood. The killers had brought nothing as refined as swords. The knife he had handed over would have been useless against battle-axes.

A sound behind made him turn. It was the guard from below. He had followed him. He edged inside and stood beside Chandler and together they measured a moment of silence as they contemplated the bloody chamber.

The stench of butchery was strong. A stool was upended. The food bowl had puddled its contents into the bed-straw. Bloodied lumps of flesh, of fabric, of hair, clogged underfoot. Chandler looked down at his feet and stepped to one side.

The guard was ashen-faced. In a dazed voice he muttered, 'They didn't expect him to put up a fight. He grabbed one of the axes and made harsh use of it. Only when he fell back near where their captain was catching his breath was he given a blow from behind that finished him.'

'You saw it?'

The guard crossed himself. 'I passed you on the stair. You pushed into us as you came down.'

'Did you know what was about to happen?'

'Something. We knew something would. It's not what you want to admit to yourself.'

'Until too late.'

In silence the guard picked up the stool and carefully set it upright.

Blood on the walls. The floor slippery with it. The smell of death deep in the stones as if never to be washed clean. Chandler was aware of an uncanny sense of absence and wondered if the guard felt it as well.

He bent down and picked up a feather from the place where the king had turned to face them. But it was black, not gold.

25

Swynford's chamberlain was a tall, stooped, hollow-cheeked, dark-visaged fellow of about fifty. His velvets were of middling grade, his gold chain of office worn smooth by much polishing. His white stick of office was crooked under one arm and he brought it out to rap three times on the floor. He was already making an announcement in wheezing tones by the time the hall fell silent.

The longbow-men at Chandler's table glowered towards the dais. He caught the gist of the chamberlain's announcement in mid-sentence.

'. . . and our lord king's dearly beloved cousin, Richard of Bordeaux, out of melancholy and in want of courage, shamed by his years of misrule, ate himself to a faint shadow of his former self through a lack of the will to live as everyone will attest.'

He gave a challenging glance around the hall.

Silence met him.

'His body will lie in the chapel to be carried in state according to the wishes of King Henry himself to the cathedral of St Paul's in the City of London.' He paused and allowed the heavy silence to lengthen before he told them, 'From there it will be taken for burial in a place gracious and sequestered enough to allow him to lie at last in peace, safe from the eyes of man.'

He finished and stepped down.

A susurration of conversation grew.

One of the neighbouring bowmen leaned towards Chandler to tug his sleeve. It was Fulke. 'Friar?' He half-whispered, 'Hear that?'

'I heard.'

'Wasted away.'

'As he said.'

The man rolled his eyes. 'So that's the story?'

'So it seems.'

'Despite the food you've been taking up? Did he not eat it then?'

'He ate it.'

'And he's not to lie at Westminster Abbey where they know him?'

'—and where his tomb is waiting,' Chandler helpfully pointed out, 'and where he hoped to lie beside his beloved wife Anne of Bohemia—'

'—not there then, no. Separated out of spite?'

The man's eyes were like two hard, shiny pebbles and he glared as if it was Chandler's fault.

Chandler countered his look by asking mildly, 'What's it to you?'

Fulke extended his shining glare then blinked and shook himself. 'We're longbow-men.' He indicated his comrades. 'We're being paid to escort the cortege on the march to London. That's what it is to us.'

Will overheard. 'I hope he's paying us as well as he paid them London bowmen he brought out the other day to go after the rebel earls. You hear what he was paying? I got it off that cellarer's boy, he said—'

'Ninepence a day, eighteen if you're a lancer, that's what he's paying.'

'He better come up with it, is what I think,' commented Will. 'All that way south again.'

They started comparing their present pay with that offered during Henry Bolingbroke's long march into the southern counties after landing at Ravenspur in the East Riding during his invasion the previous summer.

'That's when he was desperate. Paying over the odds to get an army together and if you refused, you got your legs broke or worse.' There had been hangings at Knaresborough by some who resisted.

'Most of 'em he called out were crossbow-men, useless against the Cheshire longbows. By the time they'd wound on a quarrel they were stuck all over with arrows like prize hogs in a ditch.'

'No man's better than a longbow-man though I say it myself.'

There were a few nods of agreement. Work, registered Chandler. That's all it was to them. He didn't understand them.

He forced himself to ask, 'So you were fighting in the Welsh Marches, were you?'

Before anyone could answer a shadow fell and he glanced up. Swynford hovered over him.

He stooped close enough to Chandler to mutter in his ear, 'Understand what the lord chamberlain was telling us, brother?' His glance darted along the table to Chandler's dining companions. 'I want a quiet word.' He jerked his head towards the door of the solar and Chandler rose to his feet, his meal, untouched, a gift for the kitchen lads.

Swynford's esquire cut a swathe for them through the swarms of serving staff to a private chamber off the main hall. Coming to a halt just inside the doorway Swynford slung an arm round Chandler's shoulders, man to man. 'It's this, brother. We have had a warning.'

'About what?'

'About a man refusing to eat.' He pursed his lips. 'We have to quell any rumour that three knights from London were here. Starting now.'

'And how may I be of service?'

'You'll travel with us when we eventually set out with the corpse. You'll bring to me anything I need to know. This current threat may be nothing more than the wild dream of malcontents. On the other hand, it may be a hint of another insurrection in the making.'

'Surely not, my lord?' Chandler's face was impassive. 'Is anyone in opposition not yet aware of the certainty of instant punishment?'

Swynford shook his head at Chandler's apparent naivety. 'When they see the coffin they will be deterred, that's for sure. They can't set a corpse on the throne, can they?' When Chandler did not respond he continued, 'Until the story of his death is bruited forth loudly enough some will believe it a lie and imagine they may put him back on the throne.' He eyed Chandler for a moment. 'He is dead. He starved himself from melancholy. We have a new, crowned and anointed king. Anyone who denies it will suffer the death of a traitor.'

He began to edge further into the solar but made it plain Chandler was not to follow.

'There would have been those who would have used him as a rallying point to bring down King Henry . . . You can have no idea of the perfidy of ordinary men.' He bunched his right hand and gave Chandler a light punch on the arm. 'Go now, brother. Much to do. Spread the word. Bring me anything you hear. You know what to say if anybody asks. Put them right. Those visitors of ours were on king's business. Nobody saw anything.'

Chandler began to turn away but Swynford called him back. 'During our march south we shall enjoy the hospitality of the religious houses along the route where we shall have the opportunity to spread the news. Our guards will invite the monks to accompany the cortege with lighted candles and prayers now that the tyrant is dead!'

Pondering the nature of the invitation offered by Swynford's guards, Chandler left the hall to make his way to his quarters near the stables.

A great lassitude had settled over him. It was done. How could it be done? And what next? Civil war?

TWO

Chaucer's house. February 1400.

Rain drumming in the yard out of a sulphurous sky, gusts of wind whining through gaps in the lattice, and only mid-morning. I tell myself it could be night. It brings me no pleasure to think so.

I lean against the sill in the strange yellow light as if waiting for someone to walk towards me through the puddles in the yard. But he does not come. He will not. I'm not such a fool as to expect him to come. How bleak it is, this absence. I'm thinking that all is lost for ever. I'm thinking, whatever shall I do? I'm thinking, he has gone. I'm thinking, all is lost.

Impatient with myself, calling myself names, I jerk away and as I do so my elbow happens to catch a jug standing on the sill, sending it flying across the kitchen where it smashes onto the tiles. Milk sprays everywhere, even staining the hem of my gown.

I scream with shock then to my own astonishment I am bursting into tears.

I begin to howl with misery. Once started I cannot stop.

The Master stands gobsmacked, simply staring at me as if he can't believe his eyes.

Adam, of course, thinks it's a huge joke. 'Silly chuck. You're not hurt. Stop your roaring!'

I recover enough to shout, 'It's not funny!' But I'm yelling at the top of my voice. I can't stop myself. 'What are you just standing for? Stop laughing!'

I'm swept up in a storm, floodgates open, and despite great gulping sobs I keep shouting, berating them, cursing them, the jug, the milk, the rain, the wind, the yellow sky. Everything.

Adam bends to pick up the shattered pieces. He stops mocking me, slowly lifts his head, gives me a stern glance out of the corners of his eyes.

The Master fusses forward. 'What's to do? It's only milk and a worthless jug, Mattie.'

Adam growls, 'It's not just a milk jug. It'll be some lad.'

I shout back, 'It's not my fault if men are faithless! Is it? Is it my fault? How is it my fault?'

Adam: 'Ah, I thought so.'

The Master: 'It's nothing, Mattie dear, nobody's cross with you.'

Adam: 'I knew it.'

The Master: 'Spilt milk. Worthless lads. Both the same. Not worth crying over.'

Later, Adam asks, as if it's anything to do with him, 'So who is he?'

'Shut up.'

Adam persists, as is his irritating habit. 'You never go out these days, unlike other lasses, so tell me who it is.'

Sniff.

'Where is he? I'll sort him out for you.'

I turn away.

Adam: 'Don't tell me then! See if I care.'

How can I tell him? I would have to reveal my utter out and out stupidity. It's getting to me though. I don't know what to do. I've never felt like this before. I can't bear it. I hate everything. Why is the world like this? Why is it so hateful?

In my little chamber under the eaves, I let down my hair and I see it through his eyes, how he untied it and spread it round me and buried his lips in it and ran it in strands over and over through his beautiful fingers and talked of angels and I stifle another bout of sobbing, stuffing my hands into my mouth so the Master will not hear and I rock back and forth on my bed, bereft, praying: O dear lady in heaven help me. What am I to do?

The Master had returned from Calais when he said he would and on the eve of Christ's Nativity we moved into our new house in the safety of the Abbey Close at Westminster. The house was still topsy-turvy come Epiphany.

Adam and Cook discussed the move, Cook, his bald head shining in the heat of his fire, his rosy face sad, of one opinion, and Adam, who had been tortured in Saltwood Castle as soon as the new king was crowned in the autumn, of a different opinion.

He scowled. 'We are safe nowhere.'

Cook disagreed. 'Within the Close we are virtually in sanctuary. They would not dare enter with drawn swords.'

'The trouble is he imagines he's immortal.'

Cook smothered a grim chuckle. 'He might very well be so.'

'Fifty how-many years? Fifty-three? Nobody but a madman would take out a lease for that long.'

'It'll be to give young master Thomas an income should things go wrong.'

'Anyway, we're wasting our breath on the whys and wherefores. He won't be around long.' Adam's expression was one I cannot describe.

'Is this the Master you're talking about?' I asked, going right into the kitchen instead of hovering in the doorway.

'Business, Mattie. Not your concern.'

'I heard what you were saying. I'm not stupid.' Not always, I added under my breath. 'Is it to do with his going to Calais?' I trace my downfall to the time he went away for a few days and left the house empty. It was that to put such wild ideas into my head. Not that Adam would know.

He said, 'Leave it.'

'Well, is it? Yes or no?'

He gave a sort of snarl. 'You don't know what you're talking about. Never mention that place. Ever. Get it?' He stood over me and gives me such a vile look as if he might strangle me that my mouth drops open.

Cook: 'Don't frighten the little maid, she's done no wrong. Here, pretty chuck, ignore him and try this.' He handed me a scone from the griddle dripping with honey.

When Adam was out of earshot, scratching away with his quill in the front chamber at the Master's tales, I asked Cook if there was anything wrong with him. 'What did Adam mean, Master won't be around long? He's not sick, is he, Cook? I would hate it if he was sick and was keeping it between himself and Adam.'

'He's not sick, no, lovey, not at all. I'd tell you if so. Stop fretting for no reason.'

His words did not reassure me. In fact they made me fear the worst because I thought it must be that other thing that made Adam say he would not be around for long. I could not imagine a place like Saltwood Castle.

* * *

You might imagine we would hear everything first, being so close to Westminster Hall, because although it's hardly anything like the market in Cheap where I used to go for all the latest gossip, especially at the time when the king, dear Richard, was pushed off his throne, enough important people flock to the palace, in and out as soon as the gates open and being where the laws are made, you'd think we'd be first in line to learn anything worth knowing. But no. We hear nothing. It's all guesswork. That's my feeling, anyway.

The first hint we heard that something was wrong was instead of staying out at Windsor for the joust, the duke of Lancaster as I can't help calling the new king, together with his sons, reappeared in a great bustle of troops and churchmen. Squads of militia started to fill Westminster Yard. You could hear the shouts even from here. It turned out to be a great muster. Thousands of men recruited. Flocking to join because they're being paid over the odds. The hateful sound of steel and arms. Morning till night men being sworn in. Armourers and blacksmiths busy.

'Is it the French?' I asked Cook.

'Not this time.' He looked worried but didn't say anything else.

As soon as the swearing-in was done, they began to move off. Then we heard that the lord Henry, as Adam still calls him, had set off back to Windsor at the head of his army. Only the eldest boy, Harry Monmouth, the prince, is with him this time, the others, the little ones, taken to Eltham by boat under the protection of armed guards.

In the days that followed Adam became more morose than ever. He was totally silent.

'Are you struck dumb?' I asked. 'It must be because of a lass.' No answer.

Even Cook, usually putting a cheery face on things, looked old and sad.

The Master did nothing but walk restlessly about the house, picking things up and putting them down. He barked at Adam and made him redo some copying, but mostly he simply paced back and forth as if waiting for a sign that might release him.

'Cook?'

'What is it, my sweeting?'

'Has something happened? It has, hasn't it?'

'Things happen all the time.'

'You know what I mean. Something untoward.'

'Something has happened, yes. But it will not affect us.'

'Is it enough to put a blight on everything?'

'You might say that.'

'Is it something to do with King Richard?'

'Only some nonsense about them trying to free him from Lancaster's castle in the north where he was taken for safe-keeping.'

I know he's trying not to frighten me. 'Is it anything to do with the visitors who were guests of Abbot Copthorne before Christmas?' I know what they were up to. I'm not the mindless little poppet they take me for.

He turned and gave me a straight look. 'It's this, dear little Mattie. I'll tell you what I know – which isn't much.' He led me to the bench and we both sat knee to knee. 'Some folk loyal to King Richard were plotting to kill the new king, Henry, and release King Dickon from his prison in Pontefract Castle.'

'To put him back on the throne?'

'That was the idea.'

'And it has come to nothing?'

'The new king heard about the plot. Someone betrayed the plotters. And that commotion you heard a couple of days ago was when Henry swore in a massive army to go after them.'

'Are the plotters dead?'

'They escaped. Scattered to the four winds. They only managed to get away because John Holand's nephew Thomas held the bridge over the Thames at Kingston for over a day with a handful of archers.'

'Then maybe we should rejoice?'

His stern expression had no hint of joy in it. He patted me on the arm. 'Maybe. Let's see what happens next.'

Dear, sweet Cook. I guess he has not told me everything. I fear it's because he doesn't want to alarm me and also, probably, because he doesn't want to believe what has happened.

It is a catastrophe.

Too horrible to contemplate.

It is the worst I can imagine. We are in deep mourning.

THREE

Pontefract Castle. February 1400.

Whether Swynford intended to set off for London at once or not, there was a delay. Nobody knew the reason.

The longbow-men, Chandler's habitual companions at the long trestle where they shared bread, were stuffing their faces with as much food as they could get down in the shortest possible time, while they discussed the delay in voices dripping with scorn.

'How difficult can it be?' Will spread his arms in mock-bewilderment, a wedge of bread in one hand, ale stoup in the other.

His comrades agreed, Fulke complaining loudly that they were ready to defend the cortege if nobody else was but anyway they had food at regular intervals and a roof over their heads so who was minding if they couldn't organize a dog fight in a kennels? Another fellow, a Saxon called Edfrith who only sat with them when he had news to impart, bit into a meat ball and swallowed it whole while glancing round to see who was listening. They were easy enough with Chandler by now, making sure he got his fair share of anything going.

He knew their names and many of the others in the garrison, not that he intended to take anything to Swynford. He liked Fulke. He was a shrewd, somewhat truculent northerner, hair cropped short to go under a felt cap, a leather guard on his left wrist at all times, and now in a lugubrious tone asking, 'And if he was supposed to wither away through lack of vittels as they're now telling us, how long is that supposed to take? By my reckoning it's four weeks or more. Are we supposed to believe this story of a sennight? Nobody starves to death in a week.'

'It must have been a miracle,' the one called Underwood commented in a sarcastic mutter. 'That is, if he started to pine away the instant he heard about the rout of the rebel earls and lost all hope right off. Do we believe in miracles, lads?'

Chandler, making the most of sharing the dole with them as a regular thing, quoted Swynford, 'It's king's business. Nobody saw anything.'

Will, still suspicious of a friar who was known to have worked at the Tower of London to drag confessions from the prisoners, had noticed Swynford take Chandler aside and seen Chandler walk away afterwards.

The look he gave him now showed they didn't trust him. They would be wondering whether an accidental oath against an archbishop was enough to get them thrown into prison or worse. They trod carefully. He didn't blame them. How could they know what was heretical or treasonable when the laws were being changed by the day? What was all right to say today up here in the north might be a burning offence down south tomorrow. They could not tell until they saw how the land lay. Was it wrong to express criticism of the new regime? Maybe they would be under suspicion themselves if they criticized Henry?

'I'll tell you something, friar,' Will continued. 'There's a story going round that the new king proclaimed that if a rescue bid was ever made King Dickon would be the first to die.'

Chandler could have said he already knew that but he kept his counsel.

'These earls, then,' he insisted, thinking he would like to hear how much the bowmen knew or guessed. 'What's the latest? Do we know who's involved apart from Tom Holand?'

'I'll tell you, as so it's rumoured.' Will checked names off on his fingers saying, 'Despenser's one. Montagu another. The other Holand, Sir John, Sir Thomas's uncle, the earls of Huntingdon and Kent.'

'And Edward, duke of Aumerle?' growled Fulke sarcastically.

Will scowled at the last named. The name was greeted with derision all round.

Underwood snorted, 'Traitor!' and followed it up with a few oaths.

'That's the snake in the grass. There you 'ave 'im.' Edfrith still sitting with them poured more ale and glanced from one to the other like an agent provocateur, making Chandler think he was in somebody's pay and trying to entice them to admit too much. He imagined it might be as well to watch his step himself.

'The latest story just brought in says it all,' Will continued heedlessly. 'It's that our illustrious duke of Aumerle let on accidentally the night before the planned coup after paying off a tart in Southwark. She told it to her next trick, a servant of Arundel's. And so it went until it reached Henry's eager little ear-hole.'

More derision followed.

'Lancastrians. Can't keep neither their britches nor their lips buttoned.'

Fulke banged his stoup on the table in appreciation of the story, adding, 'Now we know what we're up against, lads!' He added something unrepeatable and they all roared.

Chandler emptied his ale jar and handed it to a passing servant as he got up to go. 'I'll leave you free to blaspheme as much as you like, fellas. Bless you all.'

He understood their suspicion with his known allegiance to Lancaster – but they were making their own allegiance questionable, weren't they?

As he left Will raised a hand. Fulke nodded. Even the morose Underwood gave him a jerk of the chin.

2

Afterwards he turned towards the chapel but as he was crossing the yard he heard footsteps behind him. It was coming on to dusk. Not many people about. Flares were being lit along the walls. At the door he half-turned and thought he saw a shadow melt into another shadow against the wall but putting it down to his own dark mood he pushed the door and went inside.

The sacristan was nowhere to be seen but a couple of candles on the small altar at the east end were already making the shadows leap.

It took Chandler only four or five strides to bring him close enough to drop to his knees on the bottom step. The candle flames wavered. A little drift of smoke curled into the air. He bent his head, folded his hands, waited for the silence to reach for him.

All that happened was that the hammering of questions in his head continued. He couldn't believe it had all unfolded as forewarned.

There was definitely a sound behind him. Had someone followed him inside? He stretched his ears to listen. Nothing.

The military, though a superstitious bunch, did not frequent the chapel except when they thought it necessary. Mornings, end of day, a quick accounting to their Lady before settling in for the long winter night of drinking and gaming – they were the most popular times. Vespers was not often deemed necessary. Too much singing, even though it was only the old castle priest with a voice not above a whisper and his acolyte off-key and shy about it.

His sixth sense made him rise to his feet the better to defend himself. He swung round. A figure wrapped in a black cloak was standing no more than a few feet away.

Chandler stepped to one side as if to allow him to approach the altar.

'Don't go, friar. I have a request—'

Chandler was poised, knife in his sleeve.

Unexpectedly the shrouded figure asked, 'Will you hear my confession?'

He shrugged. 'I don't often—' He spread his hands to emphasize his reluctance.

Archbishop Arundel was beginning to encourage the friars to pick up what they could from among the usual banal confessions about adultery and bad faith that burdened so many. He was setting the friars against the parish priests who wanted sole authority to hear the secrets of their flock. But Arundel was clear about it. He aimed to prise out unorthodoxy and punish any sign of Lollardy from the populace. Friars were invaluable. Passing lightly through close-knit communities throughout the land they were notorious for their ability to inveigle their way into many a household of loose-tongued wives or disgruntled labourers. People felt, not unreasonably, that what they confided to a friar, a passing stranger, would be unlikely to reach the ears of those concerned to cause unnecessary trouble at home. Thus their popularity.

The man was still waiting.

'I don't often—' Chandler began again. 'I'm not a priest – nor a pardoner. I have nothing to sell. No pigs' bones . . .' He smiled to take away the sting of rejection.

'Hear me, brother,' repeated the man in the cloak. An edge of desperation had entered his voice. 'They say we'll be leaving at crack of dawn. I want to set out with a clean slate.'

Chandler peered into the fellow's face but he wore his hood over it, putting it in deep shadow. He could have been anybody. Then he put his hand to his hood and Chandler recognized him as one of the longbow-men, the quiet one, Underwood. He gave Chandler a desperate glance and said, 'I have to trust you. I know about your saint. I seek his protection.'

With a gesture towards the stone bench against the wall Chandler went to sit down. The fellow came to crouch at his feet and pushed his hood right back. He looked even younger, away from the others. He seemed frightened. Nervous. Burdened.

Chandler settled to listen. 'Your full name—' adding awkwardly, 'my son?'

'John Underwood.'

'Proceed, John.'

'Almighty God, merciful Father . . .' He hesitated as if suddenly regretting his decision then, heaving a breath, he continued in a dark and hurried tone, scarcely audible, so that Chandler had to lean forward to make sense of the scrambled words.

'I, a miserable sinner, confess all my sins and iniquities by which I may have offended you and deserve your punishment now and for ever . . .'

He began with his first sin, pride. His God-given skill as a bowman was not his to own. It was a blessing from God – for the defence of the weak. He himself should not glory in it.

This was followed by a confession of a second sin, one of unmitigated rage at what had been done to his beloved wife and little son when Henry the invader had despoiled his vill with his army while scavenging for food and punishing those who would not come out at once to help him in his treachery but – he continued rapidly – he could not go into details such was his grief . . . His voice dropped so low at this point that Chandler thought of asking him to repeat what he had said but then he was going on to other things that he also raged against, acts that had taken place at that time during the first weeks of the invasion, acts too numerous and beyond understanding to be spoken about and being denied by the perpetrators to their everlasting damnation.

And he also admitted blaspheming against the Holy Spirit which he knew could not be forgiven because it was the worst of sins but in honesty he stood by his curses despite his resolve to amend his ways with God's help. Should he be let.

After a sufficient silence, during which Chandler saw tears streaming down the fellow's face, he reached out to take both his hands in his. Suspecting that he knew the answer he asked, 'Is there more troubling you?'

Another pause followed. When he eventually shook his head Chandler murmured, 'May our Lord and Christ Jesus by the mercy of his love absolve thee from thy sins . . . and I, his unworthy servant, in virtue of the authority committed to me, absolve thee and declare thee absolved . . . in the name of the Father, the Son and the Holy Ghost . . .'

Underwood scrambled to his feet as soon as the words were uttered. Averting his glance and pulling his hood over his head again he hastened down the nave to slip through the door into the yard without a backward glance.

Chandler watched him go with a bemused expression. That was not all the fellow had wanted to say. He wondered about the burden that weighed on him and sorrowed that something held him back from making a full confession. Maybe it was enough? Then he asked himself whether he himself had access to any sort of power, divine or secular, that could absolve the fellow's grief? He doubted it. He was plunging into heresy himself. He had witnessed the depths of grief and rage that had driven the man to beg for absolution. Yet he had no faith in absolution. It was impossible now the king was dead. He wondered if Underwood would be back.

3

Things had quickened after the regicide and yet still they did not set off on the long journey to the City of London with the bier.

The carpenters, having worked through several nights to knock together a coffin suitable for a king on a long and rattling journey of over two hundred miles, and the plumbers having fixed the lead lining over the body to allow anyone and everyone to see a little of the face of the corpse to recognize it, if they could, as their one-time king, and the cart with its hooped awning having been prepared, the black horses chosen, and everyone, knights, guards, esquires, kitcheners, servants, sumpterers, wheelwrights, blacksmiths, armourers and diverse other necessary folk skilled at their craft, along with a wagon heaped with candles suitable for the burial of a king, were summoned and counted and prepared, and the cortege was prepared to move off.

It was dawn. A pewter-coloured sky hung low over the towers

of the castle and the crag on which they were built. Rain threatened again. They were poised to leave.

Then a valet from King Henry himself, now back at Windsor, arrived in haste. He ploughed his flagging mount to a rearing halt in the bailey and called in a loud voice for the constable of the castle.

Swynford, ready for travel in a thick cloak lined with ermine, swaggered forth.

When he heard the valet, sweating after his overnight ride, confide some message into his ear he whisked him into his solar while everybody stood about in the yard asking each other what it was about and what more might have happened down south.

'All that hurry and shove for nowt, to get it finished in time,' a carpenter was heard to complain. 'And now we're standing round after cutting corners.'

'He won't know we've cut corners. He's dead.'

Someone muttered at this outright disrespect. A corpse was a corpse after all.

'I never cut corners,' somebody else answered back, sharpish, and a scuffle ensued.

When Swynford's esquire appeared he made straight for the Chamberlain and those nearest could hear what he whispered clearly enough. 'We're to stand down until tomorrow.'

Puzzling over the reason for the delay, Chandler joined the others in the hall and the cooks rustled up enough eel pie and ale to keep everybody happy. The reason for the delay was discussed at length but to no avail. Nobody knew anything. No announcements were made. They settled back to drinking and dicing and talking things over.

'Something must have kicked off again down south,' remarked Will. Nobody disagreed.

Another night, thought Chandler, bedding down to sleep.

4

Next morning, before dawn, well before they could reasonably be expected to be alert, they were summoned again. With many of them still half asleep they were ordered out into the wagons. The elite were able to bed down under cloaks and furs and shut their eyes again but the mere foot soldiers were not so lucky. At last, however, the whole contingent was again ready to leave.

This time, setting an energetic pace to make up for lost time, they rattled down the crag side onto the long snaking road to the south.

First out were the harbingers, mounted on frisky ponies, then the heralds, accoutred in red and gold, then the militia, armed, marching in a jangling mass in two squadrons before and aft of the black-canvas-covered bier bearing the body of the king.

Bets were placed on the likely time they would take to reach the gates of London.

5

That first night they camped on abbey lands. Those not invited to sit at the abbot's table, mostly everyone, were left to spread out across the demesne, over the lanes and meads and common land, and light their cooking fires where they could.

Soon spits were dripping with the fats and juices of meat, pies were warmed, ale barrels rolled out, dice thrown, and eventually the light drinkers began to bed down beneath the wagons and under bushes with their cloaks over their heads.

Guards took up their places round the bier for the night, their braziers stuck into the ground beside them so that the flames glittered on basinets and burnished leather. The wagon bearing the lead-lined coffin was the still-point of the whole cavalcade. Whenever the awning was pushed aside the king's face was visible from brow to chin. They said he seemed to be gazing up at the moon.

News had spread of his death. From all the vills and granges within a day's walking distance people emerged throughout the night. Their black shapes moved in silence, with caution, as if any sound would break the spell of majesty that briefly touched them, as they came to see for themselves what a dead king looked like.

Chandler, sharing dole from the common pot with Will, asked him, 'How many over there,' gesturing towards the bier, 'have actually seen King Dickon? Anybody?'

Will glanced over and crossed himself. 'Not many. Mebbe from a distance if they bothered to look up.' He cocked an eyebrow. 'You're thinking what I'm thinking?'

'It depends what it is.'

'We could have anybody in there?' He looked thoughtful. 'I've never seen him in real life. That'd be a play all right!'

Chandler thought about it. 'It would,' he agreed after a pause. 'It certainly would.'

Their speculations were abruptly curtailed by a shout. It was followed by a selection of oaths that rang out across the camp. The reverential silence was shattered.

Will glanced across to where the sounds were coming from. 'Somebody found a rat in his ale?'

Both men rose to their feet. Others were already running from beside their fires, shadows jerking, dark then light, and by the time they reached the source of the outcry a crowd had gathered. Between the heads they could make out a shape lying on the ground. A log? An animal of some sort?

A bit of shoving brought them close enough to make out that it was a man. He was lying face down near the fire, so close that one foot was in among the embers exactly as he must have fallen. Flames were already beginning to lick the leather toe of a boot but had not yet scorched it.

More pushing brought them to the front of the crowd and then they drew back like everybody else.

In the middle of the man's back was a single arrow.

Some were staring over towards the woods and one or two men ran as far as the shadows then hesitated, glancing about. Others peered warily to where the light from the campfires could not penetrate. There was much confusion. One man, heedless of danger, ran right into the woods. In ones and twos others began to follow.

Chandler knelt down beside the stricken man. When he crooked his fingers underneath him to turn him over his eyes stared up at nothing and a gout of blood gushed from his mouth, seeping into the hairs of his beard and trickling down into the grass.

Will knelt beside him. 'Got him straight in the lung.'

Chandler agreed. 'You can take that arrow out now, Will. It's nothing that'll make any difference to him.'

Men from other fires were crowding round.

One of the captains came up. 'Who is it?'

'Never clapped eyes on him before,' said Will at once. He rose to his feet, put one foot cautiously on the man's back and worked the arrow free. He turned to the captain. 'Don't you know 'im?'

Before he could answer one of the men from another campfire spoke up. 'I do.' He was still eating and waved a chicken leg in one hand. 'He's one of the relief garrison. He's with us. Was,' he added.

The captain scowled. 'Better get up to the abbey and tell Swynford.'

Into the silence Chandler said, 'I'll do it. I have to go up there as it is.'

The captain stood for a moment looking down at the body without speaking. Then he roused himself and addressed his men. 'I want to know who did this. Anybody see which direction it came from, this arrow?'

His lieutenant glanced off into the darkness. One or two men were already dragging their hauberks off the cart and pulling them back over their heads ready to join the search.

'It came out of the night without warning, Captain,' somebody said. 'We were just sitting here having a last drink – I mean—' He tailed off, glancing round but nobody made any jokes.

The captain glared at the blank faces. 'Any of you lot have any argument with him?'

There were sidelong looks and a general shifting but they shook their heads. 'Nowt special,' one of them admitted to general agreement.

The few who had chased off into the woods were returning. 'No sign of anybody. But it's pitch black in there. Can't see your hand in front of your face.'

The captain ordered men with flares to search the woods, every bush and tree if their lives were worth anything, and bring the murderer out. 'Drag him forth before Swynford creates hell!'

Will began to walk away.

Chandler followed. 'So you didn't know him?' He glanced at the arrow in Will's hand when he didn't reply. 'May I see that?'

Will reluctantly handed it over. 'Nothing to see, friar.' He gave him a challenging glance. 'Blood. Red like any man's.'

Chandler handed the arrow back. 'You laying claim to it?'

'Can't let good arrows go to waste, can we?'

At least, Chandler felt, he would know where to find it should it be necessary. He wondered if this was anything to do with the warning of rebellion Swynford had mentioned. It was not something he had given much credence to as it was too soon to hear what support the earls had managed to arouse in their attempt against Henry. Something might come of it. But was this part of it? Shooting an ordinary garrison man?

'Didn't you recognize him?'

Will shrugged but didn't answer.

6

If the life of all beings is equal to every other life then the death of the militiaman in Swynford's army and the death of the king should be equal. So judged Chandler without satisfaction.

But surely, he argued with himself as he accompanied Will back to their campfire, the death of a king was worth more than the death of one man in a thousand men?

This was because of the influence a king could bring to bear while he lived. He had the power of life and death through famine and warfare by his governance of his realm. A mere man-at-arms had scant power in that respect. In the scale of things he could generally make little difference to anything, being only one and powerless and alone.

Did that mean it came down to a question of numbers? The more men you were capable of slaying the more powerful you were? If so, where did that put Christ?

Dissatisfied with his thinking Chandler sat down with the men beside their fire, finished off his interrupted meal, now not only charred but cold, and listened to Will explain to the other two what had happened. With no news about the murderer and no more alarms of men being shot at random out of the dark, he set off to report to Swynford as he had been going to do anyway. He approached the abbey gatehouse and pushed his doubts aside.

The porter let him in.

He turned out to be an elderly fellow, ready for conversation with a stranger and a friar at that. While he sent a lad off to announce the arrival of their visitor from the cortege, he said, 'My lord Swynford has been told about the unfortunate man-at-arms—'

'Already?' Wondering who had been so quick off the mark he asked, 'I was at the other side of the encampment. Has the murderer also been run to ground?'

The porter shook his head. 'Not that I've heard, brother, but it won't be long. The lord Swynford is determined the rebellion will not take hold as long as *he*'s a king's man.'

Rebellion? Was that what he was choosing to call the loosing of a single arrow out of the woods into the back of a powerless castle guard?

It made one ask what else might be classed as a sign of rebellion. An oath at the name of Arundel? A besmirching of the king's arms, the way they reversed Gaunt's arms in the City when he had Wyclif tried for heresy? Yes, that might suggest treason. Would they burn you for it now? Or merely strip a man of his house and livelihood?

Pulling himself together he said, 'It is most probably a personal quarrel by someone with a hot temper and a resentment at being crossed. You know what the military are like.'

The porter nodded. 'Anyone could have done it.' He shook his head in sorrow. 'Too many of those devils carry longbows, save them—' He shrugged. 'Still, what would we do without them?'

That was all he had to add. Evidently he didn't yet know it was a war arrow that had been used. The bowman must have thought his target worth it.

With little necessity to say much more Chandler was directed towards the abbot's lodging where Swynford was spending the night in more comfort than his men.

Guards were everywhere. Perforce, unarmed within the abbey precinct, he hoped, although he suspected the presence of concealed knives inside many a boot and sleeve if anyone had taken the trouble to search.

He eyed the guard at the ornate arch over the door of the abbot's lodging with caution. 'My lord Swynford is within?'

'You're the friar he's expecting? Pray enter.' The guard stepped aside.

7

He decided to keep a chronicle. It would be a record of these unprecedented times as they unfolded. Somebody must keep an accurate account.

Swynford had planted the seed of the idea in his mind.

It was reported, as he heard last night from Swynford's host, the lord abbot, that the royal clerks were being sent round the scriptoria of the abbeys and other religious houses, to comb through their chronicles for anything written to the detriment of the usurper or in praise of the murdered king.

'We cannot be seen as supporters of King Richard. It is now regarded as treason.' The abbot looked worried. Swynford had nodded and murmured, 'I'm sure your scribes would not be so foolish as to praise a tyrant. My own clerks will have a look at the scriptorium before we leave, if we may.'

So, he thought, if the monastics would be busily writing what they were told to write and rewriting anything that did not fit with the new monarch's lies, why should I not write my own account? The times were unprecedented, as the abbot had said. A true record should be kept.

Swynford also repeated the story that the king had starved himself to death from melancholy.

After this lie he glowered at Chandler as if expecting some objection but when he saw no change of expression in his eyes he continued with a more confident huffing and bracing of his shoulders as he paced the abbot's chamber.

The night's murder of one of the men had been duly noted, he told him. They were working on the theory that the fellow must be in the service of a lord from somewhere up near Northumberland's territory whose son, Harry Hotspur, was causing his father trouble.

There was also trouble down south, he told the abbot, hence our delay in leaving yesterday as planned. He frowned and said he would not impart the details to Chandler – he would understand that – but it could be something that turned out to be a contagion and the last thing they wanted was to have it passed onto their own forces. So far his men were loyal. He intended to do all he could to keep it like that.

After a general remark about the slowness of the pay being made to his men and a narrowing of his eyes when Chandler had nothing much else to report, that was it.

With the intention regarding a chronicle uppermost in his mind Chandler obtained a stack of over-scraped vellum from a monk who worked in the scriptorium at the next abbey that offered them hospitality, found a suitable quill which he sharpened with his own pen knife, and set to whenever they came to a long enough halt.

Chandler's Chronicle

With the murder of the garrison man on the first day of the journey unsolved, we had to leave, perforce with the murderer still with us. There were hostile glances and many stared nervously into the trees that lined our route. Men moved away from each other as if fearing the plague. A shroud of suspicion descended on us all and no one was exempt.

Other views of the matter were more cheerful, if that's the right word, reassurance being found in the smallest sign. Some believed the murderer was a disgruntled outlaw who happened to be lurking in the woods when we set up camp and decided to take a pot-shot at us for mere amusement, others said he was a bonded labourer with a grievance against the harsh treatment meted out by his overlord, or, for some reason the most reassuring opinion of all, the murderer was said to be a madman who took against a random stranger and had then done away with himself out of remorse. Further, it was claimed that his body could not be found because he had thrown himself into the river and been swept to his death on the rocks downstream where he had cried piteously for help for many hours before expiring unshriven and in great pain and so had descended unto hell.

This fruitless speculation about an unsolved murder was not the worst of things. News filtered back to us in a disjointed fashion from the south to account for our delay although it was difficult to make any sense of what was going on as no story matched any other. Nevertheless, it was all bad, or at least it could be considered so from a stance which itself would be too dangerous to express.

Thus the first of these stories to come to our ears was that the earl of Huntingdon, John Holand, stepbrother of the murdered king, and uncle to the unfortunate Thomas, was alleged to be one of the rebel earls despite the fact that he was not known to have played any part in raising an army against Henry.

He was in London and had remained there throughout the rebellion, so it was said, not riding with the others. The question was then, how could he have been involved in the plot to get rid of Henry? It was nonsense. Many thought so.

He was pursued by Henry's men nevertheless and it was generally understood that Henry was setting out to purge the realm of anyone in his kinship with a possible claim on his throne.

The story was elaborated and it was said that when earl John tried to escape the city by boat the Thames was whipped by the hand of God into such a ferment of easterlies that his hired boat was driven back onto the quayside and he had to take horse instead. In all this he was accompanied by an esquire called John Schevele.

'If he had no part in the rebellion why did he flee?' I asked in a general sort of way when this story came to our ears.

'Because Henry is in danger as long as Richard of Bordeaux's kin are at large,' said Fulke, bluntly, confirming the earlier opinion. 'And God appears to be on Henry's side, with his harsh easterlies and so on.'

We had bartered a lift for a few miles to take the weight off our feet and were jogging along among sacks of meal, knee to knee, neither of us averse to talking about the latest developments down south.

Fulke grunted but without humour.

I believe we both suspect a plot to keep us ill-informed so that news will not spread from us to the villagers and field-labourers for fear of causing another rising, one scattered and more difficult to put down than heretofore. I did not share this view with Fulke, for safety's sake. Instead I asked, 'So if they want rid of him because of his family connections where is he now, John Holand, this earl of Huntingdon?'

He leaned forward as if to impart a secret. 'They say he's escaped into Essex where he tried to get another boat to take him right out of the realm, to Flanders or somewhere similar, but again the weather was against him. They know not where he is now. In hiding somewhere, that's for sure.'

The waggoner was listening in and now said over his shoulder, 'I'm told he ran to Hadleigh Castle but when they went to drag him forth he'd already gone from there. But you're right, master. He's in hiding and nobody knows where.'

'I hope he has friends in Essex,' I murmured, thinking of Aubrey de Vere. Then I glanced up and saw Fulke watching me closely. 'For our own sake, not for his.' I crossed myself for good measure.

Hadleigh, I knew, had been one of old King Edward's defensive works at the mouth of the Thames. There was another fortification on the opposite bank of the river. It belonged to the earl of Oxford, Robert de Vere, one of Richard's chief supporters. In the old days he used to frequent Hadleigh with his wife. It made me wonder if the present earl had given shelter to their ally. Ill fate for him if he had dared to do so.

Chandler flexed his fingers and considered what he had written so far. It was all speculation but some of it must hit the mark. In all these conflicting accounts the seed of truth would be found. It was a question of getting it down and then later, perhaps in calmer times, sifting through it to separate rumour and speculation from the truth.

He picked up his quill again, saw it was blunted, and spent some moments sharpening it before continuing.

The next event of note was when we reached a large town, I forget its name, it is of no moment, and camped outside the ill-made wooden walls on some common land.

We ventured inside through the postern, confident that we would be seen as men on king's business, as so we were in a manner of speaking, and would be treated accordingly. I felt, however, that the inhabitants did not regard us with much respect but were too cowed by our men-at-arms to reveal their true feelings.

Despite this we managed to find a glove-maker eager to tell us the latest. He made no effort to suppress his glee.

It was not comforting.

When my companions heard that it was another story of defeat and humiliation they returned to camp. I, however, stayed to find out as much as I could.

I was told that the search for John Holand was still on. He was believed to be hiding somewhere in Essex. This we had already heard.

Henry's army, meanwhile, was now after his nephew, young Tom Holand, who had so valiantly held the bridge against them at Kingston. Henry and his army had pursued him and the rest of the rebel earls to Oxford but by the time they got within sight of the town their quarry had flown.

'Gone on to Cirencester,' my informant told me. 'Not that it did them much good. Imagining themselves safe the men camped in the

fields for the night while their leaders bunked up at an inn in the town. Sadly for them the town's folk were too frightened to be seen offering them refuge and a mob attacked the inn with them still inside. Arrows flew, you can just picture it, the doors studded with them. The windows were too much of a target for anybody even to risk looking outside, I'm told.' He gave a smug smile. 'I have it on good authority that one of King Henry's men stirred the townsmen to lay siege to the earls, urging them to arm themselves and going so far as to hand out weapons from the town armoury, with the promise of a bounty to everybody involved in their capture and execution.'

I tried to show no emotion at this dire news but asked simply, 'So who was involved at this time?'

'There was young Thomas Holand, of course, and the earl of Salisbury, John Montagu, and a few others.' He shrugged.

'So what happened next?'

'That's it,' he replied. 'They forced them out of their hiding place when somebody started a fire in the town as a diversion. Without more ado they dragged the leaders to the market place and cut off their heads there and then.'

I couldn't square the fellow's cheery expression with the facts he was laying before me. 'And this is God's truth, is it? They are dead, all of them?'

'True as I stand here, brother. A victory for King Henry, say I, and he hasn't had to lift a finger.'

When I returned to the wagon where Fulke and the others had gone I saw by their faces that they had heard something similar. They looked confused, shocked, and somewhat disbelieving.

'Do you think it's true?' I asked without greeting.

'About Tom Holand, the earl of Kent and his men?'

'And John Montagu, so I hear.'

'If it is true, and who's to say it's not, it's a fair day for King Henry.' Will turned away. His face was set in stone.

Underwood had his hood pulled half over and I could not gauge his reaction. Only Fulke expressed what amounted to a seditious response when he muttered something about the gates of hell being fully opened. I was pleased to see that our shadow, Edfrith, was nowhere within hearing.

The journey proceeded.

There were more rumours as we approached the middle country where news from the south was more quickly heard than in our northern fastness.

It was good, if anything was good, that Richard had known nothing of any of this. If he had ever had hopes of the country folk rising in his support he would have been disappointed. They were like sheep waiting at a gate for the shepherd and his dog. I am reminded of someone once likening the shepherd to a fox. Bad luck for the sheep in that case.

As for many folk in the towns, their glee at lawlessness and bloodshed makes me grieve for the realm of England. I see it sliding ever more deeply into barbarism.

The cortege is accompanied every step of the way by changing squads of Benedictines. Their black habits especially with their hoods pulled up render them the very image of death. Smoking flares carried through the night hours add to their sinister appearance so that I might even begin to believe in the devil myself if common sense did not pull me back from the brink of superstition.

Chandler paused to gather his thoughts. It was halfway through the night, the hour when, in more predictable times, he might have been preparing for the night office. Sometimes this felt like the most rewarding time of all. The call of the material world was less insistent. Now, the entire camp was silent. Not even a dog barked.

As ever the guards on duty round the hearse were leaning on their staves, probably sleeping as best they could. Light flickered and played over the black canopy of the hearse. Sightseers had dwindled to very few at this time of night. I must press on, Chandler told himself looking down at his pages in the candlelight. There is so much more to say.

In our masters' haste to reach London we walk until near midnight, stopping for a few hours' rest, then on again. Everywhere we go people throng the route. By the light of day and even by the dark of night they swarm from the fields and vills, drawn, no doubt, by the long serpent of flares winding along the dark lanes. They appear from everywhere in a silent, moving mass to observe the spectacle of the king's corpse passing by.

Is it threatening the way they gather on both sides of the track? They stand among the scrub where the King's Highway has been cleared or on the edge of field strips and on the verge of the wildwood. We cannot gauge their mood. Should we fear them? They stand like dumb beasts, sheep, as I say, staring in silence as we pass.

After the rains we encountered ever since we left the brooding walls of Pontefract, it has been heavy-going. Frost greets us most mornings but does not last.

Often comes the shout, 'Dun's in t'mire!' It brings the whole cavalcade to a halt while some unfortunate mule or sumpter pony is helped back into its shafts or, with a broken leg, knifed and left by the roadside, or a wheel, damaged in the ruts, is hammered back into place by some muscular brute. No wonder we are ordered to keep going for as long as we can put one foot before another with such regular delays.

He called it a night then, put his quill away, re-stoppered his ink, and lay down where he was, cloak over his head, and fell asleep at once.

8

So the journey continued. Before long Swynford sent an esquire back down the line to conduct Chandler to where he sat nested in furs under the cover of a char at the front of the cortege.

'Brother,' he greeted him. 'Tell me, how are the men faring further back?'

'In the usual manner, my lord, as best they can.'

He beckoned him closer. 'Anything to tell me?'

'Nothing, my lord.'

'No murmur of what we spoke of among your bowmen friends?'

'Nothing that I have heard, my lord.'

He raised his eyebrows. 'And?'

'More interested in the state of their feet and the quality of their ale, my lord.'

He sent him back after offering him a sweetmeat of some honeyed type from a dish beside him.

Chandler's growing self-disgust made anything bestowed by Swynford's hand impossible to digest. He gave it to one of the kitcheners who appreciated such titbits.

Still, he had not lied. His sense of shifting secrets was his own and was not fixed in dogma. Indeed, rebellion seemed to be the last thing on anybody's mind. What the silent onlookers were thinking was another matter and one not to be plumbed by anyone.

All Chandler could think of writing about this encounter was: *'London is a far-off dream of ease and corruption, a chimera none of my trio of bowmen believe in. Their thoughts go no further than the next mile and the meal to follow.'*

FOUR

Westminster. February 1400.

They are trying to scry the future in a dish of clear water. The Master and Adam are no doubt hoping for a sign that the old days of King Richard are coming back. I, in the hope of . . . well, that goes without saying.

There are five of us. Enough to form a pentagram, we are told. Present, apart from myself, the Master and Adam, of course, Cook and the mage.

The only light comes from a thick beeswax candle shedding a glow over the dish of water but leaving the rest of the chamber in shadow. The four men cluster round the dish in silence.

I stare hard but can see nothing in the water except the ripples of light across the surface caused by our breath. We sit very still for what seems like an age. Somewhere out beyond the Close a dog barks.

When he judges the time right the mage sighs with something like satisfaction. I can't see why because nothing has changed. He lifts his head and turns shining eyes on us one by one.

I try not to hold his glance and break away first but when I look back at him he is staring at me and gives a small smile I take to be one of triumph at getting me to look at him again.

To my astonishment he says, 'There is one here among you who has given of their power without stint. I think you know who I mean.' He pauses. 'Matilda, Queen of the May.'

I'm embarrassed. I'm no Queen of the May! Does he know the truth? The others are staring at me and I can do no else than give a small shrug to disclaim any involvement. Adam is smirking. I give him a black glare.

The Master leans forward and peers into the bowl again like a blind man. Catching his expression the mage makes a sign of some sort over the water again and mutters, 'Hush now.'

He starts to moan and his eyeballs go up in his head and he begins to shudder and moan some more and in an ethereal voice intones, 'Aaah . . . I see a man . . . I see him strike another on the side of the head with the flat of his sword . . .'

He moans again and begins to describe a scene as if it is passing before his eyes, his eyeballs flicking back and forth behind his lids and he goes something like, 'I see a blade of shining steel . . . I see it slice through the air with the speed of a hawk . . . I see it strike the man's neck, cut skin, flesh, innards, piercing to the bone . . . I see his head tilt, he falls, the stump left headless, blood spouting . . . man shivers, standing . . . blood . . . much blood . . . man falls, his head rolls on the ground, is stilled by the boot of . . . dark, all is dark . . . the fire is built . . . bells toll . . . a man's hands, tied to a stake and flames – flames . . . smoke . . . I cannot see . . . too much smoke . . . wait! . . . another man, headless—'

Adam puts his hands over my ears. 'Desist, now, brother, you go too far!'

He glares at the mage who jerks back as if punched in the face and starts to writhe and groan in his chair and then his breath begins, very fast, and I fear he is having an attack of some sort but little by little his breathing becomes more normal and while we all stare without daring to speak he eventually opens his eyes and blinks round.

He seems not to know who we are but gradually he becomes almost lively, smiling, shaking his head as if to clear it, flexing his fingers. 'Did anything happen?'

FIVE

On the road. March 1400.

Swynford rode back along the line to establish his authority after a scuffle broke out among the Pontefract men. A pikeman's nose had been broken and he was asking to stay in the next town to get it fixed.

All three longbow-men were sitting with Chandler as Swynford rode past. He glanced briefly into the wagon but made no sign of recognition although he must have noticed Chandler.

Fulke nudged him. 'What did he say to you about this murdered garrison man when you went to see him that night, brother? I bet he didn't feel happy at having him picked off.'

'He didn't share his thoughts with me.' Chandler frowned. 'What do you think he felt?'

'Damn all. One down. More work for the others.'

'I expect so.'

'What's a man to him?'

'Indeed.'

The wagon rumbled on again as Swynford made his way back with his horsemen clustering protectively round him.

'You reckon he's afraid of us?' Will asked, his glance following after them.

'Wouldn't you be?' Underwood suddenly realized he might have spoken incautiously and looked down to study his hands.

To ease the situation Chandler gazed deliberately towards the river that ran alongside that bit of the London road and changed the subject, mentioning the murdered man and the lack of clues as to who had seen him off. The searchers who had gone out into the woods in the hope of apprehending the murderer had come back with nothing. If anybody knew anything they were keeping quiet.

'It might be, as some are saying, a madman,' Chandler mused. 'Or somebody with a grievance against all the military and taking a chance. Or it might be somebody with a personal grudge.'

'You're not accusing us, I hope?' Fulke interrupted in a somewhat belligerent tone, despite his attempt at a smile.

'I can hardly accuse you and regard myself as a rational being,' replied Chandler, equably, as if preparing for a monkish debate about what was or was not rational. 'Where is our evidence to give us cause to accuse anyone? . . . I would solve the mystery for its own sake,' he added when no one responded.

'Look no further than the man himself,' Will interrupted. 'It turns out he was the fellow who stabbed and kicked that poor hound half to death. He might have aroused thoughts of revenge in those who were fond of the creature – or so they're saying,' he added quickly.

Chandler's own thoughts flew back to the little kitchen lad who had been so moved by the dog's plight. He had not seen him since leaving him to continue caring for the animal the morning they left. He wondered if he had been brought along with the cortege and decided to find out. Not that he believed such a little fellow could wield a bow. But maybe his grief had prompted someone to avenge the dog on his behalf?

He climbed over the side of the wagon and dropped down to his feet. 'Need to stretch my legs,' he announced.

To his surprise Fulke followed him.

The sumpter wagons were at the back of the cavalcade, still laden high with feed for the men. They waited until they drew level. It gave Chandler the opportunity to glance at the line of kitcheners walking alongside. He did not recognize many of them. The master cook was seated in some comfort with his chief assistants and his clerk but the rest took what respite they could by clinging onto the sides of the wagons for a few miles before having to drop to their feet to allow others to have a ride. The dog boy was not among them. He must have stayed in Pontefract.

'Was that pike-man known for his cruelty to animals?' Chandler asked when Fulke gave Chandler a quizzical glance as if to say, what are we up to here.

'A bad lot. Best avoided. Vicious to man and beast. Good riddance.' Fulke crossed himself. 'Nobody will be bothered he's gone. They'll close ranks. You'll never find out who did it.'

'Nobody boasting about a job well done? Maybe I'll curb my curiosity then.' Chandler turned to go back up the line.

Fulke's purpose in following him became clear when he kept pace with him and asked, 'Swynford gives you noticeable attention.'

'More than I would wish.'

'They say you're in his pay. Are you?'

'You're very blunt.'

'I'm a Yorkshireman. It goes with the territory.'

'I'm half Castilian. I'm not sure what territory that leaves me in at present.'

'King of Castile,' Fulke remarked in a derisory tone. 'Only a duke of Lancaster would dream that one up! Old Gaunt, calling himself king!'

'Or King of England if it comes to it?' Chandler looked sidelong. Fulke was watching him.

'Right,' he said when he caught Chandler's eye. 'Greed and ambition. What will Swynford make of that when you tell him?' He paused. 'You have, if I may say so, a certain sleight of mind when it comes to deflecting a question.'

'Blame it on being brought up at court. I will answer you. I thought everybody knew to whom my fealty is owed. It's straightforward. I did not choose to be made a ward of John of Gaunt nor be obliged to be part of his retinue nor that of his son. I am bought and sold. Ham-strung. Is that plain enough for you?'

'Once in their pay, never out of it?'

'Isn't everybody in the pay of a master of some sort?'

'I'm a free man. A simple bowman. What do I know? I'm hired to do a job. If I like it, I do it. I'm paid. I move on.'

'Fortunate and free. Many must envy you.'

'I see we're going to get nowhere today. I'll leave you for now. Be careful how you tread.' He raised one hand in an enigmatic farewell and walked off to join some acquaintances he had caught up with. His bow was as usual slung across his back and a quiver of arrows hung from his left shoulder. He sounded like a man who never had any doubts about anything. Enviable, if you were given to envy.

Chandler's Chronicle

As if summoned by demons listening in to what Fulke had told me, that I would never find the murderer of the garrison man, and deciding to teach me a lesson, they provided one. Another corpse, I mean, as well as another lesson in the ways and customs of demons.

It was a lesson given without delay.

Almost at once, after leaving Fulke with his friends and as I was walking back towards the middle of the cortege to pay some unobtrusive respects to the body of the king, the lesson came.

The procession was winding downhill into a wood at the time. Trees grew densely beyond the verge ten feet distant, tall oaks behind and a thicket of alders and ash nearer to the track, their leafless branches wound as thick as threads on a tapestry. They provided good cover for anybody up a tree with a bow and arrow.

As so it proved.

I heard the winnowing sound of feathers as an arrow flew through the air above my head. I heard the thud as it hit a target. Silence. Then screams. Next, shouts. Oaths followed. Then uproar.

A mad scramble ensued as men tried to take cover while others ran towards the scene or into the woods where they guessed the arrow had come from. I was close enough to see everything except for the bowman wherever he was.

His victim was one of Swynford's seneschals, an elderly official approaching fifty, with a wispy grey beard and a parti-coloured cotte open at the neck. He stood straight up like a house-pole in the wagon he was travelling in, clutching with both hands at the arrow in his chest. His expression was one of surprise more than anything else. Perhaps shriven that morning he showed no fear of death.

When it dawned on him that he was shot his eyes flashed with rage. Then he toppled slowly from the wagon into the crowd of foot-travellers massed alongside. They were the first who scattered and created uproar. Their commotion rippled along the line like a stone thrown into a mill pond.

It took only moments for the wagons to lumber to a halt. The horses were plunging and rearing in alarm. A message must have flown like lightning up the line because Swynford himself and his bodyguards arrived swiftly at the scene.

I thought it might be useful to go over to the trees to see what could be seen, if anything, but by the time I reached the other side and walked back near to where the arrow must have come from there was of course no sign of the perpetrator. Others had had the same idea and the woods were thick with men.

I returned and walked up towards the wounded man. He was in fact more than wounded. He was dead. Whoever had shot such a straight arrow had an unerring eye and an almost godlike knowledge of where to place a dart in order to kill a man. My thoughts naturally flew back to the conversation we previously had concerning the possibility of one arrow being able to set fire to an entire vill. The power wielded by the longbow was awesome.

There was nothing much I could do here but Swynford caught sight of me and beckoned.

'Is it the same murdering bastard?'

'I would not know, my lord.'

'It has to be. We have a murderer with us.'

I might have pointed out, purely as a matter of philosophical interest, that we had many murderers with us and that is what he, as their lord, paid them to be. But I restrained my retort and waited to see what he would ask of me next.

'Find him,' he grunted. 'I don't care how you do it, but find him. Earn your keep.'

Some swearing response occurred to me about not being God himself, Knower-of-All-Things, but I considered it best to clamp my lips together and bow my head. He dismissed me with his usual snarl.

Men were still swarming into the woods but their chances of catching anyone were slim by now as the bowman would already have had the sense to leave his perch and mingle with the searchers. I followed, nevertheless, and met up with a group of pike-men standing round an oak.

At first, thinking I was mistaken and the fellow was still up there, I hastened forward. It was, however, merely the fresh scrapings of boot marks on the sodden bark where he had scrambled up to a branch that offered a steady platform and a bird's-eye view of his victim. The heels of a pair of boots had been driven hard into the mud underneath the tree where he had presumably jumped down after the deed was done. I followed them a little way but soon lost them in the undergrowth.

Certainly one thing was clear. The steps led directly back towards the track.

The others were still beating about in the woodland but it was too dense to allow anyone to get far without leaving an obvious trail of broken branches. Some others were aimlessly walking along the verge where no man could have hidden. I should have told them not to waste their efforts. The bowman would be back already, sitting in a cart or mingling with a group of friends and nobody the wiser.

I took out my ink and quill and a much-scraped piece of vellum from my scrip and made a rough drawing of the print under the oak tree but it was like a hundred others and I do not regard it as having any real importance.

After that, with a final glance round about as if in the childish hope of finding the fellow's name carved into the bark, I returned to the wagon where my three friends were sitting in silence. In fact every man-jack of us was silent for several miles after that, busy with our own thoughts and perhaps speculating about retribution.

The dead man was lying on the tailgate of one of the wagons to be conveyed to where he could be decently buried, while all eyes searched the trees, more for personal safety, to catch sight of the killer before he sighted them, than in any hope of apprehending him, I doubt not.

And so the journey of the king continued towards its destination.

2

Despite exhortations to earn his keep, Swynford was as like to have Chandler disposed of as to pay him the arrears Henry Lancaster, king, had owed him these last three months. At the next stop to water the horses Chandler therefore headed for the ale wagon where a dozen or so guards were hanging about.

'Bad business,' he observed as he held out his mug under the spigot. 'Who's the culprit. Any idea?' He glanced round at the group standing round the barrel.

'If we knew, brother, do you imagine we'd be standing here supping this swill? We'd be dancing round his head on a pike by now, believe me.'

'And collecting pay for a job well done,' somebody else added.

'Not many bowmen could get in such a shot,' Chandler continued. 'Even that first killing by the campfires was skilled, finding his target in the dark aided only by the light from the fires.'

'Not so skilled,' one of them objected. 'The fellow he got was lighted up like a beacon by the fire where he sat. A child could have hit him.'

'What about this last go?' Chandler countered.

'Depends where he was shooting from,' the same man objected.

Another fellow joined the discussion. 'If he was close enough to the road he could have reached down and put the arrow in by hand.' He downed his ale and wiped the back of his hand across his mouth as if that proved his point.

'Do you think he was close to the road?'

He stared back at Chandler for a long moment then shook his head.

'But near enough?'

'What we mean to say,' interrupted the first bowman, 'is that – as we weren't present ourselves, brother, we guess it wouldn't take any great skill to kill two men the way he has done. But—' he paused, 'it would take some skill – likely no more than any man worth the name of bowman . . . in my opinion.'

Chandler adopted a puzzled frown. 'You seem to think it was the same man as before?'

General chuntering followed and a few arguments and counter-arguments flew back and forth arriving at no very fixed conclusion. It could be the same man, it could be two men, either in collusion or separately. Nobody present could agree on which was the most likely. All they knew was, it was nobody they themselves knew of.

Chandler finished his ale and moved on. He doubted whether he could find out anything this way but at least it would appease Swynford to see him at work.

He was up near the front of the column by now and chancing to look up he noticed Swynford's eyes on him.

Chandler's Chronicle

Next comes more news from the south. It is a variation on what we have already heard, about the barbaric events in Cirencester.

As in the earlier rumour it involves the earl of Kent, Thomas Holand, who, escaping into the west after his small victory at the Thames bridge, had persuaded a knight called Walter Hungerford to join his army.

Apparently, when they reached the town of Cirencester, this Hungerford, whose father happened to be a former steward of the Lancasters, deceitfully alerted the town bailiff who promptly gathered his men and, as we have already heard, besieged the inn where the rebel earls were lodging for the night.

This adds little to what we already knew.

However, there is more.

We had been told that after they were captured, my lords Holand and Montague were beheaded by the good people of Cirencester in the market square.

The latest messenger supplied a variation on this rumour and went on to tell us that John Norbury, whom I've always understood to be Henry's chief fixer, Treasurer of England, has sworn to attend the king himself to bring the captives including Holand and Montague to Oxford a week hence.

This is a great puzzle to us. Does it mean that the two earls are safe and merely awaiting Henry's pleasure in Oxford? Or is the earlier information true, that they have already met their fate, offering Henry the honour of greeting only their bodiless heads?

We do not know the answer to this without further intelligence coming our way.

I must add that various other victims were mentioned by the same messenger. Several rebels, he explained, had likewise been taken by the bailiff and awaited the king's pleasure in Oxford.

If, indeed, their expectations have not already been satisfied, these men are Sir Ralph Lumley, Sir Benedict Sely and Sir Thomas Blount. Everyone of them is a known supporter and long-time, loyal retainer of King Richard.

No one here can give credence to any of this as the closer to London we approach the faster contradictory reports fly in.

SIX

Westminster. March 1400.

After Chaucer threw the scryer, the so-called mage, out of the house he and Adam spent a long time closeted in the front chamber where Adam does the copying. I could hear the Master pacing back and forth, his voice going on and on and then for a while Adam's voice as he repeated what he had written. And then the noise of shuffling pages as they were put away out of sight.

Nobody will come here into the precinct to check on what he's writing. Surely we are safe here within the abbey walls, as Cook says?

Yet day by day we hear of more horrors from the north.

The scryer predicted none of the details, only general violence which we ourselves could have imagined without looking into a saucer of magic water.

His biggest blunder was not to mention the worst of what we feared.

It is more than rumour now. A proclamation on the steps of St Paul's and here at Westminster confirms it as fact.

King Richard is dead.

Westminster Abbey is in mourning.

The altar is draped in black.

All day and most of the night we can hear the monks singing the tenebrae, the requiem, the mass for the dead. The big bell tolls without cease.

Adam, newly returning from the City, tells us that out in the streets all the way along the strand and past Charing Cross and down to Westminster people are blundering about like dumb beasts as if they don't know where to go. When the mayor made the announcement on Mansion House steps a great howl of grief went up. Men as well as women were openly sobbing.

Now, every day that passes we hear about more of King Richard's supporters being hunted down, more beheadings, unlawful hangings, and the quarterings of human beings like beasts in the shambles.

A story that shakes through London is that Sir Thomas Blount and twenty-five others were forced to walk from Cirencester to Oxford, barefoot and in chains, where they were butchered and their bodies quartered and slung in sacks to be brought here to London. The pieces are going to be hung at every gate into the City, at Aldgate, Aldersgate, Ludgate, and on the bridge.

While they were being marched to their deaths in Oxford a group of men tried to rescue them but they were butchered as well and their bodies were thrown into the Green Ditch near the castle.

I cannot bear to think about it.

We are struck dumb. We go about our necessary chores, speechless and sightless with grief.

When did he die? we ask. The soothsayers cannot tell us. Some say the French announced his death on the day of St Valentine. Others say it must have been later than that, in March, because it is only now that it has been officially announced. There is great confusion. Those in charge are lying to us. What can we do?

Were there comets? Yes, the soothsayers insist. It was foretold. The Prophecy of the Six Kings has come true. The Mold-Warp reigns.

Plans are being made for us by the Master but I have no idea what they entail. I dare not ask.

SEVEN

Chandler's Chronicle

Another story comes to my ears. I hardly dare make record of what has happened. Only the urge to bear witness gives me the courage to place one word after another.

Things went badly with the rebellion after Cirencester. It was worse than we had at first been told.

There are several versions of these events. One is that a fire was built in the market square and this must have been at Oxford after Sir Thomas Blount was made to walk in chains from Cirencester. When he arrived they say he was dragged through a rabble of onlookers so dense that armed men had to force a path through the crowd ahead of him to allow him to take his punishment.

The executioner, with a sack over his head with slits for eyes, was handed a butcher's knife by one of his assistants. Sir Thomas was dragged right up to the fire when the flames caught hold. As they began to rage up to the height of a man the crowd jostled and bayed for blood.

Sweating from the heat despite the wintry weather, the executioner ripped open Sir Thomas's shirt and breeches so that the knife would not be impeded as he plunged it into his prisoner's belly. With practised dexterity the executioner, a local slaughter man, reached inside to pull out Sir Thomas's intestines while he lived. These he threw onto the fire and the stink and crackle of body fat must have been overwhelming to those standing nearest.

As you can imagine, a bunch of youths from the town would be as close as they could get in order not to miss the fun as they would see it.

While Sir Thomas lay on the ground in his agony the executioner asked him if he would like a drink of ale to ease the pain. Able to speak and having lost none of his courage, Sir Thomas replied, 'I would welcome a drink, except that you have unkindly removed the wherewithal to enjoy it.'

Even the brutes standing close by, yearning with animal lust for his death, were impressed by his spirit. Mayhap it made some of them think twice about their allegiance.

So, Sir Thomas Blount and his allies are the heroes of this rebellion against the usurper, with other men of courage, and women too, the lady Constance taking as full a part as any of the men, as it is rumoured, and now imprisoned for her loyalty.

It is my constant fear that I must keep these notes secret until I find a safe place for them or it will be my guts burned before my eyes if they fall into the wrong hands.

2

By now London was only twenty miles away and St Albans was the last town on the great north road where they would make a halt.

Exhausted by the continual rumbling of wagon wheels over the ruts in the dryer country of the south they were all eager to reach their destination. The men-at-arms, some of whom had walked the entire distance, looked as strong and sound as ever, no doubt made even more hardy by their physical exertions. Others were near exhaustion.

The bowmen who shared the wagon with Chandler were mostly silent as they approached what, for them, was the unnatural habitat of the market town. Open fields and woodlands were more their style.

Fulke admitted he felt uneasy. 'All those buildings with their windows on high. Who can tell what enemy lurks out of sight? In open country an alert fellow can predict danger before it can do for him.'

'It wasn't much help to Swynford's seneschal, the countryside,' Chandler remarked.

'That's because he spent his life as a courtier passing on orders and had lost the ability to scent an enemy,' Underwood muttered in a bitter tone.

'So have many of us,' Chandler couldn't help observing.

This drew black looks, a warning, as if he needed it, that they were in the midst of enemies wherever they went in these dark days and didn't need telling.

'It's a gracious town,' Chandler remarked to deflect the undercurrent of hostility. 'By looks only,' he added. 'The St Alban monastics were unfriendly to the followers of John Ball back in the Hurling Time, if you remember, and there's doubtless still much animosity between them and the towns folk over the matter of flour mills.'

He was referring to a scandal everyone knew about concerning the banning of hand-mills used in people's homes to avoid the extortionate rates demanded by the abbey miller at the large windmill within the purlieus.

The abbot had been so incensed at the obstinacy of the townsfolk and their refusal to pay his exorbitant fee he had sent men to gather up all their hand mills and had them levelled into the entrance to the church so that they would have the humiliation of being forced to walk over their own now useless mills whenever they were called to prayer.

'They won't be unfriendly to Swynford,' muttered Fulke. 'The monks, I mean.'

'So I believe. They're a Lancastrian endowment and are unlikely to speak against their paymasters. In fact their abbot's scriptorium is overseen by one Walsingham, the author of a most biased chronicle in which he blames King Richard for every ill conceived by man and every fault the human soul is heir to.'

'How do you know that?' Fulke asked but Chandler merely shrugged and murmured something about him having read it for himself.

Chandler's Chronicle

As soon as we settle into our quarters we discover what has happened to Huntingdon, John Holand, King Richard's stepbrother. It was his mother, don't forget, who was known as the Fair Maid of Kent because of her beauty and charm and it was no surprise that King Richard, her son from her second marriage, should be so handsome they called him the new Absalom.

Be that as it may, the story went that John Holand had fled London to take ship for Flanders or some other safe haven across the sea but had been driven back by January storms.

Now a new messenger arrives to inform us that the earl has taken shelter with Sir Aubrey de Vere, the earl of Oxford, whose own elder brother, Robert, the ninth earl, had been one of Richard's most loyal supporters. It was Robert's doom to be a victim of the Appellants in the Merciless Parliament when the barons banded together the better to curb the king before he curbed them.

It was that period, remember, when there was the first bloodletting and the barons thrust aside the rule of law to behead King Richard's allies without trial. These so-called Appellants, Gloucester and his crew, included Henry Bolingbroke and poor Mowbray whose alleged fears for their own safety brought on the present barbarism. Fortunately, Robert the ninth earl, escaped their cruelty for a short time by fleeing into exile.

His youngest brother, Aubrey, happened to come into the earldom when the middle brother of these three died – one assumes of natural causes, although who can tell in this time of unprecedented cruelty? Aubrey was not much involved in events at court, choosing to live peacefully between his castles at Hedingham and Hadleigh with his wife, Alice Fitzwalter as was.

It was in the latter stronghold, Hadleigh, built as a sea defence by Edward III during his wars with France, and lying right by the mouth of the Thames where it opens out into a wide, marshy estuary, that the earl of Huntingdon, John Holand as I should say, had sought safety, no doubt hoping for a ship and a change in the weather to effect his escape out of the realm.

Our messenger smiled round at us. 'The traitor,' he added and was unfazed by our blank stares.

Of course I replied not a word to his remark about traitors but black kettles and pots sprang to mind. Tu quo que, as the monks would say.

He went on to tell us that Lancaster's blood-hounds had tracked Holand to the house of an esquire called John Prittlewell, from whence they dragged him back to the castle at Pleshey. From there they no doubt intended to convey him to London to stand trial.

However, such was Holand's ill luck, the countess of Hereford, Lady Joan Fitzalan, was at Pleshey. She was kin to Thomas Arundel, the new, self-appointed archbishop, and she also happened to be mother-in-law to Henry himself as well as to no less than Edmund of Woodstock – I mean The Fox, the traitorous and ambitious duke of Gloucester, Richard's arch-enemy in former days.

No doubt motivated by a feeling of vengefulness after his unexplained murder at Calais that sparked Bolingbroke's banishment, she encouraged her servants to fling open the gates to the clamouring locals and urged them to do what they would with poor John.

The horrifying scene can be imagined. It ended when Holand was beheaded in the exact spot where the Fox had been arrested on a charge of treason three years previously and finished up in the Calais prison from which he never emerged alive.

One imagines that the courtyard at Pleshey was tainted, in the view of the countess, by the death of the Fox despite his having started this whole sorry business of ambition, murder, double-dealing, revenge and the downfall of the rightful king and incipient destruction of the realm of England.

3

It never ceased to bother him that he was no nearer discovering the murderer of the two men in Swynford's retinue than when he was ordered to do something about it on the way down.

He wondered how he was expected to go about it when everyone dispersed when they reached London, with the bulk of the army being sent to an encampment at Five Fields near Ebury Manor. It would make it nigh on impossible to take things further.

Did he fear Swynford's threat? Only in the sense that a prudent man might fear assault on some lonely road and take steps to avoid it.

He had decided he need look no further than the trio he was travelling with for a likely suspect or two. Any one of them might have drawn his bow in a fit of self-righteous rage at what was taking place. He had grasped where their affinities lay. Underwood for instance. His truncated confession suggested there was more to come.

All three were morose at any mention of Henry and his Lancastrian ilk, although, to be fair, they seemed no more cheerful at being tainted with the same brush as the rebels. Proud, maybe, to owe allegiance to neither house? Who could tell? The rest of Swynford's men exulted in wearing Lancaster's colours. They didn't care as long as they were on the winning side.

The arrow interested him, of course, the one Will confiscated at the first murder. Those feathers. He wondered about them. They were quite distinctive. He knew it was a matter of pride for the true experts to fletch their own arrows.

He distracted himself with all this not only because he couldn't fob off Swynford for ever but also because the image of a young woman with golden hair only twenty miles away taunted him. Was she waiting for him as she promised? He knew he had no right to expect such consideration. And yet, to his surprise, he longed for it.

Underwood happened to catch him staring at the arrows in his quiver while these thoughts fluttered through his mind and asked him what he was looking at.

'The f-fletcher's art is one I admire,' he stammered, putting out a finger to touch the feathers as if stroking a hawk. He tried to remember where Underwood was when both victims were shot. 'What are the fletchers like who travel with us?'

'They suffice.' Underwood was never one to use more words than absolutely necessary, doling them out like hard-earned coin.

'I suppose you fletch your own?'

When he said nothing he gave up and walked off towards the cloister.

4

Shortly after arriving at St Albans he got into conversation with a young monk who came out to greet them.

After a few preliminaries, the fellow announced, 'Things are looking lively down in London. Dissent against the Church is being seen increasingly as dissent against the—' he paused as if to correct himself and continued, 'against King Henry.'

They both searched deep into each other's eyes in the hope of plumbing the other's soul to discern the truth, neither of them apparently willing to risk an opinion that might land them in the conflagration of Arundel's orthodox fires.

Eventually Chandler conceded that, 'The Archbishop is ever keen to stamp out heresy.'

'And now he has found a monarch willing to back him in his endeavour,' the monk riposted.

Fearing a trap, for who was to say the young fellow was not ambitious enough to draw heretics to their deaths the better to earn his abbot's esteem, Chandler said nothing. Who am I? A friar of an alien cult. This is not the place I expect to find allies, he thought.

'Are they still considering the need to bring in a burning law?' he asked in a tone seeking information rather than offering criticism.

'We heard rumours on our way down here that they hope to have something on the statute books by the end of the year.'

The monk remarked that it seemed likely.

Eventually he directed him to the guest refectory and Chandler thanked him and following his instructions was brought out in a wide, fair court with the refectory close at hand from which already came the noise of men celebrating the near conclusion of their long march.

Pontefract was like a world apart, a bad dream, except for the knowledge that its very real consequences would resonate for decades to come.

Reluctant to enter the hurly burly of the hall and an army of men drinking and eating there he took a seat on a stone bench and gazed out across the grass to where a fountain placidly cascaded into a stone basin and waited for an explosion of grace to carry him forward.

EIGHT

Westminster. March 1400.

'Adam,' I begin. 'I have something to confess.'

He jerks his head up from his writing desk. 'Do I look like a priest?'

'Not with your long hair tied back in that leather boot lace,' I tell him, to sound light.

He sighs and puts down his quill. 'Come on then, out with it. You've nearly made me wreck this page for the master. It's only taken me all day.'

'It looks fine to me.'

'What would you know?'

'Don't bother then. I've changed my mind. I'll tell you some other time. I can see you're not in the mood.'

I walk off into the little herb garden at the back of the house. Last autumn we stood out in the yard at the house in the Vintry, the neighbours who shared the water from the pump with us, that is, and while we filled our jugs we talked about the imprisonment of King Richard at the Tower and what would happen if they made him abdicate.

It seemed impossible then that any such thing would ever really happen. But that was then.

Now we know.

Anything can happen.

Adam never talks about it.

I fear that if I start weeping I shall never stop.

The Master says little but I know he is worried. They are working at his pilgrim tales to make them less dangerous.

'What was I thinking—' he cries in despair. 'The whole set of them show pilgrims for what they are. Sinful and sinning. Hypocrites all. The Church nothing but a leech on us. Are we to blame the mirror for the images it shows us? We all know folk go on pilgrimages to indulge their lusts in the pleasures of the world, swyving and drinking and all that. Now it's a crime to say so and to call the whole thing a sham, is it? Is Arundel going to line us all up and accuse us of what he calls heresy? Is he going to pitch us all into his fires? Are we not flesh and blood with everything that entails?'

He goes on for some time in like mode and of course there is no answer any of us can offer that will pacify him. We are walking on broken glass and we know it.

The Lollards are being pursued because of what they believe about the saints and pilgrimage, and the Eucharist and the corruption of the Church with its continual demand for tithes and taxes, and the luxury in which so many churchmen live while others starve. Anybody with the courage to speak out is accused of being a Lollard and suffers the consequences. I think it's reasonable to want to read the Bible in our own language instead of having the Church tell us what it says to suit itself. But every day people are more scared that they'll be overheard saying something forbidden and be reported to their parish priest, knowing that from there it's but a short step to the bishop, to Arundel and to the Tower.

How can they stop us speaking what is true in our hearts? How can an incautious word lead to your death? It's not right.

This isn't what I wanted to say to Adam. That will have to wait. Maybe for ever.

Why do I need to confess anything anyway? What I did, I own. It's for me to find a way out under my own efforts. What use would Adam be? Or a priest for that matter. Or anyone.

While I'm picking some rosemary for Cook, Adam comes outside. He walks up to me and stands off just looking at me.

'Don't frown, Mattie.'

I look at the ground and can't stop a tear sliding down my cheek. He comes close enough to put his arms round me and give me a hug. 'He'll be all right.'

I say, 'You can't know that. You don't even know where he is.'

He releases me and steps back, looking puzzled. 'Last time I heard him cursing he was in his chamber.'

I stare at him. Tears simply cascade from my eyes without my being able to stop them.

'Oh,' he says after a long moment while he stares at me, 'you mean him?'

I nod.

'Who is he?'

'I can't tell you.'

'Because you wanted to confess and I refused to listen to you?'

'It doesn't matter.'

He looks uncertain. I pull at some stems of rosemary and hold them and stand in a drift of scent. Nothing seems real.

'You can tell me his name – I promise I won't do anything against him if you don't want me to.'

I take a breath. I'm tempted to tell him, partly because I long to speak his name aloud. My desire to hear it spoken like a magic incantation persuades me that somehow, it can, it must bring him back to me. Wherever he is in the world he will be drawn here by the sound of his name. That is my hope and belief. *Dolt.*

Adam reads my uncertainty and urges me to name him. 'It'll make it easier to bear,' he says. 'I expect he lied to you and didn't tell you he was married. Is that it? I won't let on. You can tell me anything, Mattie, you know you can.'

And I think, why not? Why not just say it? My fingers twist a stem of rosemary and I scatter the dark spikes on the ground before I dare look at him.

I brace myself and whisper, 'It's Rodric.'

I can see it means nothing to him so I add a little louder, 'Rodric Chandler.' Even then he doesn't get it so I say, 'Brother Chandler – who came to the Master's meeting of alchemists before Christmas.'

He looks at me in stupefaction. His face goes white. 'Say that again.'

'It's Chandler. I don't know why you have to look like that—'

In reply he grips me by both shoulders and I struggle to get away as his fingers dig in, yelling, 'Stop it! You're bruising me!'

He shakes me as if he wants to kill me. I've never seen him so furious.

'Let me go!' I kick out.

He thrusts me away as if he hopes I'll fall to the ground and vanish.

'What have I done?'

He comes close to me again and grabs me by the hair. His teeth are gritted. He doesn't speak. His lips are white.

'I don't know what I'm supposed to have done!' I shriek, struggling to get away, but my hair has fallen down and he grips it and yanks my head about while I kick out at him and then he releases me so abruptly I fall to my knees. I clutch my stomach.

'You don't know what you've done, you empty-headed, witless child! You've placed a death sentence over us!'

'What? . . . What do you mean? I don't understand . . . I haven't done anything!'

'Are you so thick-headed you don't know who he is?'

'He's—'

'He's one of Lancaster's spies! You know that! . . . I spent three weeks at Saltwood being tortured by Arundel's devils! Look!' He removes the glove he has started wearing on his right hand and for the first time I see why he wears it.

I stifle a gasp. His nails have been ripped out. The ends of his fingers are swollen and sore. They look like little stumps. I wonder how he manages to hold a quill and write all day and whether it causes him as much pain as I'd imagine.

I can hardly speak. 'They did that to you – as well as the wounds you showed us on your back?'

'I stood against them and pretended I knew nothing. I did it for the Master. I knew what Arundel was hoping for. He wanted something he could destroy him with if he didn't come out on Lancaster's side and now you tell me about this betrayal!' He turns away in disgust.

I'm cut to the quick. I rise slowly to my feet and follow him. Grasping his sleeve I ask, 'How could I know it wasn't just a rumour, Adam? Why would I even imagine such a thing? And anyway, how can he be a spy? Did he tell you? If it's true why did the Master invite him here? I don't understand! You must be wrong.' But in my heart I know, as I have always known.

'What can I do?' I whisper when Adam turns and gives me a scorching look. There is no doubting the truth. 'I didn't tell him anything that would harm anybody. I don't know anything that could lead to harm.'

He goes to sit on the wooden bench with his head in his hands. After a moment or two he rubs his hands over his face with the damaged one held like a paw and looks up at me. 'Tell me exactly what you said if you can remember any of it.'

'Of course I can remember. Every word is carved in my memory.'

'Here.' He indicates the place next to him. 'I want it all.'

I sit beside him. 'We chatted the way a man and maid do when they—'

'Yes, and?'

The memory of lying next to him in the bed-straw floods over me. 'I saw an inscription over the door,' I mutter.

'The door where?'

'In his chantry.'

'You went there?'

I nod, blushing, shame-faced.

'So much for the holy friar. What did it say, this inscription? Virgins enter here if you dare?'

'It said "St Serapion" – that's his cult – "St Serapion, martyr for God." It was in a curly script but quite clear.'

'And it was I who taught you to read. Did you tell him that?'

I shake my head.

'What did he say to you when he discovered you were so erudite?'

'There's no need to be sarcastic. He just said something joking like, "I like a girl who can read."'

'I bet he does. Did he ask you what the Master was working on?'

'No.'

'Are you sure?'

I hesitate.

'Which one did you mention?'

'Don't be mean to me, Adam.'

'Archbishop Arundel will be more than mean to us if he gets the chance.'

'I didn't know the Master was a Lollard. I thought it was only Lollards Arundel was going after?'

'Don't be naive. What did you tell Brother Rodric?'

I speak in a small voice. 'I just happened to mention that he was translating the Book of the Lion.'

Adam makes a sound like a cry being ripped from his throat. He jerks to his feet. 'Is that it?' He strides halfway to the door.

I nod. 'I don't know anything else. You know I don't.'

'What did he say when you told him?'

'He asked me what it was about.'

'And what did you say?'

'I told him . . . I told him it was about a king beloved by his people and a prince who was jealous and wanted his crown – Adam, I told him it was a French story the Master was translating. That's not wrong, is it?'

'Think about it. A story like that? Then imagine how a usurper might regard it.'

He gives me the blackest look and with his head lowered hurries indoors. I hear him slam the door to the Master's writing chamber and it is ages before they both come out.

NINE

St Albans. March 1400.

Chandler was sitting by the door of the refectory, his beaker of ale supplied by the monks from their own brewery now empty in front of him. He had drunk it off in one draught and was feeling the effects when Will sauntered over from somewhere in the crowd and sat down beside him.

'Giving us the cold shoulder now we're nearly back in London, brother?'

Chandler matched his jocular tone. 'Not at all. I didn't see you and the lads. Have you eaten?'

'We have.' He indicated Chandler's empty beaker. 'Good stuff. Are you having another?' Before Chandler could answer he clicked his fingers to bring a servant over and two beakers were taken off his full tray and placed before them.

'Where are the others?' asked Chandler.

'Coming over.'

'Is something up?'

'What do you think?'

It wasn't like Will to be enigmatic and he said so.

'There's another one. And Swynford is looking for you.'

'Another what?'

'Where have you been for the last hour?'

'In the church.'

Will chuckled. 'I'd forgotten you might be there. Then I'll explain. There's another killing. Same thing. An arrow from out of nowhere. Dead shot. Some bowman, eh? Nearly as good as us!'

'Did he kill him?'

A look at Will's expression told him yes. 'Who was it?'

'One of Swynford's guards. He's erupting all over the place like a volcano. We're all going to be caught in the burning coals. Just thought I'd warn you.'

'And he's asking for me?'

'As I said.'

Chandler glanced up when Fulke and Underwood appeared. 'Are you in the front line because of your—?' He indicated their bows.

'We weren't anywhere near. We can prove it.'

'I hope you can. So you haven't come asking for my help?'

'It might be you wanting ours,' Fulke said.

They sat down and explained. 'He's keeping us all here until they lay hold of the murderer. He vows to have him tried at the abbey court before being turned over to the town gaoler and punishment.'

'God help him,' muttered Underwood.

He gave Chandler a wary glance but didn't say any more. Chandler thought he might guess what he wanted to say. It would be about his half-made confession back at Pontefract. Given his suppressed rage that was motive enough to get rid of a few Lancastrian regulars. He tried to convey the fact that a confession ended with him but Underwood turned away looking nervous.

'So where is he?' Chandler rose to his feet. He wanted to get out of here. Out of the whole scheme of things. As he stood uncertainly, trying to make up his mind whether to go and find Swynford or go somewhere and let him find him himself, one of his esquires hurried up.

'There you are, brother. Will you attend my lord presently.'

It wasn't a question. The lad pulled at his sleeve as if to wake him from a dream then plunged off into the crowd in the expectation that Chandler would follow.

'Better do as he says, brother,' advised Will with a sardonic smile. 'He needs somebody's brains to pick. It might as well be yours.'

'He won't find much there,' Chandler rejoined. He drained the beaker of ale Will had called for, shook his head to clear it then followed the esquire.

2

'Have you heard?' Swynford was more red-faced than usual.

Deciding not to play any dumber than he felt he nodded. 'I have, my lord. Pray tell me the details, if you will.'

'It was as the men were unloading the wagons down by the guest quarters where my personal guard are bunking down and, as before, out of nowhere an arrow—' He glared at Chandler. 'Your intimacy with those bowmen must have yielded some suspicions by now? Surely a word has been let slip hinting at disloyalty? They're not Lancastrians. I can vouch for my own men but I know there are those we had to take on, mercenaries, and mayhap there's disenchantment with our new king among such riffraff?'

'I've heard very little, my lord.' It was true. Hints and raised eyebrows meant nothing. 'As I've already mentioned, their chief gripes are about the ale and their feet. The latter should be less of a concern now we're near journey's end and the former seems to have met with approval which will last until it stops flowing. Who was the victim this time?'

'That's the point. It was one of my personal bodyguards. A man I trusted. He'll be a sad loss.'

'Getting closer to yourself, my lord—'

'I don't need to be told that!' he snarled. 'I want the devil found and strung up. That's what you're going to devote every minute of your waking life to, brother – find him or you will be held responsible.'

'I'll do my best,' he bowed his head, adding for luck, 'my lord.'

They were in an ante-chamber off the refectory and Swynford strode over to the door and kicked it shut. 'Listen, I'm instructing you to coordinate our information. My men are at work even as we speak, questioning every half-competent bowman travelling with us. We should have done it earlier but – on the road – difficulties – it's only now we have the leisure to seek him out.'

3

Chandler was provided with a stool and a table in the ante-chamber and after a brief discussion with Swynford and his captains it was decided that all mercenaries known to have uttered the slightest seditious remark would be brought before Chandler to be questioned. They would be ordered to account for their movements on three occasions, and also to produce three witnesses who could not have colluded in their testimony.

'That last's a tall order,' objected Chandler. 'What if some fellow says he went into the woods for a piss? Do we expect him to have taken a couple of escorts with him?'

'I don't care,' Swynford shouted, losing his temper after too long holding it in check. 'He's laughing at me. Me? He'll be laughing on the other side of his face when I get hold of him.'

4

Before they started dragging in the poor lunks under suspicion Chandler had time to return to the refectory to grab a drink. He told Swynford's esquire where he was going so there could be no misunderstanding.

While he was there he passed the trestle where Will and the others were talking and without stopping said, 'Make sure you know where you were the three times this bowman struck. You might be asked to come up with witnesses as well. I assume you were together except for that first time when Will was with me.'

He walked on.

Word spread like wildfire that there was going to be an interrogation and Chandler knew his name had been mentioned by the way people stood aside to let him pass. Taking a filled flagon and a pie or two for sustenance he made his way back to the ante-chamber.

It was already set out and the captain, a black-bearded drinker by the name of Studley, was already lounging in a chair he had brought in for himself.

'Do you have the necessaries, brother?' he greeted.

'If you mean pen and ink, yes. If you mean a crystal ball to scry which man is lying, no. We'll have to use our wits.'

Studley gave a little smile. 'We'll do that. My lord has decided somebody will pay the price.'

'Let's hope we find the right man for him.'

Studley sniggered. 'I see you're new to this game.'

The first suspect was dragged in between two escorts.

He was cowed, somewhat bloodied about the face, and without a bow slung over his shoulder he looked defenceless.

'I've told them,' he began at once, 'I only said, "I hope the king appreciates us the wear of our shoe leather." Everybody was saying the same. Look!' He lifted one of his feet and it was true the sole was well worn down to its inner lining and nearly falling off.

'What about your movements at the time?' Chandler asked. He waited with pen poised.

And so it went. Six men were brought in, some obviously having resisted more fiercely than others. Any one of them could have done it, assuming they were as profligate with the truth as everybody else – especially the king, thought Chandler, seditiously – think of last summer at Flint Castle – and when Swynford came in to check on how things were going he shook his head.

'Their alibis will need to be double-checked but according to them none of them were anywhere near the place where the arrows might reasonably have been let loose.'

Swynford asked him to read out his notes and listened with one hand stroking his beard.

'There's a fellow waiting outside,' he announced when Chandler came to the end. He looked irritated that so far there appeared to be no firm suspect if the testimonies were to be taken into account. 'Bring him forth, guard!'

It was John Underwood.

He stood in front of Chandler warily but with the pride to which he had already confessed and for which he had received absolution.

Chandler put down his quill. 'You fellows,' he glanced at the captain and the escorts who had brought Underwood in, 'you may tell me your grounds for bringing this man before me and then I will tell you why you are wrong.' He waited.

One of the escorts began to sweat. 'It's obvious why we picked him up. He's a crack bowman. We see him shooting arrows with some of our lads and he has them goggling. Who else but a crack shot could have pulled off three murders like this? Three of our men dead. It could have been us. Any of us, dead without warning. It could have been my lord Swynford.' He cuffed Underwood on the side of the head. 'This is the man!'

'Except that I was with a crowd of others all the time,' broke in Underwood, bunching his fists. 'Ask them. They'll tell you.'

'I bet they will! All mates together! You mercenaries are nothing but a nest of traitors!'

'Surely,' intoned Chandler, turning a face like stone towards the escort, 'you have checked this man's alibi?'

The escort sneered. 'These northerners stick together, you can't trust a word they say.'

'In that case,' Chandler made as if to rise, 'I and my colleague here have wasted our time.' He flicked at the pile of vellum containing the witness statements. 'I see you have in fact brought us a selection of northern mercenaries. If we can't trust a word these northerners say then their testimonies must be a pack of lies. Is that what you're telling us? That you and your fellow men-at-arms have been wasting our time?'

The escort stared at the floor.

'Come now, brother,' Studley urged as Chandler gathered the folds of his robe as if about to leave. 'Will you remain? I can see there might be doubt about the man's story.'

'I can vouch for him myself, as it happens.' Chandler sat down again. 'He's one of the bowmen who shared space with me in a wagon on the journey from Pontefract. I never heard a seditious word out of him the whole way down. At the time of the first death, I admit, I was not with him but I noticed he was in the company of others in his unit while I myself was talking to their captain. I was with him in person on the second occasion when we were sitting in the wagon at the time in question. And for this last murder, I assume he was unloading the gear along with everyone else, a fact that can be properly checked. Even if there is doubt, one out of three is enough to exonerate him, is it not? Release him and stop wasting our time.'

5

While Swynford laboriously read through the statements to see which one of them was most likely to give him chance to produce a scapegoat, Chandler walked out into the cloister for some air.

Somehow or other he found himself approaching the inner court of the abbey and when he saw one of the monks walking by he went over. After a few pleasantries he asked about the scriptorium. 'Its fame is known throughout the land,' he flattered.

Without saying anything he conducted him to someone higher in the abbey's hierarchy and Chandler eventually found himself face to face with the portly monk in charge.

After giving him an up and down look and firing a few questions at him he eventually said to an older monk, 'Show our Castilian brother our clock and see what he makes of that.'

Only after marvelling at the arrangement of ticking cogs and wheels and expressing his amazement with the response, 'Quite befogging,' was he led briskly along to the scriptorium to admire what they possessed there too.

It amounted to an impressive display with several lecterns bearing chained books on them and several carrels where scribes were working in silence.

He gave a sharp glance round and peered at the list of books he was handed. He could see nothing resembling a seditious tale about lions, nor even a page about the princes they represented.

After leaving the inner precinct, he found Fulke in the garth with a few companions, and indicating that he should let them walk on ahead for a moment as they seemed to be heading somewhere, he asked, 'Where were you, in fact, when that first fellow was shot?'

Fulke did not answer at once but stared off into the distance.

Chandler continued, 'When Will and I went to see what had happened you were nowhere about. I didn't see you until we came back to the campfire afterwards. I noticed Underwood and a few other familiar faces near the man who'd been shot but not you. Where were you?'

'I heard you didn't let them pin it on John.'

'Good. So you know our procedure. It's the truth I'm after. Answer my question.'

'I was there. Prove I wasn't.'

'A study of logic will tell you that you cannot prove a negative.'

'Good job I know nothing about logic then, isn't it?' He gave Chandler a sidelong glance. 'Where do you think I was?'

'That's neither here nor there. I could think you were on the moon but it wouldn't put you there, would it?'

Leaving Fulke to work things out he went to find somewhere quiet where he could think things over until Swynford sent for him again. They were their own worst enemies. Innocent or guilty? He had no idea. Was their resentment of Henry and his Lancastrians strong enough to be called hatred? Was that enough to lead them to murder?

6

It was not much later while he was gazing at one of the barns where the conversi stored the abbey grain that he managed to get a good look at the upper level.

As expected when told about the location of the shooting, a wide opening, about six feet by six and about ten feet above ground level, was where the sacks of grain were hoisted inside. A hook on a chain would be attached to the sacks but while it was not in use the chain hung down over the opening and looped back on itself like now. It jutted out on a beam like a gallows and was heavy and thick enough to give some slight cover for anyone standing up there with an arrow at the ready.

It was a perfect vantage point for a bowman wishing to shoot anyone in the yard.

Assuming nobody looked up, unlikely, as they were busy unloading, even an average shot could have hit a target from there.

Chandler strolled over for a closer look and as he did so one of the conversi appeared.

'May I have a look inside your barn?' Chandler asked.

'Connected to this shooting?' He nodded. 'Go ahead. I'll open the doors for you.'

Before going in Chandler asked, 'Could anyone have got up there without being seen?'

'Not officially,' the conversi frowned. 'But you know how it is? We usually keep it locked.'

'They tell me there were plenty of people about.'

'Aye, we were busy on account of the guests. I assume you're with the lord Swynford's retinue?'

'For my pains.'

'I hear he's set on finding the man who did it.'

'That is his aim.'

'And maybe you're the friar they mentioned?'

'Maybe I am.'

'Then I'll tell you this for nothing.'

Chandler raised his eyebrows and the man leaned forward. 'It wasn't one of us.'

'Why would it be?'

'You might have heard which side they're on?' He nodded over his shoulder towards the abbey precinct where the monks could be distantly heard singing from inside the church.

Chandler nodded in agreement. 'There can be no doubt that King Henry has the whole-hearted support of Brother Walsingham and his confreres.'

The man glanced over his shoulder towards the precinct again.

'Them, yes. Worth bearing in mind, brother.' Before Chandler could ask him to explain, he took out his keys, turned the lock then walked away with the words, 'Some think: let a hundred schools of thought contend. Some don't. Take a look round, by all means. That's the only place where the shot could have come from.'

7

So hostility between town and monastery still lingered.

It was dark inside. A narrow passage between high stacked bales of what was probably the wool clip led to a flight of stone steps against the far wall. Edging towards them he went up and found himself in a store under the roof. It was lighter here because daylight entered through the wide opening where the hook and chain were hanging, but even so it was gloomy enough because the open side faced north. Dust covered the wooden floor and was scuffed by many footprints.

Chandler stood at the top of the steps without moving. From this position he could see across the yard to other barns but he could not see down to the ground. It would take several paces to a place where he might observe anyone in the yard below.

At this moment he heard the sound of voices as some conversi walked round the side of the building opposite and he heard them go inside where they were presumably engaged in various chores. After only a moment he heard them come outside again.

He took several careful paces towards the opening, just far enough to see half a dozen of them carrying sacks. None of them looked up. In fact, he doubted whether, even if they had, they would have noticed him where he was standing in the shadows.

The murdered man was in the middle of the yard when he was shot, a prime target.

Why shoot him? Chandler wondered. Was he merely in the wrong place at the crucial moment? Why the other two, come to that, he asked himself for the hundredth time. He had been unable to discern a link between them other than that they were vassals of the king.

The first, shot at night sitting near a cooking fire, happened to be the fellow who resented dogs. The second victim was remarkable for his office. The third? He seemed to be just another man-at-arms, appointed to keep his lord safe from danger and engaged in a menial task while the cortege was lying within the safety of the abbey purlieu. Or so he must have assumed.

His mistake was to have discarded his hauberk. The bowman had shot him through the heart.

Chandler stood for some time in the sweet-smelling grain store watching the coming and going of the conversi below. He had taken care to tread to one side in order to avoid the scuff of prints in the dust but had decided there was nothing to see there.

When he reached the bottom of the steps he heard the sound of more voices, northern ones, loud in their badinage, and by the time he reached the doors at ground level a group of men were going past. They wore the Lancaster badge and he remembered one or two from Pontefract. He saw them head out under the stone arch towards the outer wall, the mead and the distant river.

8

Swynford had something planned to appeal to his men he discovered when he returned to the abbey. The first he knew about it was on his way back into the precinct from the barn when he was almost sent flying by Swynford's remaining bodyguards sweeping out of the refectory with Swynford tightly guarded in their midst.

When he saw Chandler he broke free, gripped him by the arm and brought everyone to a halt. 'We have to choose one as an example to demonstrate that I do not tolerate indiscipline, brother. It'll be that mercenary you defended. He'll do. I'll not touch one who owes fealty to Henry without good reason. Where is he?'

Chandler stared at him. 'That man you're referring to is part of a unit of good bowmen.'

'Precisely.'

'There is no evidence against him. Such men are skilled and too valuable to lose, my lord. May I suggest you reconsider? If the king calls out the army, as he will, he'll need men like him.'

About to march on, Swynford stopped in his tracks. 'Hold on, men!'

He turned to Chandler but before he could speak Chandler said at once, 'They're mercenaries, not likely to put their livelihoods in jeopardy by doing a little private work. They're useful men, my lord. They do what they're told without question. They are at the top of their skills. They cannot be faulted . . . Worth their weight,' he remarked for good measure.

Swynford looked uncertain when he heard all this. 'Of course to make an example of one of them might—' He rubbed his chin.

'Might not go down well with his comrades?'

'And we would not want them to seek employment with our enemies. True.'

'Exactly what our lord king would say,' Chandler spoke with certainty.

Abruptly Swynford dashed him aside saying, 'In that case you'd better watch them like a hawk, brother, all three, and ensure they are faultless in their allegiance. That's what I demand. See to it.'

9

Will noticed Swynford stamping away with his guards and remarked to Chandler as he approached, 'Still on the trail, brother?'

'And for some time if Swynford keeps trying to pin it on the wrong man.'

Will looked askance. 'You must have suspicions if you think he's after the wrong one?'

'You don't know how close to the edge you three are.'

'Because we work for pay?'

Chandler let it go.

Will took the hint. He hitched his bow more comfortably across his shoulders and made as if to leave as well.

Before he could do so Chandler asked, 'I hear some of the town bowmen have challenged our men to a shoot-out?'

Will grinned. 'They've not a chance against us but they don't know it yet. If it's your fancy you might come to watch? We're down in yon mead.'

'It looks as if we're not for Westminster yet. I've finished my business in the abbey.' He didn't mention he had failed to find the Book of the Lion. He shrugged. 'Lead on.'

Together they strolled down towards the gate where earlier Chandler had noticed some bowmen going out. As they crossed the barn yard he remarked, 'It wasn't such a difficult shot from up there, was it? What's your opinion?'

Will followed his glance. 'Your main risk would be if you were seen. But a good shot could be in and out quick enough not to be noticed. It's no great distance. A blind man could get a line on a target from there.'

'That's what I thought, as a non-bowman.'

Amicably they went under the arch into the meadow on the other side of the precinct. The butts were at the lower end in the long grass going down to the water meadows. While they walked down Chandler thought it might be an opportunity to find out more about what was biting John Underwood. His confession had only alluded to wrongs in a general way, profound though they seemed, and there was clearly much more that grieved the young fellow than he had admitted. But Will was circumspect. He deflected any invitation to gossip.

Not wishing to press the issue Chandler suggested that he show him where to stand for the best view of the action.

As they waded through the grass Will said in an offhand tone, 'They're good lads. A loyal squad.'

'Loyal to whom?' Chandler raised his eyebrows.

Will didn't answer apart from offering a small, knowing smile. Instead he led him to a hillock with an uninterrupted sight of the butts. 'You'll see everything you want from here, brother.' He left him there and went off to join his men.

Chandler had a good look round while everybody was marking out the range and deciding the order of play. He could see over the whole site as Will had told him, being on a slight eminence facing south. It made him feel vulnerable to be so prominent. Other men were grouped further down the slope. Chandler was more noticeable than he liked.

While he waited for things to begin he considered Underwood and his own uncertainty about whether he would be back to bring an end to his confession.

Was he relieved to have shifted some of his burden off his back? Or was he frightened, that after a little thought Chandler might let slip something that would point a finger at him in the present situation with a killer on the loose? His anger was justified by the sound of it but not necessarily focused enough to make him seek revenge for what angered him. And why those three?

Henry's reputation had not been enhanced by the ruthless way he had called men out to fight for him. Many had suffered by their refusal. Many more would have refused if they had known they were being ordered to fight in the overthrow of the king. Their loyalty to the man they called King Dickon often went against their allegiance to their feudal lord. A king was a king after all.

Except, Chandler reminded himself, when he illegally stole the crown. Then what was he?

Underwood had sought absolution. Wiping the slate clean, as he had called it. That should be the end of the story. But there was another question about regret and whether he now blamed himself for coming so close to pouring out his soul to Chandler.

Of course seditious comments were made on the way down here despite what he had told Swynford. They were men, weren't they? The grumbles of an army on the march, a cortege, no less, was bound to be an occasion for complaint even to toughened men-at-arms impervious to physical hardship.

Their arrival in Westminster was becoming urgent. Rumours about the changes Archbishop Arundel wanted were reaching them more frequently as they neared the capital and although they were surely too extreme to be credible, it was obvious changes were afoot.

Burning at the stake for not believing in the Eucharist? That had never been a threat during King Richard's reign – despite the pope's urging.

Could such a barbaric punishment be in the offing, now Henry was on the throne?

In the old days it had been up to the individual to choose what to believe, or to seek guidance from a priest if troubled, but not to be made to pay with their lives in such a cruel manner for merely thinking for themselves.

Nobody wanted to be caught mouthing criticism of the new regime unless they had a taste for martyrdom. They were right to be wary. He himself had persuaded several Lollards to change their tune by recanting in public. Better to keep your thoughts to yourself, he told them, than to risk the flames. He agreed with the Bishop of Durham on that one.

The rumours coming up from the south must be exaggerations, Chandler decided, standing on the hill in the fresh breeze from the river, the scene tranquil in the clarity of a fair day, now, at the beginning of spring. They could not burn alive the living for what they believed. Not here, not in England.

Until they reached London and judged the situation for themselves, nobody could know what to expect.

He noticed that the first archer, a fellow from the town by the look of his fustian cotte, had already taken his turn with creditable skill and Chandler tried to push his speculations to one side for a while. There was simply nothing but hearsay to go on at present. Everything would become clear once they were back in the City.

Clear for me too, he thought as an image of Matilda's unloosened hair claimed his attention for one disconcerting moment.

10

It was a good contest. The townsmen did not shame themselves but they were clearly no match for the professional bowmen, the elite in the royal army.

'Aye,' mocked one of the St Alban's contestants afterwards, 'pay us nine pence a day and you'd soon see us hammer you into the ground.' They all moved off to find ale in the town in a spirit of camaraderie.

Alone Chandler made his way back to the precinct. What had surprised him most was Fulke's moderate showing.

11

A few days later, Swynford's ad hoc thinking about scapegoats soon became clear.

While the cortege was stalled in its departure for London by the endless crowds who came to pay their respects to the dead king, he acted.

Despite a long wait in the rain outside the abbey gatehouse before being allowed in to view the corpse in its lead-lined carapace, the crowds showed no sign of decreasing.

So that the hangman did not feel thwarted, therefore, and so that Swynford's men did not lull themselves into imagining they could get away with anything, and to show that Henry was the law nowadays, he concluded that he needed to make good his promise and someone should be punished for murder. A scapegoat was needed. Anybody would do.

One of the prisoners waiting in the town gaol was brought forth and to the jeers of the townsfolk and the weeping of his kin, he swung high on the town gibbet for his misdemeanour, whatever it was, while a couple of friends pulled on his legs hard enough to break his neck to shorten his agony.

Chandler felt sick. Swynford had insisted he be present as if to lend authenticity to what in truth was nothing to do with him.

As the body hung limply from the noose, Swynford himself concluded with satisfaction, 'That'll show 'em.'

12

While everyone gathered their belongings and negotiated space on the wagons, Chandler, having little with him that was not always habitually carried in his leather scrip, decided to bring his chronicle up to date in a quiet corner of the cloisters. Much news had come in since his last entry.

Chandler's Chronicle

All the conspirators are dead by now except for the lord Despenser and the egregious son of the duke of York, Aumerle. I do not count the latter's sister, the lady Constance, still mewed up in the nunnery at Reading. Suffice to say, I pray she is eventually freed and does not suffer the fate of her co-conspirators.

Of these only the lord Despenser was for long unaccounted for and all we heard was that he had fled after the debacle at Cirencester to his castle near Cardiff. It took some time before reliable news reached us and we were already here at St Albans before his fate was made known.

It so happened that the lord Despenser had agreed to join forces with the earl of Huntingdon, John Holand, but unaware of his ally's brutal fate at Pleshey, the lord Despenser set out to fulfil his side of the plan. This led him to take ship across the Narrow Seas to Flanders.

However, even in this, Lady Fortune chose not to offer her grace.

The shipman whose vessel Despenser boarded with a handful of men was as duplicitous as so many others in this chronicle and no sooner was the ship at sea than the captain turned back towards the shore.

'Where are you going now?' Despenser is imagined to have asked.

'Back to Bristol, my lord, by your leave.'

'Oh no you're not,' replied the rebel, 'I've paid you to take me to Flanders.'

'And I've had a better offer from King Henry,' the shipman might have answered. 'We're returning to Bristol so I can hand you over to his captains.'

An argument ensued which we may imagine was heated and at that a swarm of militia burst from below decks where they had been hiding and attacked the good lord who defended himself right valiantly. Outnumbered, however, he and his men had no choice but to submit.

In chains they were returned to Bristol into the keeping of the mayor, Thomas Knappe.

The next day, while the council debated what they were to do with them, the ordinary people in the town were stirred into a mob by the king's men-at-arms who, with dire threats of vengeance against every man, woman and child if they refused their support, forced them to gather outside the mayor's house and bay for Despenser's blood.

Chants of, 'Bring out the traitor! Bring out the traitor! Put him to death!' must have frozen Despenser's blood.

Against such a violent mob Mayor Knappe was unable to maintain the rule of law or save his captive from their clutches. Despenser was snatched from the safety of the mayor's house and dragged to the market cross where, without any sort of trial, he was beheaded.

Thus ended the rebellion against the usurper that started and ended in the month of January.

Chandler reread his account which was as true to the facts as he had lately heard them. He knew that if it got into the wrong hands it would be his undoing. Yet it had to be written. He saw it as a marker in the shifting sands of rumour. The facts should be brought into the light.

He was alerted by the rumbling of the wagons as they began to roll out of the precinct. A group of black-robed Benedictines came to stand out on the foregate to sing a hymn. Seeing them Swynford rose to his feet on the tailgate of his covered char leading the cortege.

Raising his sword in full sight of everyone he shouted, 'And now, men, to London and King Henry!'

And so they set forth on the last leg of their journey with the body of Richard of Bordeaux lying in state on the bier.

TEN

Westminster. March 1400.

The Master shows me much kindness, patting me on the shoulder, urging me to cheer up, even though he knows what I've done. 'It's a case of spilt milk again, Mattie. Life is full of enough challenges to tax the wisdom of a Solomon. We must do the best we can.'

They are both busy, Adam and the Master. I scarcely see them. Cook supplies them with meat and drink at all hours. The big bass bell tolls from the tower to mark how swiftly time is passing since the king died and is unavenged. The sound fills me with constant dread. I thank the angels for the high walls that surround the abbey and its demesne here on Thorney Island.

It is all very well the Master trying to reassure me. I know I did wrong in mentioning that accursed book. I did it out of sheer ignorance but that is no excuse. Worse, there is no way of making it better. I can't now say I've never heard of it. Lion? What lion?

When I try to say this to Adam he gives me one of his black looks. 'You should think before you open your mouth, Matilda.' He walks off. He will not talk to me. I hate it when he calls me Matilda when I've always been Mattie to him and to everyone who knows me.

I decide that if ever I meet Rodric Chandler again I will do as he does and pretend something else, for my own ends. I can't believe he would betray the Master. But facts speak for themselves. I can't forget poor Adam's fingers. It makes me shudder to think of them. I have made up my mind that if I ever see Rodric Chandler again I will beat him at his own game. I'll make everything right for the Master and send the friar to his doom with a smile.

How to do it is unclear to me – especially as the likelihood of seeing him again has gone. He is probably dead in a ditch, his throat cut just as his housekeeper suggested that time when I went to his lodgings to slap him across the face – for what good that would have done any of us.

It's strange how she disappeared after the steward at Comberton's house was poisoned, if he was. She said, 'I'm taking this baking to Comberton's. Come with me.' She'll probably never be seen again.

But I will do something.

In this confusion I'm beginning to long for somewhere to call home. Maybe it might be in Guelderland but I scarcely remember it. I was too young when I was brought to England in Sir Roet's household. No more than a child. Home is here, like it or not. I have to face the truth.

I was horribly sick this morning but it soon passed.

ELEVEN

London. March 1400.

The cortege laboured up a rise above the Thames valley and halted at the top near a small vill called Hampstead. There below was their destination in all its mystery, regality and corruption: London, towers and palaces and ancient walls, and a thousand churches, their bells tolling a hollow greeting at the arrival of the body of the king.

Every step of the way beside the steep road down through the heath people lined up to pay tribute with garlands of evergreen. And every step of the way the usurper-king's men held them back with threats and violence. Jeers reached the wagons and the king's horsemen plunged into the crowd to silence the critics with cuts and whips.

And at last they came to St Paul's.

2

Chandler knew he would have to visit the house in Seething Lane. It could not be put off. First he had to attend the requiem mass in St Paul's where the body was lying in state surrounded by a hundred candles and afterwards he walked up to his own lodging above Aldgate.

As expected his housekeeper had gone. He did not blame her. He looked in the casket he had told her about and saw with satisfaction that certain banes, a gift from Brother Daniel at his herb gardens in Hackney, had also gone. Chandler remembered how the old herbalist had warned him to use them wisely and his message had been clear – use them to punish the enemies of King Richard.

When he went out to the communal pump for water a by-stander told him that the man who had murdered the little novice at Dowgate the previous year had died suddenly.

'Not plague as we feared, brother. He was the only one to die. It's believed it was something he ate.'

So Beata, his housekeeper, had understood him and acted on his covert instructions.

He went into his chantry.

It was full of memories of the last time he had been here. Dust covered every surface. Plaster had fallen off the walls like scabs from a leper.

He pushed open the door into the vestry where the straw he slept on between the night offices was as rumpled as one would expect. It was as they had left it, never imagining they might never return.

A rat scuttled across the floor but did not obliterate the memory of her spread hair and he bent down to pull a strand of red-gold from among the lighter gold of the bed-straw.

He knew he was only putting off his meeting with Knollys, the spy-master. It had to be faced.

3

'My dear Rodric, pray enter, and then, dear boy, tell me all your news.'

He followed as the ancient old man shuffled upstairs to his solar.

When they were comfortably seated in the bay overlooking the wife's little garden on the other side of the street, and after the servant had poured some of the potent wine they sent him from Aquitaine, Knollys, looking more ancient than the last time Chandler had seen him, invited him to bring him up to date with news from the north.

'I gather,' he said, 'things went well up there?'

'They went to plan.'

'As I heard! As we have all heard!' He added maliciously, 'So it seems my lord Swynford has done his utmost to impress his stepbrother?'

'I believe he desires ever to be in the king's kind regard,' Chandler told him.

As the conversation was batted back and forth about events at Pontefract, Knollys, sharp as ever, filed away what he could use later and Chandler had a searing memory of what he had not mentioned last time he was here.

The old man had been in bed, lying next to his snoring wife, it being the middle of the night, and, insisting on some entertainment to while away the sleepless hours, Knollys had kept Chandler talking for some time. Despite this, Chandler had held his tongue.

Now the question of the chronicles being written up in all the scriptoria in every abbey up and down the country became Knollys's theme.

Chandler recognized his technique at once.

It began in the light, lulling, gossipy tones he used at these times, mentioning that it was a sore worry to the king that so many of his subjects had learned to read while lacking the knowledge to make sense of what they read.

'Think of the Bible that blundering fool Wycliffe started to translate into the common language of the peasantry! Think of the consequences if that hadn't been stopped!'

Chandler murmured something that could have meant anything while Knollys continued.

'Likewise, what if these chronicles, such as they are, written by monks who know nothing of life outside their abbeys, write up Henry's acquisition of the throne in such a manner as to reflect badly upon him? There was enough discussion over the legitimate way he could establish himself as king, without an army of ignorant monks writing it up to their own fancy. It can only cause unrest and we have all seen enough of that these last few months. Wouldn't you agree, my boy?'

Knollys gave a practised smile as if to convey to Chandler that nothing like a warning might lie hidden in his words. 'And now,' he continued, 'we have the famous poet and his incessant writings doing who knows what harm with his mockery. We cannot have it.'

Chandler seemed to see in letters of flame the title of the Book of the Lion blazing between them. He had withheld his knowledge of it either because of a residual shame over his method of obtaining the information from Matilda – when straightforward torture of the poet's scrivener had brought them no result – or whether it was for some other reason he had not yet framed in words to satisfy his conscience.

Knollys was still talking.

'We have been unable to get anything on him to bring him to our side by persuasion. So far he has refused to pen a eulogy for Henry even though his friend and rival John Gower is busily rewriting his *Confessio Amantis* in praise of the new reign. I hear,' he leaned forward as if to impart some deep secret, 'he is erasing all mention of Richard even though it was originally dedicated to him.' He sat back. 'I fancy our more famous and illustrious friend thinks too much of his poetic integrity to stoop to a retraction of his early more seditious work. You, dear boy, might think of a way of getting him to see our point of view? I remember you told me last time you were here that you had found a way of being invited to his house. Does that arrangement still stand?'

Ah, thought Chandler, so now he's got to the point. 'I cannot tell, my lord.'

'A woman?'

Chandler gave a deprecating shrug.

Knollys: 'I'm sure you'll find a way in. You handsome young devils with your sweet tongues never have difficulties in that direction. We need her master to honour us with his allegiance, just to pacify any doubts as to Henry's popularity.'

There followed a little more inconsequential chat and another generous offer of wine and as he got up to leave, Knollys remarked, 'You know, by the way, that last quarter day they retreated to a rented house in the precinct of Westminster Abbey? If proof were needed of his allegiance there it is. We must get him on our side without delay – or find some other way of drawing his sting.'

4

Afterwards he retraced his steps through the winding streets towards the twin towers of St Paul's to pay his respects before compline.

Crowds of townsfolk, making the most of their freedom before curfew, were flocking in the same direction. They snaked all the way round the side of the church and through the yard to the canopied pulpit of St Paul's Cross, where some priest or other was warning of serpents belching flames. When he passed in front of the line of stationers' stalls to reach the west doors he saw nobody to arouse his notice.

The two towers housed a ring of bells. Today only one bass bell tolled its doleful reminder of death.

Inside, when he was let through, he noticed that the army and his other companions on the road from the north had already left.

Clouds of incense made him cough. Candles blazed round the bier and rows of monks sang constantly while from behind the screen the boys' choir added their own ethereal descant.

Chandler knelt on the steps below the catafalque. As always he was overcome by the war within himself between what his senses perceived and his mind's yearning for something ineffable, the thing, the fact, the evidence, of what lay forever out of reach of experience.

Glancing round at the bowed heads he wondered if others were racked by the same questions, or whether they were merely inventing shopping lists or planning what to eat next. He would never know because that was also the problem, we could never see inside the secret recesses of another's soul.

The coffin was open for the purpose Henry had proclaimed, to make sure everyone could see that the previous, useless king, Richard of Bordeaux, was now dead of his own hand and could therefore not be reinstated.

'That should put paid to any more rebellions,' someone said close by as Chandler got up to go.

'I can't persuade myself to believe it,' came the rejoinder. 'It's scarcely to be credited that he should starve to death so opportunely.'

Richard alive and Richard dead were two separate entities. Lying peacefully he might be asleep yet it was clear he was not. Something lived on.

It was said to be the animation of the soul that made the difference, Chandler pondered as he walked away. But what was the soul? No one could see it, touch it, talk with it. It was a chimera. Or was it enough to have a simple word, a name indicating something that otherwise could not be perceived? Old John of Gaunt in this very place had raged at Wycliffe's intransigent and impeccable logic, shouting, 'Out, nomen!' And had thereby defeated his own argument.

5

Next morning to Westminster. He took a water taxi. Crossed over the bridge near Palace Yard. Bought a pie from a stall and stood eating it while he watched the passers-by, their comings and goings.

He wondered how he could summon her. And if he did so by means magical or prosaic, would she acknowledge him?

In one way he hoped she would refuse. In another he knew she would not. It might take time but she would not refuse him. Could not.

He joined the tail end of a small group of pilgrims from the West Country – or so he assumed from their accents – and entered the abbey church where the building works to Richard's extension to the nave were continuing slowly now Henry was having to fund the work himself. The church was already fine and high and impressive to make the most confirmed heretic feel holy enough to praise whatever the being with the power to hold the universe, earth and firmament, together.

The group of country-folk now standing round the portrait near the entrance gazed in justified wonder at the painter's skill in showing Richard as if alive in all the beauty and regality of his youth.

Chandler considered this. Even then, when the painter made his brush marks on the panel, Richard had worn a wary expression as if expecting assassins. How could the painter have suspected what was in his mind? How caught such a hint of fear? How prophesied the end?

Subdued by the confusion of his thoughts, he turned away and was crossing the yard outside when he noticed the scrivener he had seen at one of the poet's alchemical gatherings at his house in the Vintry before Christmastide. The lady Constance had been present, he remembered. Her young, dashing husband, the lord Despenser, had arrived after everyone else, touching her hand softly under the cover of his cloak when they met, and they sat with fingers secretly linked all evening.

The scrivener, whose name would probably come back to him, was striding along with youthful energy, his hair swinging as, with a bag over one shoulder, he headed for the far end of the close where a few houses stood. Tenancies. He was going to work, was he? Heading for the house where Chaucer was hiding?

He sat down on a wall to wait. She would eventually come out. She must.

6

The bell for sext was long past. He wondered if he was going to have to sit here all day. Eventually he rose to his feet, set off towards the pie man and was already rooting in his pouch for a farthing or two when suddenly without warning the door of the house flew open and she came hurrying out. He waited until she reached the path near St Margaret's chapel then strode after her. He caught up with her before she went inside.

'Matilda! . . . Mattie?'

She turned.

He said quickly, 'I was on my way to see you.'

She looked the same, that hair crammed into a coif, her neat figure, the little cross she wore on a silver chain. He had forgotten that.

She was looking him up and down. 'How did you know where to find me?'

'Someone mentioned it.'

'Who?' Suspicious.

'I can't remember. One of the market women.'

'Are they all back, then?'

He countered, 'Were they ever away?'

She looked confused. 'Don't you know what's been happening here?'

'I was sent north. News didn't reach us easily.'

She looked at him without expression but said nothing as if wanting him to say more.

He felt a need to add enough to make things sound normal. 'I have – er – I have an elderly aunt in – er – in the north country.' He pulled himself together. 'You're very sharp with me, Mattie. I can see I've earned your disapproval.' He made a half-turn as if about to walk away but as he hoped she called him back.

'I never expected to see you again.'

'Did you find my message in the chantry – I left a message for you on a piece of – I wrote something – I thought you might find it.'

'I know. I got it.'

'Because you said you could read.'

Her lips trembled. 'And you said you liked a girl who could read.' She looked suddenly defiant.

'And so I do. Especially this girl.' He lowered his voice. 'Mattie, forgive me?'

She stiffened. 'For what?'

'For anything I may do.'

'That's a lot to ask.'

As her face crumpled she tried to force a smile and as he remembered from before, it was her courage that disarmed him. He felt an urge to fold her in his arms but instead he reached out and pulled a tendril of hair from under her coif and held it.

She drew back with an angry swish of her head. 'Don't! You'll have it all down!'

It could have been meant as a light-hearted rebuke but her voice wobbled and he knew everything was so changed that it could never be the same again.

In a rush he asked, 'Can you come and see me at the chantry? I must open it again if there are any believers to open it for. Come by water taxi. If you let me know I'll meet you at the steps.'

When she said nothing he said, 'Tomorrow? I'll be there before nones? Like now?'

So I made a mess of that, he thought, angry with himself as he walked away. She had simply left him standing there, hurrying into the chapel without a word as if the hounds of hell were after her.

Would she come to him? To hell and damnation with her, he thought, deflecting the wish from his own sorry performance where it rightfully belonged. How inept he was at this sort of thing. So much for Knollys's belief in his sweet tongue. How else was he going to get into the poet's enclave? He was bereft of any practical ideas whatsoever. Disarmed in every sense.

TWELVE

Westminster. March 1400.

I am mortified. I made such a fool of myself. So much for my resolution to make amends and put him on the wrong track. It was the way he suddenly appeared from nowhere as if I had cast a spell to bring him to me. As if, in truth, the spell I did cast had worked. Which is shocking enough. Am I a witch?

Later I allowed St Margaret, patron saint of women, to take me in her arms and forgive me if she will. She is the protector of women such as me.

Now the house is filled with the sound of Adam and the Master at work. Their voices. All hours. Urgency. Never resting.

Adam brings in new vellum. Constantly mixes ink, sharpening his pen with the little knife. Quills are delivered by a stranger who will not give his name. He is not your usual pedlar. Under a rough cloak he had silk sleeves, a ring on his finger.

Cook peels and scrapes and seethes and throws fat in the skillet to make it spit and never stops and never says a word.

The bells toll. The crowds, thousands of them, twenty thousand they say, flock into the City to wait outside St Paul's in the pouring rain. Townsfolk, folk from the countryside, everywhere about, coming out here to throng the Close, peering into the Great Hall to glimpse the new king and his council. Two kingly visits in one. I don't know. What do they hope? That King Richard will suddenly spring to life again and call everything back to order?

I venture as far as the top of the water stairs to gaze downriver towards the City. A ferryman calls up to me. I shake my head and turn back to the house.

After much struggling with myself I take my courage in both hands and ask Adam, 'Will you give me your advice?' I explain what my plan is and he frowns.

'Keep away, Mattie. He's dangerous. You'll only make things worse.'

One morning I slip inside Westminster Hall where they're discussing the introduction of a new statute and to my horror I discover what he means.

How can they? How can he? My flesh crawls. These are his people.

Next time I see Cook throw a log on the fire I can't take my eyes off it. I watch it burn. Sap runs from it like body fats.

THIRTEEN

Aldgate. March 1400.

Will and his archers were quartered in the Five Fields by Ebury Manor and came every day to fulfil the hours of their watch at Westminster and to keep order by the fear their mere presence in the yard aroused. People were cowed enough by the trials of daily life without causing trouble over the added horror of knowing an anointed king had been murdered.

Because of where they were quartered Chandler saw little of them. He remained in his rooms above the gatehouse at Aldgate, rode out to Hackney to see Martin, his sacristan, still living in secret behind the high walls of Magister Daniel's herb garden, but mostly he tended the chantry and offered what regularity he could to the interrupted worship of St Serapion.

Afterwards he usually picked up a meal in the Fleece where he met up with his old friend, City coroner Sir Arnold Archer, who greeted him warily these days. An impassable rift now separated them.

As he walked in on this particular day a man was already on his feet. With Archer not here yet Chandler found a space and, greeting one or two acquaintances, sat down to listen. What he heard appalled him.

The fellow was part-way through his thesis and it went like this: '. . . make no mistake, friends, everyone knows he cannot have starved himself to death. The dates do not tally. There is no way for Henry and Arundel to argue their way round the facts despite their efforts.

'First, it is known by the French – far across the Narrow Seas with the weather against the easy passage of their couriers – and lacking, we doubt not, the magical powers necessary to scry into the future – the French, as I say, had already broadcast the fact that King Richard died on the fourteenth day of February – not a week later as Duke Henry claims – a day, by the way, dedicated to a saint, Valentine no less, celebrated by Richard and his beloved Queen

Anne at their pleasance on the Thames isle of Neyt. God rest their souls—'

A growl of approval rose up but a heckler interrupted. 'Get on with it!'

'I will,' the orator continued, 'but it is a fact I wish you to note and it is this – and I repeat myself – the French knew of his death *before* the spurious announcement by Henry and his court of assassins.'

He glared round at everyone but there was silence so he repeated, 'They knew before the announcement by the English court! So how did that come about?'

Again silence.

'I repeat, the French knew before we, the English, knew of it.'

Somebody muttered, 'Clever folk, the French.' The man's irony was not lost on the orator.

'The truth is, as you have guessed—' he continued, with their full attention, 'Harry and his lackeys dared not announce his death too soon for fear of encouraging support for the rebel earls. Only when the remaining rebels were safely dead dared they announce that our king was dead also.'

He gave a stern glance round the chamber. 'Second, the French, again, have it on good authority that King Dickon did not go quietly to his death in a spirit of melancholy resignation as we are told – can you imagine that? – no, he took the axe from his nearest assailant and laid about him with good vigour, killing at least two, maybe three, of his astonished would-be assassins until a cowardly blow from behind forced him to fly this earth and join the heavenly choirs above – where, we can be confident, he has been made right welcome.'

The entire chamber was still locked in an unbroken silence.

'Thirdly, friends, is it or is it not true that no man can pine away for want of food in only seven days?'

Rumbles of agreement greeted him this time.

'The story put about by the henchmen of Henry Bolingbroke – for thus I must name him – that it was only when King Richard heard of the lord Despenser's barbaric and illegal beheading in Bristol that he accepted that the last of his rebel earls was dead – and only then refused to eat . . . This is the story we are being told. This, friends, is Bolingbroke's *big lie*!'

In the past Chandler had enjoyed sitting in the Fleece swapping yarns with any and everyone. His allegiance in those days had not mattered. It meant nothing. That things were changed now beyond all reckoning could not be avoided. It seemed as if years not months had passed since he had been on his usual bench listening to the speeches of whomsoever chose to take the floor. He was sharply aware that he was now surrounded by men who would regard him as a servant of the Devil.

This present orator was one of the regular drinkers, a weaver by trade, and eloquent in the manner of one who could read and took pride in doing so.

When he paused in his oration growls of agreement rumbled up from all sides. It showed that nobody believed that Richard, doughty young hero of the Great Revolt during his early years on the throne, had meekly given in to physical threats.

'A swordsman par excellence,' somebody commented. 'He would not go meekly. He was a true king.'

'And not without a fondness for the higher arts,' an old book-binder added. 'Never have music and poetry flourished so abundantly as during his reign.'

'And don't forget cloth,' said the weaver. 'It has been my great delight to live through the reign of a man so discerning about a good piece of fabric, with an eye for line and colour, and the nous to further our interests in Flanders and elsewhere. Opus Anglicanum, even, would not have had the prestige it does today without the support of our blessed Dickon.'

'And that's all kings should bother themselves with,' somebody else remarked. 'Leave wars to fight themselves. We want none of them.'

The man who had begun to list the ideals and pursuits of Richard's court mentioned poetry again and a great sigh went round when somebody rose to their feet. Removing his cap he held it in both hands over his heart.

Without the need for encouragement he began to declaim a poem Chandler did not recognize. It was short and brought shouts of applause when he finished.

The weaver demanded somewhat belligerently whether the Lombards or the French threatened their own poets with imprisonment and book-burning as was happening here.

Chandler turned to the stranger sitting next to him. 'And who wrote that?'

'Master Chaucer,' the stranger confirmed. 'Good, ain't 'e?'

Shaken to the core he eventually made his way outside. He did not doubt that the weaver was destined for a shorter life than he might anticipate. The same might go for every regular at the Fleece. Archer had not been present. Coroner or not he would be cautious about revealing his allegiance under the new regime. And if Chaucer's name was getting round to link him with the wrong sort he would have to tread very carefully indeed.

2

As for himself, she did not come. He went to the water stairs every day after nones and the boats nosing into the wharf from upriver were full but she was never in one. The Book of the Lion was forgotten until he forced himself to a decision.

He would approach the scrivener and tell him face to face some story about having heard of such a book and was wondering how he might get hold of it.

Is it in English? he would ask. Is it in French? No matter. I can read and speak French. Or, he might ask in all innocence, is it maybe in Spanish? Is it a story my saint Serapion might have known? Is it a story from the east? I ask in a spirit of shared scholarship, he might add, aware that you are a lettered man. And out of curiosity. And having heard of such a story in a tavern. Or in the North country. Or somewhere. And having heard of it I yearn to read it for myself. Surely a scrivener, a man such as yourself, can understand?

It was a ploy that would not work. He saw that at once. The fellow was not a fool. He would guess at once that he was being asked to lead him to a copy of a proscribed work. Especially after Saltwood. And if it wasn't already on the list, and if what Matilda had told him about the subject was true, it soon would be. Arundel's blood-hounds would make sure of that.

Such a book need not be connected to the Master, he argued with himself. Anybody might wish to read it. Not guessing its seditious content why would they not?

Stricken by indecision he again let the matter slide. His daily walk to the wharf to see the Westminster ferry arrive continued. No harm in that. She was never there.

3

Over the next few days in the City and in the country beyond the walls, in the towns and vills throughout the shires, a settled peace seemed to reign. It was ominous, like waiting for an explosion by an arquebus that delayed and withdrew then began to lumber forward in renewed threat until again it withdrew.

During this time a scandalous attempt was made on Henry's life in the castle at Windsor. It was the talk of the London taverns.

A strong poison such as huntsmen might use to kill a bear was smeared on the saddle of Henry's horse, so they said. It was enough and potent enough to kill a man in moments. Nobody knew how it got there. And nobody put it to the test. It was yet another rumour, the overt wish of those who denied the big lie and longed for justice.

Lady Constance, who might reasonably have wanted revenge for the murder of her husband, could not be blamed. Now under house arrest, she could not but be innocent.

Who else would wish Henry dead from among the remaining cousins in his family? A few names were mentioned, of course, a bastard son of the duke of York, often ignored, who might have borne a grudge or two, but nothing proven.

The story was even put to good use by Henry's supporters that here was another instance of royal forbearance: he chose no one as a scapegoat.

4

Chandler was still taunted by the earlier mystery of the random murders on the march south. He had no hard evidence one way or the other. No more killings took place. The murderer appeared to have got away with it. The sprawling camp at Five Fields behind its picket fence near Ebury Manor ran its orderly course.

Now and then he saw Will and the others on guard at various locations, mostly at Westminster Palace where Swynford spent his time trying to remind his stepbrother of his existence. Then, sometime later in the month, he saw them on duty outside St Paul's.

The great building was echoing to the singing of a requiem mass before the body of the king was finally put out of the way.

With Henry himself briefly – very briefly – making his obsequies, the banks of candles were finally doused. People, contained in the yard, were pushed back to make an avenue for the official mourners, and, draped with the gold embroidered arms of a king of England, quartered with those of France, the coffin was brought forth.

In silence over a thousand people stood with bared heads to watch it shuffled into place on a black-draped wagon. Some wept. The older ones were in awe that the golden child they remembered could come to this.

A team of black horses, with plumes drooping in the rain, stamped and rattled their bridles. A dog howled dismally in the distance. The loudest sound was the voice of a marshal intermittently shouting orders to his guards.

Slowly the horses began to move off. Their iron shoes were muffled in velvet. People dropped to their knees as the cortege passed from the city.

Will was on duty at a high point overlooking Ludgate as the dark wave of mourners streamed after the hearse. Chandler found himself being swept towards him. 'Hail, fellow, how goes it? Are you back to the north after this or up to Norfolk with the cortege?'

'Staying put,' he acknowledged, eyes flickering over the bowed heads as people walked by. 'Westminster. Work to do.'

'My regards to the men.' Chandler slipped back into the stream of mourners on the way to Charing.

It seemed to him that they might even be laughing at him, the squad as he thought of them. There were questions. Set too much apart to fit in with the Lancaster regulars, mercenaries were often a force apart. A brotherhood.

They had adopted him at Pontefract, inviting him to share their dole, looking out for him as soon as he set foot inside the refectory. They knew what he was doing, attending the king, Richard that is, and yet it had made no difference to them. They never mentioned what his duties might entail. He couldn't help thinking he might serve as cover for them. What was more acceptable to the Lancastrians than one of their own interrogators eating alongside a group who might otherwise be suspect?

Underwood had half-admitted his allegiance in the early days when he made his confession, such as it was, in the chapel of St Clement's, but had never enlarged on it. That he was angry enough to have a motive for killing three Lancastrians was not in doubt. His skill was such that all three targets would not have taxed him.

Fulke was somewhat ambiguous. He gave nothing much away. His showing at the archery contest had been lacklustre.

Will, despite his affable manner, was a closed book.

None of them could safely be put at the scene of any of the crimes. Their alibis, each other, had to suffice.

He pondered again his own advantage to them. A holy friar wearing Lancaster's badge? It was protection – orthodoxy, the word now being bandied about. To be seen with him was useful. It allayed suspicion. The idea confirmed his feeling that they had been playing with him.

Such was the progress of the hearse and the brutality of the guards in clearing people out of the way, it was now far ahead and beginning to move at a faster clip past the barons' palaces along the riverside. It would pass the royal mews at Charing until, turning off towards Westminster, it would make a short stop before taking the road to an out of the way chapel in Norfolk. There the royal corpse would be interred in a place where it would be unlikely to become the focus of pilgrimage.

No fomenting of more trouble, Chandler concluded. You had to hand it to Henry's advisors. They thought of everything.

Or rather, *he* thought of everything. Arundel. Brooding over the legal execution of his elder brother as a traitor, maybe, or more likely driven by his own monstrous ambition. Bishop of Ely at twenty. Strings being pulled by his war-rich family. His sense of entitlement unassailed.

A tug on his sleeve made him jerk to a halt, hand already reaching for his knife. Then he stepped to one side with a laugh. 'Underwood! John, well met, fellow.'

The bowman nodded towards the entrance to a nearby alleyway, empty while the river of mourners wound down hill. 'A word, brother?'

Chandler glanced to left and right, remembered a previous passing idea that Underwood might be happier if he wasn't a witness to that foolish confession, then followed him into the alley despite his misgivings. 'I've just seen Will. Where's Fulke?'

'Coming along.' Underwood gave him a derisory glance. 'No need to go for your knife. It's about what I said to you at Pontefract—'

'Ah!' Chandler put his hands by his sides.

'You didn't mention it to anybody?'

'Do you think I did?'

Underwood grinned, for once changing his dour expression. 'If you did it hasn't come back to me.'

'The point of confession is that the confessor holds his tongue.'

'That's what they say but in practice I reckon it might be somewhat different. Depending on the confessor.'

Chandler put his head on one side. 'With some, maybe. What do you want of me?'

'Hear me again?'

'Is there more?'

'You know there is.'

'Come to my chantry then. Do you know how to find it? It's by Aldgate.' He explained how to get there. 'Where are you billeted now? Still at Five Fields?'

'For a bit longer. Swynford hasn't been invited into Henry's magic circle. He's fuming. "After all I've done." But there's nothing he can do about it. He's relegated to being the commander of a middling battalion now his use is over.'

'Is that so?'

'That's what we all reckon. We're on duty at Westminster. Some ructions with the King's Council and the Commons. When this is all over—' he broke off and nodded down hill after the hearse, 'we reckon we'll be there until they can hammer out their differences.'

'Shall I come out to Westminster instead?'

'Will you?'

He wore a look of relief as he took his leave with an agreement that he would see Chandler at Westminster on the morrow. As he slid back into the crowd he lifted one hand. 'Palace Yard, brother. See you there.'

5

Knollys was in black velvet. His mourning garb. He had clearly been up at St Paul's earlier. He wore a silver chain and several rings including the one with the blood-red stone he always wore.

Firelight flickered over the rafters and glinted on the glass he raised to his lips. To Chandler everything was the colour of fire and blood.

The lane had been deserted as he made his way there after high mass and later the prayers that followed the king's funeral. Such was the darkness of his mood he felt a million eyes watching him through every shuttered window as he strode between the houses towards Seething Lane. He imagined night-hawks in the livery of the king vanishing before each step he took into the night.

'A sad day,' the old spy greeted with a duplicitous smile. 'News?'

'A book.'

Knollys lifted his white head. 'Go on.'

'Tavern talk. It may be of interest.'

'And where may one read this interesting book?'

Chandler spread his arms. 'I have not been able to discover that, my lord. It seems to be a French book. Untranslated as far as anyone knows. But the contents seem to give encouragement in certain quarters.'

'Untranslated?' Knollys raised his eyebrows.

'So I believe.'

Knollys considered him as if expecting more until he put down his goblet.

'If that is so, my boy, you can do no better than to talk to a young fellow called Adam Pinkhurst.'

When Chandler made no comment he wrinkled his face into a quizzical expression, forcing Chandler to adopt an expression like someone searching for a name and eventually finding it. 'That must be the scrivener attending our poet?'

Knollys refilled their goblets.

6

Of course Knollys would know of Pinkhurst. Saltwood. That connection.

Even so it shook him. Knollys had come to it at once. He inferred, therefore, that he was letting him know of Matilda. And of himself, such as he was in that regard.

As he took the boat up to Westminster the following morning he wondered why Knollys thought he might succeed when the torturers had failed.

It might be because of a mistaken view that he was again a regular visitor to the Chaucer household despite its move to the abbey close. He had been careful to show the old spy-master no surprise when he first mentioned the move and it might mean that he was again seen as a useful link with the household now he was back in London?

First he would see Underwood on that other matter. Next he would look in on the proceedings of the Commons in the Great Hall. Then he would pay a visit.

7

It was beginning to rain when he walked up from the quay into Palace Yard. Crowds were already jostling at the doors to the hall. There was no sign of Underwood. Guards from another unit were on duty with not a bowman among them. At the entrance marshals were manhandling the crowds trying to get in, picking and choosing who they would allow into the council chamber against a barrage of ineffectual protests.

With no sign of Underwood's detachment Chandler pushed his way through and found a place at the back where he could hear what was going on.

As he strained to see who was speaking he felt a tug on his sleeve and when he glanced down an old fellow in a grubby brown cloak was looking up at him through rheumy eyes in a nest of wrinkles. He crooked one finger at Chandler to bring him closer.

'It's this, young fellow,' he croaked. Under cover of his hood he lifted one hand and, eyes on Chandler, opened it slowly like a trickster to reveal something lying in his palm. It was a badge of some kind.

Chandler bent his head. 'What's this?'

'I thought you might be interested.' He closed his fingers over it.

'Maybe I am when I know what it is.'

'I found it at St Albans.'

'What were you doing there?'

'Visiting my grand-daughter. She lives in the town. I thought I'd go and have a look at some old friends of mine in the graveyard while I was there.'

'And did they tell you much?'

'No more than usual.' The old man revealed his gums in mirth. 'You want this or not?'

'How much?'

Chandler was already reaching wearily into the pouch on his belt but the man clawed his hand over his to stay him.

'I don't need coin at my age. Take it.'

'Why have you brought it to me?' He weighed the badge on his palm when the fellow insisted. It was heavier than pewter. Not a common pilgrim badge then.

'I heard you know about things and wanted to know more.' He gave him one long considering look then turned, inserted himself in a brief gap in the crowd, and was gone.

Chandler considered following but decided against it. He looked closely at the badge again but it was damaged and he could make nothing of it so he put it in his scrip for later.

After a frustrating hour listening to the discussion in the chamber by a handful of shire knights that didn't seem to be going anywhere other than to express outrage at the possibility of a clamp-down on freedom of speech, he went outside again.

Underwood was waiting for him. It was still raining. He had his hood pulled down half over his face so that at first Chandler didn't recognize him and thought it was some other old fellow come to show how mysterious he could be, when the bowman stepped into his path and lifted the edge of his hood to reveal his face.

'Oh, it's you. I looked for you earlier. I thought you were on guard duty this morning?'

'They changed our routine. Anyway, it's wet. Strings,' he added cryptically. 'Come on. Let's get out of this pissing rain.'

For once he wasn't wearing his bow across his back.

He made towards the inn used by those attending parliament and when they reached the overhanging eaves he hesitated. He looked edgy, bouncing on his feet with glances side to side and his hands first in then out of his sleeves.

'I'm not listening to your confession in an ale house, John, so you can forget it if that's your idea—'

'I know, don't mind all that. Nor am I going inside. I've had second thoughts about being seen with you. There's been developments.'

'About what?'

He ran his fingers across his throat in a slitting motion, adding, in case Chandler didn't get it, 'About them murders.'

8

Chandler sheltered under the eaves with his hood up. 'What sort of developments?'

'Swynford. He reckons we're the only bowmen he's taken on he can't trust. Mercenaries. Driven by a lust for gold,' he added, 'not by love for him. Fancy that!'

'So what's he doing about it?'

'Nowt yet. Will had his ear to the ground . . . We thought you might know more?'

'I wouldn't worry. Even he has to have some evidence against you.'

'What, Swynford? He wants to fix somebody for it. He's got Henry to please. He's jumping round like a tom cat, sees his pension disappearing if he can't keep in his good books.'

'I'd imagine his pension is the least of his worries if he's fallen out of favour. If he wants my advice he'll lie low, "yes, majesty, no, majesty," that's if he wants to keep his head on his shoulders after what he's done.'

'You tell him that if you're bothered. I'm more bothered about my own head.'

'There's nothing to pin it on you or the others for that matter. I'll say so.' He remembered the badge the old fellow had just handed to him. He felt in his pouch. 'Tell me, John, and put my mind at rest, is this yours and did you lose it at St Alban's?'

Underwood glanced at it then backed off. 'Where did you get that?'

'One of your admirers gave it to me not an hour ago. What is it?'

'If you don't know, I'm not telling you. Never seen it before in my life.' He glanced out at the rain. 'Got to head back to my unit.'

'Wait. What makes you think Swynford's after you? He can't afford to lose you. He knows that. I told him so. He's not a total sotwit. He needs good men.'

'Something Will says he heard.' He looked frightened. 'A rumour. No more than a curl of smoke.' He gave Chandler a crooked smile. 'Maybe better watch your own back, brother?'

Then he too, like the old man earlier, slipped away with nothing more than an ambiguous lift of his hand. Chandler watched him disappear into the murk.

9

Fingering the badge inside his scrip where nobody could see it he considered the cause of Underwood's alarmed recognition.

As he was standing in the doorway of the inn it seemed logical to enter and have a drink while he was here. Taking a seat in the corner a few minutes later with a flagon in front of him he bent his head to peer at the badge again.

It was mangled as if trodden on by a mailed boot or something else heavy enough to press it out of shape. Could it be one of Richard's white hart badges? It might be anything. It certainly looked like an animal of some sort. A saint's badge? Who had animals as their symbol? St Francis? It wasn't a bird. A lion, maybe? St Mark? Maybe it wasn't even a lion despite that curling shape. It could be a tail, a wyvern? A serpent even? It was impossible to tell.

What would be helpful was to know exactly where it was found, whether dropped by the murderous bowman in the abbey barn yard or simply picked up in the street. He cursed the old fellow's reticence. Without somebody answering a few questions nothing suggested even the wisp of an answer. He finished his ale and went outside.

It was raining worse than ever. Gusts billowed across the yard sending people scattering for shelter.

Many were still trying to gain entrance to the Commons chamber to hear the latest on Arundel's set of proposals for tightening up the heresy laws. The current draft was facing a rough ride but he didn't doubt that it would eventually become law. That's the way things were going now. Gone were the old days when Richard held power on a pleasantly loose rein.

Ever since last autumn the nature of the new regime had been made clear. Straight after Henry's coronation in the September a fellow called John Hall had been dragged into court to answer charges over the death of Gloucester in his Calais prison cell.

Hall had the misfortune to become the scapegoat used to taint Richard's name with murder. Making an innocent man pay for

Gloucester's death allowed the real murderers to go free and the rumours about who was guilty were officially silenced for good.

In fact all Hall had done was obey orders and hold the door for Henry's men while they pressed the pillow over the old Fox's face. Now Hall was dead, executed without trial, and another obstacle between Henry and his stolen crown was silenced.

People were flattening themselves against the wall under the overhanging thatch as rain cascaded off it while the guards sheltered grimly inside the porch. What a thankless task, thought Chandler, with a glance at their morose expressions. At least he was free to find shelter in some more congenial spot. Briefly wishing he was still inside the inn he set off with long strides towards the nearest chapel.

It happened to be St Margaret's and he bundled inside in his sodden cloak, the hem of his robes clinging wetly to his boots, dripping puddles onto the tiled floor. He knelt at the first shrine he came to and shut his eyes.

10

A strong scent of incense and the feeling that the place was filling up eventually made him open them. A couple of acolytes were swinging a censer and trying to adapt themselves to the grave pace of a priest as he processed down the nave.

A crowd had entered since he arrived. A swift survey made him drop his glance at once.

She was here.

For once she had been far from his thoughts.

He risked another glance in her direction, saw her lower her eyelids. She had noticed him. Was pretending she hadn't. He would do nothing now but bide his time.

It was the midday office, usually sparsely attended but today attracting a full congregation because of the rain. It was battering against the window-glass and every time the doors opened gusts ran the length of the nave, blustered at the hems of cloaks and swept wet leaves between everybody's feet. The altar candles guttered. The little acolytes halted for a moment to grip the censer-chain and stop ash falling to the tiles.

As soon as everything was righted the service began. He did not look in her direction again.

11

It was still pouring. Nobody wanted to be first out. They jostled in the porch until some began to push their way through the press. He followed until he was brought up beside her.

Rain already beaded the inevitable loose strands of her hair turning it to the dark gold of molten bronze. When he spoke her name she turned with an exaggerated exclamation of surprise.

'I did not notice you inside, Rodric.'

He considered matters. The fact of her duplicity. She knew he had seen her just as he knew she had seen him. And now the unexpected intimacy. *Rodric.*

'I thought I noticed you but dare not hope it was you,' he replied blandly, watching her expression.

A darkening deep in her eyes may have been in his imagination, or not. It could have been a trick of the light. He trod carefully as if over quicksand when he spoke again.

'As we have met, by chance, perhaps you will do me the honour of allowing me to walk with you, Matilda, if you're going back towards the house? Here, look, I have a cloak.'

An attempt to hold the edge over her to protect her from the rain. A slight bridling. A submission, the cloak over her shoulders. They began to pace between the puddles towards the row of lease-holds.

To break the silence he murmured, 'How convenient for you, to have the chapel of the blessed St Margaret close by.'

She gave him a startled glance. 'St Margaret's—?'

Then she walked on, looking straight ahead as if he wasn't there.

It made him remember the time at Aldgate when he had led her, unresisting, to the chantry that first time. That only time, as he now reminded himself.

He framed various platitudes without uttering them. None of them sounded innocent. A question about her master? Too loaded. About Pinkhurst? Suspicious. What she was doing next? Too inquisitive. The fact that she had not come to visit him at Aldgate as he had suggested? Too much like an accusation.

When they reached the house she removed his cloak from her

shoulders with a small, false laugh. 'Now your hair's wet. And it's my fault.'

He ran a hand through his hair and wondered if she might use it as an excuse to invite him in but she did not. She merely smiled like a woman under some constraint. Still angry with him, he supposed. Pretending otherwise.

No wonder, to be fair. Leaving her with only his scribbled text about alphabets of love, like a philandering courtier. Leaving it where she might find it. Like an afterthought. It offered no excuse or explanation for his disappearance.

Well, in truth, how could it? He could not drag her into things. Not then, at any rate. Now it was different.

He said, 'You do understand that I had no choice but to leave you when I did? It was not my decision. The lord I serve gave me no time to reach you.'

She gave him a blank look.

'You remember, you told me the Master was away and I said I would come to the house? And on my way back to Aldgate those men you saw earlier, those men-at-arms . . .?' He had still not managed to bring a spark of recognition to her expression. Surely she had not forgotten?

'Remember the men-at-arms who tried to disarm me in the street? And you ran across the road to me? And called my name,' he added, lamely.

The corners of her mouth lifted a little. 'Of course I remember. There were four or five of them against one. It was so unequal.'

'So,' he replied.

She waited for him to continue.

'So their lord came along later. He was waiting for me with his bodyguard outside my house that night when . . .' He faltered. 'I had no choice. I had no idea where we were going. No way of letting you know.'

He considered matters. So far he had not needed to lie.

His air of honesty may have beguiled her. She put out a hand to rest it on his arm. 'Rodric,' she sighed. To his astonishment she lifted her mouth as if to receive a kiss but there were people about and she sighed again. 'Now here you are.'

Again he considered matters.

At last he said, 'But you have not been to see me as I hoped you would. After we met again not more than – not long ago—'

'It would be impossible for me to make that trip downriver as you suggested. I am bound to my Master and his authority.'

'Does he never let you have time off from work?'

'I will think of something.' She hesitated. 'Trust me. I will send a message to the chantry.'

With a quick turn of her head she hurried towards the house and in moments she was inside and closing the door between them.

He lingered, expecting, hoping, that she might appear at the window to see if he was still there but if she did so she was taking care to stand so far back he could not make out her shape in the shadows.

Thoughtfully he walked away, now oblivious to the pelting rain.

Chandler's Chronicle

It is some time since I added to my pages. Not since St Albans, since the story about the lord Despenser and the barbarous folk of Bristol. Not since then. I have found it difficult to continue this account. Because of the burden that has started to weigh on me. How do I separate rumour from fact? There are so many rumours. So many versions of the facts. Can that be right? Can truth have many versions? If I write what I see, then I offer only a partial story, a splinter of the truth. There are versions that are plain lies, designed to deceive. Others not so designed. I also wonder if this is my true voice. Where is it, I might ask? It disappears as soon as I sharpen a quill and set to work. The facts are as I witness them but something changes them as soon as I start to write, like alchemy, blending my meaning to suit a different law, facts themselves struggling for life through the labyrinth of invented words – truth, shifting to some other realm. Or is it words themselves, belonging to neither God nor the Devil but inhabiting an unknowable region between the two?

I fear to set anything down in case the truth becomes distorted. Lies set in stone.

This morning the old man handed me the badge as if it meant something and I might be interested.

But for the existence of the badge itself I half-believe I might have invented him.

I begin to wonder if the murders are something invented by myself and no mysteries at all.

Look at it. At what it is.

He found a pilgrim badge, he said, and saw me, a friar, he said and, as it happened, thought to hand it to me. 'I thought you might be interested.' Very well.

And Underwood. The look on his face. Was it invented by me? Was he merely thinking better of making a confession of some trivial sin, deciding against wasting my time and his own with his concerns? Feeling like a fool claiming importance for something nobody else would find shaming? Gossip about his commander, maybe. Rage at Swynford being his usual irascible self and no schism between him and Henry? In short, nothing serious. Underwood. Hardly even looking at the badge. 'Watch your back, brother.' Simply what men say to each other, all the time. No mystery there either.

And Knollys. I mention a book with questionable content. He tells me about someone who may be able to help with a translation. Fact. Nothing to it.

Why does it bother me so much? Why do I imagine it means anything more than what I write now? Nothing to it. Why does it bother me?

And Matilda. Her look.

He replaced the quill on the stand and watched the excess ink pool under the sharpened point.

FOURTEEN

Westminster Abbey Close. March 1400.

I am forced to a decision. They are frantically busy. Adam is scribbling away with rapid glances at a sheet on the stand beside him. Copying. The Master is sorting through a pile of vellum, putting them into some sort of order. He places finished pages in stacks on a side table. Now and then Adam hands him a dried sheet to add to the pile.

To be hoped Brother Chandler as I now think of him does not appear or it will be a scene from hell.

I begin, 'Master?'

He glances up. 'Not now, Mattie—'

Before he can return to his sorting I say, 'May I have some time off to visit my friends in Cheap?'

He is peering at one of the pages and looks dissatisfied. He murmurs without looking up, 'When would you like to go, my starling?'

'Now . . . unless you need me for anything?'

He places the page on top of the other ones and looks up at me as if seeing me for the first time. He glances across at Adam, all this while pretending not to be listening in, and the Master catches his eye then beckons me, saying, 'In return will you do something for me while you're out, my chick?'

I stand before him. He knows I will. 'What is it, Master?'

'Will you be as much like a little shadow as you can manage and take a message to someone for me?'

'In the City?'

'Aye, in the City quite near Cheap. I'll tell you the address and you must remember it and as soon as you leave there you must forget it. Can you do that?'

'I expect so.' I give him a haughty look. 'It sounds easy enough.'

'And you must remember that no one must see you enter the house.'

'I have remembered. I'm not likely to forget.'

'I know that. I know I can rely on you, dear Mattie.'

'What's this message I have to take, Master?'

'Nothing more.'

'What do you mean, nothing more?'

'Ask for the steward by name, Master Whitlock, and wait until he appears. Tell him who sent you. That's all you have to do. He will reply. This is the point of the matter. You must remember his words exactly.'

'It sounds easy. Are you sure you wouldn't want some messenger lad to do such a simple errand for you?'

'I'd rather send you because I know I can trust you to do exactly as I ask.'

I've decided I'll do this first and then go onto Cheap to see Izzie and the others and then, fortified, I shall make my third call because he mentioned St Margaret.

As I turn to leave, Adam half-rises to his feet. To the Master he says, 'I think I ought to go with her, the way things are—'

The Master shakes his head. 'No, no, not necessary. She can slip through the crowds with less notice than you, you great hulk. She's an elf, nobody will bother about an elvish girl. Take a shopping basket with you, Mattie,' and he smiles at me.

FIFTEEN

Aldgate. March 1400.

He forced himself to put her out of his mind and give the other matter some serious thought. It had to be one of the three. He couldn't see Swynford's longbow-men shooting their own, knocking them over like pigeons. Not possible. They were handpicked for loyalty. Staunch followers of the red rose, with no illusions about what would happen to them if they stepped out of line.

The way the crowd had been so easily turned against the rebel earls like brutes of the chase showed what mood people were in these days. Blood lust was in the air. The military knew it. They played on it. They were like fire-raisers setting a spark to tinder. They would not want to be its victims if the house came down. He grieved at the thought of what they had done to Montagu in Cirencester, a most kind and gentle knight – only beasts who had lost touch with reason could have torn him physically apart in the toils of such ferocity.

He knelt in front of the small icon to St Serapion but no prayers would come. It was meaningless. Nothing there.

He got up, wishing that his sacristan was back with his cheery face, to jolly him out of this dark mood. Anyway, he thought, it was better for Martin that he was still safe with Brother Daniel out at the herb gardens in Hackney. Arundel would not get at him there. He could be as Wyclifite as he wanted, the young rogue. His presence would go unnoticed under the guardianship of the herberer in his walled enclave. Just another gardener stooping over his cures.

He gnawed away at the problem without respite.

The doors to the chapel stood open and one or two worshippers came in to pay their respects and plead for better times.

The streets sounded rowdy again. The few who turned up were grateful for Serapion's sanctuary. He recognized them all. They lived close by. He exchanged a few words. Did not explain his recent absence. Noted only that they were glad he was back.

They were mostly merchants, praying for the safe voyage of their ships, or a wife or two, praying for a husband's return from overseas. All with the usual needs and despairs of ordinary, powerless folk who wanted nothing more than to lead quiet lives with a shred of dignity and only minimal need for dishonesty in their trading practices.

After the last one left he closed the doors and caution made him drop the beam into place.

SIXTEEN

The City. March 1400.

The address I have to find is near Bread Street.

Before I leave, pulling up my hood and looking as much like a shadow as the Master would like, I tell myself that it is not an out-and-out lie to say I want to see Izzie and other friends in the market at Cheap. I do. It's just that that's not all.

I'm at the door when Adam comes out of the front chamber still holding a quill.

'I don't like this, Mattie. I can ask him if I can have time off to come with you.'

'There's no need. Nobody will notice me. I'll do exactly as he says.'

'I know you will. But things are getting rough in the streets. There's much unrest today.'

'All the rowdies are down here at Westminster now the new king is come from his castle in Hereford to sit in on the parliament.'

'Even so, they won't all be here. Make sure you don't draw attention to yourself.'

'I won't.' I open my scrip and show him the hilt of a little knife I've borrowed from the kitchen.

'Carrying a blade, you naughty girl?'

'What else would you expect.' I slip it back out of sight.

He smiles. 'I wouldn't like to be on the wrong end of that.'

'Behave yourself then you won't be.'

'I'll not forget.'

He gives me that leering look that always makes me turn away before I can stop myself, like somebody who can't think of a reply to cut him down to size. As if. It just seems fairer to hold my tongue. So I do.

He comes to watch me leave.

When I look back he is still watching from the doorway. He sees me glance back and shuts the door.

2

I alight without incident at Wood wharf and walk up Garlick Hill in the direction of Cheap until I reach the turn off towards Bread Street. Making myself as invisible as I can I find the place I want easily enough.

Nobody takes any notice when I enter the courtyard where some horses are waiting. I ask one of servants where I can find Master Whitlock. A jerk of the head directs me towards the main doors of a fair-sized mansion running the length of the yard.

Somebody is standing in the doorway when I mount the steps and I ask again and am directed inside. It is much grander than the outside would suggest and I wonder who lives here.

There are plenty of servants about and an imposing fellow who can only be the steward is already coming towards me. He looks me up and down. I do the same, noting his good quality velvet, his ring, his staff, his clipped grey beard, his assessing blue eyes and receding hairline.

'I come from Master Chaucer,' I say, expecting a blank look but instead he glances over my shoulder into the courtyard then smiles down at me. 'Then tell him my dear, that the serpent is scotched and the child awaits.'

We gaze at each other for a long moment and I want to ask him what he means but guess there will be no answer. Job done then. I thank him and turn away.

'Here,' he calls me back. 'For your trouble, little maid.' He hands me a russet from a nearby dish. His rings flash.

Cheapside looks busy as I approach from Queen Street and there are plenty of stalls with the usual goods on display. What is lacking is the old bantering atmosphere where you really have to be on your toes to parry the thrusts from the marketeers. A heavy, dark, dead dullness hangs over everything and instead of wit and smiles I feel as if I'm moving among stones.

Nobody looks at me except cautiously when they recognize a familiar face and when I ask about Izzie the fellow on the fish stall tells me she's still in Kent with her three strong sons. 'Given up her trade here. Along with that friend of hers.'

'Annie?'

'Aye, she's not been seen since before Christmastide.'

They were my two friends, Izzie with her lovely cheeses that always pleased the Master so much and Annie with her gifts of orchard fruit, always secretly adding extra to my basket for my own self. My sorrow at missing them cuts through me and is a penance for using them as an excuse.

'Will you tell them I was asking after them if they turn up again?'

The fishmonger gives a doleful smile. 'They'll like to know that. Here.' He reaches under his counter and pushes a small herring wrapped in leaves towards me. 'Get yon cook to make something of this.' We talk for another moment or two, catching up with the latest clamp-down on the City, and as he turns aside to a customer he says, 'Come back and see us again when you're sick of Westminster.'

Two gifts, the russet to be saved for later and shared with the others, and a fresh fish to delight Cook's heart.

The serpent is scotched and the child awaits.

Now for my third encounter. I turn towards Aldgate.

SEVENTEEN

Aldgate. March 1400.

He left the chantry long enough to go out to the pie stall at the top of Cornhill and then refilled his water bottle at the pump. While he was doing so the sound of discord reached his ears. Troublemakers. He glanced along the street. All morning he had been aware of the intermittent tumult of street-fights. First it was near, then it drifted away, but the City was more febrile than ever and the sounds of incipient violence never really stopped until curfew.

When he could see no particular rout he turned towards his chantry but had gone no more than two or three paces when a running, heaving mob erupted from a side street and began to tumble down the short length of Aldgate towards the walls. It caught up with him and quickly swept him up but managing to fight his way out after a few yards he pushed back into the chantry without harm.

The beam banged into place and he stood listening as the shouts and running footsteps receded. By the sound of it two rival gangs had clashed and it was not difficult to guess who they were, apprentices mostly, one side with the confidence of winners, the other full of the grievance of losers.

He finished his pie while sitting on the altar steps with his long legs outstretched. *I should clean this place now I'm back*, he thought as he restoppered his water bottle and glanced round at the dust and peeling plasterwork. He knew he hadn't the heart to do it.

Outside the gangs were surging back and he heard them banging on the doors as they passed. Let them, he thought. But when it continued as if somebody was trying to get inside he got to his feet with the intention of shouting at them with some suitable oaths they would understand. But halfway to the door he paused.

He imagined he heard a woman's voice above the rabble. It seemed to rise on a note of desperation. As he listened it came again and something familiar about it took him in a few swift strides across the floor.

Soundlessly lifting the beam he jammed one boot behind the door and edged it wide enough for a single person to squeeze through.

It was not one of his parishioners as he might have expected.

It was Mattie.

As soon as the door was wide enough she fell inside.

He slammed it behind her and stared in astonishment. 'I thought I must be dreaming. What are you doing in the City?'

'I came to see you.'

She glanced towards the door. The mob outside was still hammering at it, shouts more aggressive. Something like a brick was thrown and there was a thump and after that the clash of what could only be weapons of some sort.

Mattie had one hand to her mouth. 'I thought I was done for.' She was breathing in great gulps, gasping for air.

He held out his water flask. 'Drink some of this.'

'Is it communion wine?'

He shook his head. He was amazed she could still joke when she was so clearly terrified. 'Sadly not, Mattie, but maybe with the right prayers I might turn it into wine for you?' He held it out again.

She was leaning with her back against the doors and staring with wide eyes at him as if too frightened to move. 'Why are they rioting?'

He frowned. 'Come and sit down. You're safe here.' He held out a hand. 'Wait until they exhaust themselves. They usually give up when it gets dark and the bailiff and his ruffians come out to beat them back to their lairs at curfew.'

'I can't stay until then!'

Instead of following him she stood where she was and in a shaky voice said, 'I have something to tell you.'

EIGHTEEN

Aldgate. The chantry.

Before I can explain he forestalls me, saying, 'Tell him he is best to do what they ask.'

At first I have no idea what he means. He? What '*he*'?

Noticing my confusion he adds, 'All he needs to do is say something flattering about Henry and all will be forgiven. The guards will be taken off. He will be free to go where he wants and talk to whom he wants. It's not much to ask. He could write a fitting eulogy in the blink of an eye.'

I don't know what to say. He seems to think I've turned up in order to betray the Master.

When he receives no response he says, 'John Gower has already complied. He made no fuss about writing a few lines of praise. He's even re-dedicating his *Confessio Amantis* written for King Richard and now he's changed the names and it's in praise of his puissant lord, King Henry the fourth.' He gives a sardonic smile. 'He's scrubbed every reference to King Richard and his magnificence from his text, they tell me. If Gower can do it, so can a poet with far more skill than Gower will ever have. He must do it to save his neck,' he urges with a grim frown when I say nothing. 'Tell him so.'

A stone is hurled through one of the windows, shattering a small pane of coloured glass, the sort probably donated by a wealthy widow. He puts out a hand to shield me from the flying splinters. I ignore them but cannot help noticing the swiftness of his gesture.

He repeats, 'Tell him so, Mattie. Do that.'

To be sure I now understand him I ask, 'Are you talking about the Master?'

'Isn't that what you've come to tell me? That he cannot work with guards standing out in the Close watching his house?'

'Guards—? I didn't know there were guards!'

He gives a sigh of exasperation as at the wittering of a dolt. 'What do you think they're doing there?'

'I didn't even notice them.'

'Is he as blind? Surely he's seen them?'

'How would I know?'

'Doesn't he talk about it? Somebody must have mentioned them. Has he said nothing about Arundel? About this new statute he's trying to get onto the law books? Don't you know anything, Mattie? Are you living in a dream?' Suddenly violent, he strides towards me and grips me by both shoulders and shakes me. 'Don't you know what's going on?'

I shut my eyes. 'I don't know anything.'

'So it would seem.'

I'm aware of him standing over me.

'Is he in danger?' I ask weakly. 'Is the Master in danger?'

'The king was murdered in Pontefract Castle . . . As even you must know. Why do you think I was sent there? Of course he's in danger!'

He flings away leaving me with the feeling that the floor has suddenly sunk from under my feet.

I know I'm staring but I cannot reconcile the way he looks – his face, so fine, like a saint on a tomb, his reckless mouth making me want to – and what he is telling me. What he has just said. His expression has changed into something hard. But even so I want him to hold me, tell me none of this is happening. One look at him and all my common sense deserts me. I weaken . . . I will not weaken.

Grasping at any straw I tell myself I misunderstood. With breath held in until it aches I plead in silence for him to explain.

Instead he sprawls on the altar steps with his long legs outstretched and takes a gulp from his leather bottle asking, 'So what do you imagine those rioters outside are arguing about? The price of fish?' He gives a sarcastic laugh. 'Not this time. Those days are gone. Now it's a life-or-death matter. Anybody writing a word that can be construed as heretical whether it is or not had better look out. Your poet is not safe. Tell him that. No one is safe.'

He gets to his feet, restless and angry, although I'm not sure who his anger is directed at. He begins to stride about. His boots crunch over broken glass.

'Have you given a thought to what they're discussing in Westminster?' He stands over me. 'You must have realized something's up?' He sounds less angry than before, more resigned, as if it is all no use.

My voice comes out as a whisper and he takes a few paces

towards me to bend his head and I repeat what I said. 'I know he will never deny anything he has written in good faith. He will ask, why should I?'

'Not even the Book of the Lion?'

When I daren't answer he straightens. 'He should do exactly what they want of him if he wants to live.'

His expression is chilling. I wonder if he is trying to frighten me into telling him something but he gives a sort of smile and closes his eyes.

'The Book of the Lion,' he murmurs. 'Is that the one he'll stand by? Or those tales showing pilgrims for the lying, irreligious, sinning folk they are? Which one is worth dying for? The Book of the Lion isn't even his own story. It's French, isn't it?'

His eyes are suddenly needle-sharp, holding my glance until I'm forced to make some sort of a reply although I can barely speak. 'I don't know.'

His voice cuts through me. 'I thought you told me you were reading it? He must have already translated it – unless you read it in French.' He raises his eyebrows.

'I don't – I don't know.'

'Come now, Mattie.'

When I can find nothing to say that won't lead to something even more incriminating he insists, 'English or French, Mattie? Which was it?'

With more urging I manage to croak, 'It was in English.'

'I thought so. And your Master put it into English, didn't he? So that anyone could read it and have a laugh at a usurper's expense. Was he writing it for a patron – or only for general amusement?'

I shake my head.

'Maybe it was for Madame de Pisan? Her son is living in the household of earl Montagu – and we all know which side John Montagu was on . . . and the price he paid for his loyalty to King Richard.'

'I don't know . . . I know nothing about any of this.'

'So why are you here?'

Before I can scrape an answer from somewhere a thunderous banging on the doors echoes round the chantry and we can hear a man yelling to be let in. I've almost forgotten the rioters in the street. They cannot frighten me as much as Chandler does. *He was sent to Pontefract. Then the king was murdered.*

He goes to the door and with his ear against the wood asks, 'Martin? Is that you?'

An answer comes and he begins to lift the beam as a young fair-haired friar pushes inside and the beam is dropped back across the doors leaving howls of thwarted rioters outside.

'What the devil are you doing in the City, you losel?' Chandler throws his arms round the stranger in an extravagant bear-hug and at the same time ushers him further into the chantry.

They sit on the altar steps and the stranger, looking unperturbed by his narrow escape, throws an arm round Chandler, saying, 'I thought it a good idea to make sure you were safe, old fellow. Daniel has been fretting about you.'

'No need to worry. Here I am. Holed up like a hawk in its mews.'

'I have information. It's a business malign beyond all belief except for Pontefract. Nothing could be worse than this now he's been murdered.' He crosses himself and is so moved he can hardly speak. I'm astounded to hear him refer to King Richard. Saying this to Chandler of all people?

He goes on, 'It's about John Aston. They've dragged him down to Saltwood. They'll keep him until Arundel's statute is law and then they'll burn him. There is no way he can talk his way out of it. He will never recant. Arundel needs a warning fire to deter the rest of us and Aston is going to be its first fine flame.'

Chandler simply stares at him.

Before he can find a reply the stranger becomes aware that they're not alone.

He glances at me, looking puzzled, turning to Chandler for an explanation. I wonder how the spy will explain me away. My mind teems with questions about this stranger wearing the robes of a black friar and his mention of John Aston whom everybody knows to be a staunch follower of Wyclif from the early days and a translator of the Bible and a well-known heretic. I want to warn him he's speaking to a spy.

To my surprise Chandler merely says, 'As soon as that mob out there goes quiet I'm escorting her to the water stairs so she can go back to Westminster.'

'They're only making a noise for the sake of it,' the stranger says. 'I'll come along to the waterfront with you. Now I've seen you I need to get back to Shadwell.'

'And how is he?'

'As always! Praise be! He's teaching me all he can. I'll soon be able to cure you of any ailment known to man. I'm his right hand and I'll soon be good enough to be yours.'

'You'll always be good enough to be my right hand, Martin, have no fear.'

Soon it is as they expect. The rioters tire of their noise and move on elsewhere. Daylight, short-lived at this time of year, is fading behind the broken glass of the little window they shattered and Chandler has picked up the shards and put them in a neat pile on the step beside him.

They have both ignored me all this while, discussing the ins-and-outs of the moment. Now Chandler looks across at me. 'I told you there was no need to be frightened.'

He is, I understand, trying to explain my presence by suggesting that I sought refuge here in the chantry. I have no idea why he should want to imply such a thing. What does it matter that we have an acquaintance of sorts? Who is this friar he pretends to hold in such esteem? What are they to do with Aston? It makes no sense and I fear for the newcomer as he clearly does not understand Chandler's allegiance.

I pull up my hood. 'I'm not frightened. It's getting late. I'll be on my way. My thanks for offering me sanctuary, brother.' I sound sarcastic. I don't care.

'Wait.' He stands over me. 'I'll open the doors and check if it's safe to leave. If it is, I'll escort you as far as the landing from where you can take the boat back to Westminster.' He turns to the friar. 'She lives in the household of Master Chaucer.'

A flicker of some thought passes swiftly over the stranger's face but I can make nothing of it.

All I want is to get back, away from here. I have not told Chandler what I wanted him to know. Maybe now I never shall. I cannot imagine ever wanting to come here again.

As we prepare to leave I'm glad I mean nothing to him.

Every gesture confirms it despite his natural swiftness at protecting me from the flying glass. He would have done the same for anyone. Every look and word and touch tells me I am nothing to him. He means nothing to me either.

The stranger is smiling at me in a kindly way and then, apparently familiar with how things are done here, he lifts the beam to open the doors to the street. He pokes his head outside then glances over his shoulder. 'They've gone. I'll come down with you both to pick up a ferry.'

The street outside is strangely empty after the rioting. Good folk are indoors. The rioters themselves have moved on leaving only bricks and splintered wood and random garments. Chandler checks everything in the chantry, dousing a candle with a thumb and fore-finger, and comes out last. He closes the great doors behind us. Turns a key. We set our faces towards the river.

The serpent has been scotched and the child awaits.

I know nothing about anything.

2

'And so I found it quite easily, Master, and the steward Master Whitlock gave me the message without any problem just as you said he would. And I hope it makes sense to you.'

He gives me a kind smile then turns it on Adam. 'I think she has done remarkably well, don't you, Adam? A treasure of a girl. And was all quiet in the City?'

'Reasonably so, with only a little unrest,' I fib so as not to alarm him.

'You were late back and we were beginning to worry—'

'I missed the ferry and had to wait an age for another one.'

Feeling that by casting my lot in with them I am defying Chandler and everything he stands for I tell him that if he ever wants me to run a similar errand he only has to ask.

'You're a good girl, Mattie. We don't know what we would do without you. There will be something, maybe one or two little errands at some point.' He nods. 'Now then, Adam, back to work.'

'A moment.' I bite my lip because I do not want to cast a shadow over things but I feel I must pass on the warning I was given. As quickly as I can I tell him about the rioters, playing it down a little, and I have to mention what happened and how I was swept briefly into the safety of St Serapion's chantry near Aldgate as I was passing and, while Adam scowls, I repeat what Chandler told me and add for good measure the mention of Aston by the stranger who turned up.

All Adam says is, 'You must have been there a good long while.'

'The rioters were running back and forth between Cornhill and the city gate but evidently they were not allowed through onto Mile End. It wasn't safe to go out once inside with the door barred. They threw a stone through the little east window. It was the only coloured glass they had.'

'Of course she was sensible to remain where she was, Adam. I would expect you'd have done the same.'

'I wouldn't have been in Brother Chandler's domain in the first place.'

'Ah, well, we are all wise after the event, are we not? I expect she had a good reason for going there.' The Master is already thinking of something else and makes off towards his writing chamber and Adam, with one dark glance thrown in my direction, follows.

Later Adam wants to know exactly what I said to Chandler. 'Did you mention where you'd already been?'

I'm outraged. 'Of course not! Do you think I'm a dolt? The Master warned me how careful I had to be!'

He is alarmed, though, when I tell him Chandler mentioned the Book of the Lion. I can't help blushing with shame. 'He mentioned it first,' I excused myself, in vain of course. 'I didn't say a thing out of place, honest, Adam, you can believe that now after the way you carried on before . . . I was on my guard—'

'Don't make things worse. What did he say about it?'

'He only wanted to know whether it was written in English.'

'So you told him. Thank you for putting our heads at risk.'

'He knew anyway. Would I be likely to read French? He knew I'd read it. I wouldn't have told him I was reading it if he hadn't tricked me into talking about books. I didn't know it was going to be on Arundel's list. How could I? It's just a story. Where's the harm in it?'

'And Aston?' He quickly changed the subject. 'He's in Saltwood now, is he? Poor devil. I hope he manages to get out before long, alive for preference, with his fingernails attached.'

3

I did not tell either the Master or Adam what had happened on the way from Aldgate to the wharf. It was this.

We had not gone far when we were set upon by four or five ruffians. Whether footpads taking advantage of a girl and two friars, easy targets in the general mayhem, or professional cut-throats on a different mission, I shall never know, nor shall I know whether I would have been safer alone as being less of a target or not, but certainly it was frightening to see them bursting out behind us from one of those dark alleys near the river, knives and fists being wielded purposefully against us.

By the kindness of providence and the protection of the angels my two companions were armed with swords concealed under their cloaks. It was something that surprised me, and later I thanked heaven for it because they drew them at once and when the gang still jeered and came on they surged against them side by side and spared them nothing.

It had been Chandler who tried to warn them to lay off first and he landed a hard punch in the face of the nearest one that almost felled him but when the others ignored him and drove on at him with more determination he struck the leader on the side of the head with the flat of his sword and when, undeterred, the ruffian raised a broadsword to strike Chandler, he received his punishment. In ignorance of Chandler's unlikely skill as a swordsman, he stood no chance of retribution.

I cannot say too much about what happened next except that there was much blood and when we made our escape leaving four men lying on the ground, cursing their misfortune, a fifth was running like a hare from our presence.

I was shaking all over with a mixture of terror and relief and Chandler stopped and put his arms round me and held me in a calm embrace for some moments.

I believe I muttered something about not knowing why I was shaking because I had already witnessed his skill when Swynford's men tried to set about him at Aldgate before Christmastide, an event that led to my recent situation, the memory of it bringing me back with a jolt to the present. It wrenched a sob from me, my misery made worse by the confusing tenderness with which he held me.

For a moment I had forgotten his companion who had himself put up a strong showing, a real right hand as Chandler had attested, and I believe I started to swoon in the tumult of my feelings.

Somehow or other we found ourselves on the wharf where the boats were jostling for trade and the friar, Martin, as I remember he was called, said, 'This is where I leave you for now, Rodric. Pray for our dear Aston.'

As he turned he seemed to remember something and called back to Chandler, 'Wait a moment, brother. I have something to show you. Look at this.'

Chandler stepped aside to see what it was he was holding up.

Martin said, 'I ripped this off the big fellow.' He held it to the light of the boatman's flare.

Chandler frowned and started to rummage inside his scrip and eventually drew out something that he showed to Martin in his cupped palm, asking, 'This one is somewhat damaged. It looks similar. Do you know what it is?'

Martin gave an odd laugh. 'I do. It's a recent thing. He's having them cast in order to hand them out to his inner circle, his personal guards, his arse-licking prelates. Can you believe the arrogance of the man, this self-styled archbishop? . . . It's meant to be a serpent.'

The boat taking him to Shadwell was about to leave and he jumped down into it, calling up to Chandler, 'So! We know who they were! Mystery solved?'

And Chandler shouted back, 'The devil's men all along!'

Then Martin was being carried away downriver as he shouted something else and lifted one hand in a gesture of benediction.

Chandler wore an odd expression as he watched him disappear downriver, distant, a little stunned, and he was unspeaking as he turned away.

I was already looking for the boat going up to Westminster and expected him to make off now he had done his duty but to my surprise he followed me to where the oarsman was settling people on board the up-ferry before casting off and, making as if to hand me into it, said, 'I've decided to escort you to Westminster, Mattie. Move over.'

'I'm sure you have no need—' I began but he was already following me although he didn't say anything else. When we were underway, to break the silence I made a remark about not having guessed how good he was with his fists.

'It's a rough place, the cloister,' he replied.

'You're not a cloister monk,' I pointed out.

'I don't claim to be.'

'To anybody who didn't know better they'd have thought you were making such a claim.'

'They shouldn't make assumptions should they, this mythical person?'

'Except that you lead people to make assumptions. I call it lying without lying.'

'A lie is something spoken.'

'So what's the difference between a flat lie and speaking to deceive?'

'Do you think I deceive you?'

'I think you deceive everyone.'

'You may be right – except for one instance.'

'Which is?' I expected him to say something sanctimonious about God but he didn't.

He said, 'The instance of you and what passes between us.' He looked into my eyes and added, 'Don't expect me to claim it's a matter of the heart but you confuse me . . . that's the one instance where I will not deceive you, the matter of my confusion.'

I tried to scry his meaning but he turned away and stared out across the river with a morose expression and said no more.

After that I had no choice but to suffer his silent presence all the way back, passing the tumult of the apprentice gangs onshore, drawing level with Lambeth rising white and commanding on the other bank, all witnessed in silence until we reached our destination.

NINETEEN

Westminster Stairs.

He had to choose between calling on Knollys in Seething Lane to demand some answers or going up to Westminster to see what he could find out for himself. He chose the latter course for obvious reasons. At first he thought they had been attacked due to a simple case of mistaken identity. Then Martin showed him the serpent badge and he feared a deeper and more dangerous reason. Knollys was hardly the man to whom to reveal his fears. Those brawlers might have followed them from the chantry for all he knew. He pushed the thought aside for now.

His immediate reason for going up to Westminster was to search out the old fellow who had given him Arundel's token and persuade him to admit where exactly he had picked it up. There was obviously more to the story than the man admitted.

Knollys, he felt, must know something but until he held a stronger hand it would be pointless to show his cards. Knowing him of old it would be impossible to persuade him to admit anything if he was under orders to keep things to himself.

These thoughts kept running through his mind as the boat made its slow way upriver. He told himself how important it was to find out if the old fellow knew what the badge was – now Martin had revealed its meaning. He did not for a moment believe it had been found by accident. The nonsense about visiting a grand-daughter in St Albans sounded implausible, given the difficulty of travel at this particular time, with Swynford's men clearing the road for the cortege and so forth, and he must have been given it by someone with instructions who to hand it to.

Was it a warning – or an accusation?

Either way, Underwood's advice to watch his back seemed worth taking seriously. It was impossible to guess how likely it was that he would find the mysterious old stranger but a few questions asked around the taverns was the most likely source of information.

With this in mind he was keen to get ashore but when they arrived at the Westminster landing it was seething with folk trying to get away and the bottom of the steps was impassable.

The boatman sculled a little way off and called out to one of his fellows in an adjacent boat about the reason for such a scrum.

'You missed it, they've got another one.'

'What's that? Another what?'

'Another murder.'

'Who is it?'

'Another of lord Swynford's lot. Somebody's been picking them off since they started out with the cortege.'

'Where did it happen?'

'Out in the yard, believe it or not. Another longbow-man? Or the same saucy devil as before? Perched up out of sight, he was. I'm off until it's safe.'

'I'll do the same. Thanks for the warning. I'll let these off but I'm not taking anybody else onboard yet. Not likely.'

Uproar came from those left stranded when they heard they were not to be taken off. Money was jingled to entice the boatman back but he refused to risk it. Chandler helped Mattie to scramble quickly onto the wharf. Curses followed as both boatmen headed out into the stream despite having to push against the tide. In the falling light they were soon nothing but shadows on the dark waters.

TWENTY

Westminster Stairs. Moments later.

Chandler gripped me by one arm and, dragging me behind him, began to shoulder his way through the crowds lining the stairs. Oblivious to complaints he managed to fetch us to the top where a jabbering mass of people were gathered in the shadow of the Great Hall.

Without saying anything he pulled me briskly along in the direction of the abbey gate and when we were almost there he stopped.

'Listen, are you able to go on from here alone? I imagine those monks will pose no threat to you.'

I couldn't help asking, 'Where are you going now in such a hurry? There are no boats taking anybody back to the City. You heard what they said.'

He shook his head. 'I'm not going back yet. I have things to do.'

With no more than a light touch on my arm he turned swiftly and set off towards the crowds jostling in and out of the Great Hall and I soon lost sight of him. He did not look back.

It was then Adam appeared from nowhere and took me in to see the Master and afterwards gave me another good roasting for blabbing secrets I didn't even know I knew.

TWENTY-ONE

Westminster.

First, the dead man. He was lying on a trestle in Swynford's guardroom.

Unsurprisingly the place was heaving with folk, some useful, some useless and present only to imbibe the nectar of excitement murder often arouses in the ignorant. Swynford had one or two apothecaries in attendance and it was clear to Chandler he would be in the way.

As he turned to leave he noticed Will, standing head and shoulders above everyone else. Chandler went over. The two men eyed each other for a moment. 'And how did this one manage to get in the line of fire?' Chandler eventually asked.

Will gave a lazy smile. 'The skill of Swynford's guards is almost God-given.'

'So presumably the perpetrator has escaped capture?'

'Presumably.' He brought himself to sharper attention. 'How come you're so timely, brother?'

'Chance. I was shown a badge that looked like the one I was given by some old fellow here and decided it was time I found out where he got it.'

He brought it out of his pouch and showed it to him. 'Says he found it at St Albans, implying it was near where a bowman must have taken his lucky shot in the barn yard.'

'Did he, begod. What was he doing there, this old fellow?' He took the mangled piece and peered at it. 'Copper alloy.'

'Seen one like it before?'

He shook his head. 'No.' He handed it back. 'Where are you going to find him?'

'I thought I'd put my head into one or two taverns. Want to join me?'

He sloped after him as Chandler began to shove a path through the gawkers round the dead man. When they were outside Chandler said, 'You must know Underwood recognized it at once? He didn't let on.'

'And that makes you think it has something to do with him?'

'He knew what it meant, that's all I can say.'

'With your connection with Swynford are you surprised he didn't say more?'

'Swynford asked me to find out who the bowman was who's slowly whittling away at his retinue. I've no choice but to do what I can. I am bound. You know that. It doesn't mean I'm going to tell him everything I find out.' He hesitated. 'The truth is I'm implicated whether I want to be or not. He'll have his scapegoat one way or another. I don't want it to be me.' He frowned. There was more he could tell him but this was not the time or place.

Will gave him a close look, eyeing up a target. It made him think he would not like to be in his sights when he put an arrow into the nock.

His only remark as they reached the doors of the first tavern was, 'What does this cove look like, brother?'

When Chandler told him he grinned. 'A little old fellow? He should be easy to spot! If we start now we might finish questioning them all by this time next year. By when,' he added, 'if he's as ancient as you tell me, he might be in his wooden bed covered by daisies!'

Despite his words he followed Chandler in and they stood for a moment casting a glance over the men lined up in front of their ale mugs on the trestles.

One glance revealed that there was no one resembling their quarry, nor were Will's two companions present. Chandler wondered where they drank when they came off duty.

They tried one or two more taverns among the ones that lined the path from the water stairs to the Great Hall, an area of tenements, taverns and traders, bustling as ever with the types drawn to the seat of government and the money to be made there.

Not for the first time Chandler saw the entire realm as nothing more than a market-place for the purpose of profit and loss, the profit being beyond the dreams of many and the loss being the fate suffered by most.

So much for Lady Fortune, he told himself. It was well she was shown blindfold like justice so as not to see the travails of the suffering as she turned her wheel.

As they left the third or fourth drinking den without finding their man, Will said, 'Let's go and have a word with the lads. It's time we asked Jack Underwood what he knows.'

Chandler was surprised by this but followed him as he led down a laup or passage narrow enough to make him assess whether there was enough room to wield a sword effectively. They came out into a crowded yard between the buildings.

Chandler noticed at once that it was full of off-duty military, many wearing the colours of their lords, Swynford's men prominent among them. A few glances were thrown his way but nobody made any remark that could be construed as hostile and it seemed that Will was a fellow in good standing with his colleagues and provided safe-passage for a friar among this mob, confounding his belief that it was he providing protection for the bowmen.

The other two were leaning against a wall at the far side in a group of several others who happened to be wearing King Henry's colours and they greeted Will with immediate offers of ale from the jug that was being passed round. Without any questions they included Chandler, thrusting a stoup of ale into his hands, and continued their war talk with scant curiosity about his reason for joining them, a paid interrogator, albeit on the right side of things. He helped matters by fading into the background as best he could.

Eventually he noticed Will gradually edging Underwood out of the group and, whispering something in his ear, glance across at him and without making much fuss they eventually appeared by his side.

'I'll tell you why it surprised me, the badge,' Underwood began. 'I'd seen that thing once before and knew who it belonged to and I couldn't understand what you were trying to get out of me, testing me, like.'

'It was a straightforward question. At that point I didn't know who it belonged to. It was as I told you, how I got hold of it. I want to know why the old fellow handed it to me.'

He and Will exchanged swift glances.

Underwood quickly asked, 'Where did he say he found it?'

'He didn't. That's another thing I want to find out—'

Will interrupted. 'All he said was he found it at St Albans where that guard of Swynford's was shot.' He glanced at Chandler for confirmation.

'Better ask him then,' Underwood jeered.

'That's why I'm here,' he replied, echoing his belligerent tone.

'Now then,' murmured Will as he sensed their antagonism.

'Maybe it proves something nevertheless . . .' Chandler continued. They leaned closer. 'Maybe . . .' He collected his thoughts. 'Maybe it's our lord Archbishop himself – picking off Swynford's men?'

Will roared with laughter as if to relieve the tension. 'Now there's another thing to tax poor Swynford's brains, brother. A plot against the plotter Henry's vassal? Ho! Good one!'

Even Underwood gave a slow smile.

But it led nowhere and he bought another jug of ale to pass round and eventually thanked them both for their interest, aware that he was being led along like a blind fool and that nothing would be revealed knowingly to him, so before he left he thought it worth a warning.

'Swynford has marked you three out because you're mercenaries. He doubts your allegiance. He thinks you'll do anything for pay. He's determined to get to the bottom of these attacks. His pride is hurt. He imagined everybody loved him. Now he knows they don't.'

As he was leaving he had to make way for more customers seeking the solace of the alehouse and as the group stepped under the light from the brazier at the entrance to the passage he noticed a familiar face.

He stepped into the shadows and watched as he and his companions joined some men taking up space in the middle of the yard. There was backslapping and shouts of welcome. The centre of this enthusiasm was Adam Pinkhurst.

TWENTY-TWO

Chaucer's house. Night.

I hear Adam leave. I think it strange that he should go out so late but then the alehouse is probably as enticing to him as to any other man despite his reading and writing. Cook has cleared up in the kitchen and damped down the fire by the time I come up to bed and soon the whole house is silent.

The Master and Adam had been discussing something in the front chamber and long after the door closed when Adam left I could hear shuffling about as the Master rearranged his pages.

All the time I'm lying here thinking about the sounds around me I know I'm trying to play a stupid trick on myself, a ploy to stop myself from thinking about Chandler. *Rodric. O fatal name.*

Sot wit.

With Adam's warning ever in my ears my thoughts drift back over the incidents of the day, the dangerous feeling of being trapped in the chantry with him and about to pour out my heart; my black fear at what he did at Pontefract; then the interruption by his 'right-hand man', Martin; the stone smashing through the little window and the way he crunched over the glass as he walked towards me; then the attack on the way to the water stairs, the increasing tumult as we approached Westminster, the panic at another murder, the fourth, they say; and the fact that even before that he chose to escort me upriver as if he cared for my safety.

I think about the way he held me after the rout of the attackers, the way he held me, the way he came to the gates of the Close when it was time to part, the way it must mean something, the way he held me, the way he held me.

I cannot sleep for the thought of it, the way he held me in his arms. *Rodric.* I cannot sleep.

It is halfway through the night when Adam returns. His very stealth as he enters creates more stir than if he bangs in roaring some bawdy tavern song.

I hear him murmuring downstairs and realize that the Master

must have been busy in his writing chamber all the time I've been wrestling with vain thoughts about Rodric.

Does he care for me, does he not care for me? Does he, doesn't he?

And I fear he cares only for something beyond me, something dangerous that will bring about his own downfall and maybe mine and the Master's and everyone ever connected to the King, and how nothing makes any sense since they murdered him, if they did, as the spy asserts.

What is the Master doing downstairs all this time?

The sound of their voices rising from the writing chamber at last lulls me to sleep long enough to give me a nightmare.

I am kneeling in the abbey church on the cold floor and trying to put back together the great pavement at the crossing. They made it long ago out of millions of small pieces of coloured stones and glass and in the dream I keep trying to fit the pieces back into place and have nearly done so when I find one more piece that sets the whole pavement into a jumble again and I have to start once more. I am in tears in my dream after several useless attempts, my fingers bleeding and raw, and when I drift awake my cheeks are wet with real tears.

Downstairs their voices are still rumbling on, first one then the other, unaware of the broken pavement and my tears falling on the stones.

Half asleep I get up with the intention of going down to the kitchen to get some water when I hear the Master ask, 'So what was he doing there?'

A mumbled response comes back then the stairs creak and it must be Adam coming up because he says something about being right glad to have somewhere to sleep out of the rain and the Master replies with something like, 'it's a bad business for Swynford,' and 'watch out for repercussions.'

Footsteps go past my door and I hear Adam enter the attic on the other side of the landing. Silence descends.

When I'm certain everything is quiet I creep downstairs, and while I'm fumbling for the tinder box in the alcove near the kitchen door so I can find the water jug to take a beaker up with me the Master finds me. The sudden spurt of flame makes the shadows slither along the wall.

'Sleepless in Arcady, my dear little Mattie?'

My fingers slip on the beaker and water spills down the front of my night-gown.

His look of surprise turns to kindness. He comes over. 'What is it? Are you sleep walking? Did we disturb you, nattering away through the night?'

I shake my head. The drops of spilled water on my bedgown might be tears. Maybe they are tears after all? I can't help blurting, 'Are we safe, Master?'

'Mop it up with this.' He takes one of Cook's clean cloths hanging to dry above the ashed-down fire and holds it out.

I mutter some nonsense about the pavement in the church excusing myself by adding that it was only a dream, as I dab at the spilled water.

'Truth lies in dreams I've often found.'

'There was always a piece missing no matter how hard I tried to fit them together again.' I add, 'It could have been such a beautiful pattern, all the different colours, the shapes, the little coloured stones, and a meaning I can't quite grasp . . .'

'Sometimes it can be dangerous to see into the heart of things. The less it makes sense, the safer you might be.'

I take my beaker of water and turn for the door. He says softly, 'Guard your tongue if you encounter our friend Brother Chandler.'

'I will, of course I will.'

'Then give no further thought to the follies of mankind. Difficulties are here to challenge us, not to defeat us. Trust in the good angels, Mattie, and all will be well.'

TWENTY-THREE

Westminster. Night.

Rain pounded on the roof of the tavern as if it would never end. The only place he could find to bed down for the night was in the straw in a backroom of the Mitre along with several other homeless drunks, not that he was drunk, or homeless come to that, merely struggling through this vale of tears.

During the long hours, to the drip-drip of a leak in the thatch and a chorus of snores, he reviewed the previous night.

It had been largely a waste of time if he'd hoped to find the bearer of Arundel's sinister-looking serpent badge. The old fellow had either gone to ground or returned to whichever manor he came from.

In some sense he had deflected suspicions from the three bowmen, although the old man could not have known that. They were hardly likely to wear a badge of allegiance to Arundel, weren't they?

It was common knowledge that Will, a Cheshireman, had teamed up with the other two last summer when Henry made his push south into Wales in order to ambush King Richard on his return from Ireland. What they thought about their vassalage to a usurper like Henry of Lancaster they had never admitted out loud. They took his silver. As mercenaries they would see their work for Swynford as just another job. That was what he assumed at first.

It was only gradually that he noticed the odd subversive remark, a few grimaces, shrugs, a raised eyebrow or two, suggesting something more dangerous than mere opinions – intentions possibly – that led him to wonder about them. Even their skill made them stand out and set them apart. They had value. It could open up possibilities for them. They must know that. They could state their price.

Sleepless, his thoughts roamed fruitlessly over what he knew, bringing no respite. Where were their loyalties? Everything hinged on the answer.

Four fatal shots.

The first night's camp in the abbey meadows when Will stuck to him and even kept possession of the arrow after the captain had had a look at it – where were the other two then? They were calmly sitting round the fire when he and Will made their way back.

The second time when the seneschal was shot at from the woods, they were sitting in the cart as he recalled, except maybe for Underwood, who came along soon after the shout went up.

Then three, St Alban's. He only had their word that they were together.

Now this latest. And the badge, Arundel's token.

He turned restlessly for the hundredth time.

The Archbishop was the last man on earth they would support no matter how much he offered to pay them, wasn't he? Would he want men loyal to himself inside the army of the king's trusted commander? Very likely. Chandler groaned to himself. It was not possible and yet everything was possible. Now, in the middle of the night, it seemed very likely that Arundel would want exactly that, a cohort of well-paid loyalists so that if – *if* – he was planning on grabbing more power he would have the means to enforce it.

If the badge had been found at the scene of the St Alban's murder – and he didn't know it had – and because Underwood happened to recognize it, it didn't mean he was the one Arundel had paid to shoot the fatal arrow. But again, why had he hurried off as soon as he clapped eyes on it?

Chandler, usually confident in his deductions, felt any certainty crumble. He wondered if he was ill. His thoughts were usually sharp enough. Now he felt he was sickening for something, with a feeling of being buffeted from one supposition to another with no sense to be made from any of it. He might have told Mattie that she caused confusion – why had he told her that? – but she was not the only one. Everyone he spoke to seemed to be lying to him. Just as he himself was lying to everyone else.

Only Martin was what he seemed. And old Brother Daniel. He thought of John Aston as well, being pulled in by Arundel's men for his honesty. He shuddered for him. The feeling of sickness persisted as he thought of Chaucer and whether Mattie had warned him about the danger he was in.

He was living in a nest of lies. He could trust no one. Only one thing was sure. Swynford would ask him to account for his failure to drag the murderer before him the moment he showed his face in the yard on the morrow.

For long hours he pitched about in the straw, taunted by fleas and the pounding of his thoughts. He only fell into a troubled sleep as the distant bell from the Abbey called the monks to Prime.

2

'So,' barked Swynford, scowling, 'we are no further on and my men continue to be shot like fish in a barrel! Who is this bowman who taunts me, brother? Do you have any suspicions? So far you've brought me nothing. It's not good enough!'

'My lord, sometimes matters have to take their own time. I am this very morning consulting the captain of your guard and other bowmen to ascertain the true trajectory of the arrow in this latest assault. Unfortunately I was not present when it occurred and have had to take the incident as hearsay until now. Everyone has a different opinion. Today I shall call on expert knowledge and we will perhaps be able to tie down the exact spot from where the arrow was loosed.'

'Perhaps?'

'I am no bowman, my lord. I can only use the expert knowledge of others. I'm surprised no one at the scene did not think to seek at once the place from where the arrow issued. They might even have caught the bowman in situ.'

'I'm sure they did seek it. Where were you?'

'I was at my chantry in Aldgate.'

'Then you'd better come up and take lodgings here where you can do some good. See my steward.'

Swynford's scowl deepened. His own captain had proved useless, blustering and denying that any of his men saw anything, even producing alibis for them which a tavern-keeper had corroborated, paid well, no doubt, for his lies.

'Get on with it, brother. I want results!'

It was his parting shot as he stormed away to see to something in council. The king, so-called king, was at Westminster in the royal apartments now and it was to Swynford's advantage to be seen about the place, defending his stepbrother's interests.

Was it true, as rumour would have it, that Swynford was in fact one of John of Gaunt's many by-blows, conceived adulterously when Katharine was still married to Swynford père – hence sharing the same father as Henry himself? If so it would also make him close kin to the powerful little coven of Beaufort offspring openly fathered outside marriage on the persistent *belle Katharine* by the lecherous Gaunt.

He vaguely recalled attempting to float the idea last night in the tavern but it had brought forth no opinion either for or against. It was just another of those stories that lie forever unresolved in the halfway house between fact and fantasy. Not his concern. It was only interesting in the light it might shine on the subtle and secret alliances forming round Henry himself.

3

The body had already been taken to the mortuary. Chandler went over as soon as he got away from Swynford. The captain of the guard accompanied him, a man somewhat worried-looking – as well he might be, given that he could be next in this murderer's delicately paced killing spree.

Chandler sought the captain's opinion as they walked along.

They were in accord that the murders had occurred at a slack time when the men had other things on their minds and tended to be off guard: lounging round a campfire after the first day's tiring march with the cortege; rattling along in the carts in the middle of nowhere as they drew towards a major halt at St Alban's, those in the carts half asleep and the others concentrating on their feet as they laboured along in worn-out boots, counting the miles covered and yet to come; and then later in the barn yard within the purlieus of the abbey itself when everyone was preparing for the next big moment when they would enter London.

Now, finally – to be hoped finally – this one, just when everyone was beginning to think they had shaken the murderer off and were safe within the royal precinct.

'The only thing in common is that the murdering bastard times it when defences are down.' When the captain made no comment Chandler continued, 'It's either coincidence and he's an opportunist, or he's a careful calculator of the men's lack of preparedness – a man knowledgeable about their routine so he can plan his moves.'

'That doesn't give us his name, does it?'

'It focuses our attention, mayhap?'

The captain had no wish to have his men under suspicion and

the rumour that they were out of his control had started to gain credibility after St Alban's. It could not be ignored. The earlier fear that it was a madman or a disgruntled villein had been discarded and the conviction that it was a bowman from within their own ranks was growing.

Suspicion coloured everything with this latest death. Chandler saw signs of it all round as they crossed the yard. Side-long glances. Every man wearing mail, their coifs pulled on, with not a bare head in sight. It was a fear that gained credence the more it was voiced. Soon the rank and file would start looking for someone to blame. It would then be but a short step to the breakdown of law and order.

They went inside the mortuary to view the body. Rigor had set in. He was no one remarkable. A reddish short-bearded pike-man, one of hundreds. The captain filled Chandler in on his details. 'Random,' he concluded. 'His own bad luck, brother. It could have been any of us.'

Chandler took a closer look at the wound. The arrow had pierced with sufficient force to enter between the links of the hauberk he had been wearing, distorting them, and had then pierced his heart. There was bruising but not much blood. The hauberk itself, damage clearly visible, was hanging on a strut beside the body.

It was either an extremely skilled bowman who knew his job or a piece of amazing good fortune for the perpetrator. Bearing in mind the earlier shots Chandler knew which view he favoured and could not help but applaud the bowman's forethought at choosing the right time to foster his deadly skill.

'And the arrow?'

One of the captain's orderlies was standing by and handed it to Chandler at once. He recognized it as similar to the war arrow used for the first murder and resolved to remark on it to Will, perhaps suggest that they were made by the same fletcher. The other two arrows had been unremarkable regulation issue. Not all bowmen made their own arrows.

To the question why the victim had been standing out in the open, looking about him, the captain grunted, 'His choice, gormless fool. I'm not a nurse-maid. He knows the drill. He must have thought he was safe enough near Westminster Hall.'

'Unlike him, King Henry is taking no chances this morning,' Chandler observed as they went towards the doors. There had been guards three or four lines deep round the building just now, even before the king was likely to put in an appearance. Nobody could get into the hall even if they wanted to without the necessary docket.

With his hand on the door he asked, 'Is it always so when the king is present? How tight are they about letting people inside?'

The captain gave a dismissive shrug. 'We always have extra guards on duty while he's in residence. Royal orders. He's not a man to take chances with his own life.'

'You mean this bowman took the opportunity when he saw it offered – before the guard came up to strength? . . . Inside knowledge?'

'Looks like it.'

If the bowman already knew about the order to post an increased number of guards it tended to confirm the likelihood that he must be one of Swynford's array. 'What's to stop him taking a shot even this morning with the king's archers lined up?'

The captain shook his head.

'So, where do you think he was when he took aim?'

'Come. I'll show you.'

He led the way to the spot where the man had fallen. It had been marked out with a chalk cross on the path. The rain had all but washed it away but it was clear enough now the rain had stopped. Someone had placed a wreath of leaves there. The captain indicated with the toe of one boot. 'Head here, heart there. Staring towards the river.'

'So, just to make sure, the bowman must have been inside the hall itself?'

'That's obvious.'

'Meaning that he was authorized to be inside for some reason?'

'There's a guardroom on the other side. He would have had no difficulty in getting inside if he was one of ours.'

'You don't doubt that by now, do you?'

'I doubt everything.'

Chandler, in agreement with the captain on the question of doubt if on little else, nodded. 'Doubt is a virtue . . . except when it comes to the Eucharist.' Narrowing his glance he looked up and measured with his eye the likely trajectory of the arrow and it seemed at a rough glance that there were two or three windows that looked likely. 'Will you take me inside?'

'I will. But you won't find anything. We had the place searched after.'

'Nevertheless, if you will.'

They went inside. It might have been enough for Chandler to be admitted without having to account for himself, accompanied as he was by the captain, but the young clerk checking dockets nervously demanded authority to let him through. The captain eyed the lad with disdain, shaking his head as they were eventually allowed into the echoing hall. 'Fool,' he muttered under his breath. 'This way, brother. First floor.'

Chandler let the captain go ahead. They took the stairs two at a time and reached the long corridor with several doors at intervals down one side.

'Audience chambers for petitioners,' remarked the captain. 'He must have known they would be unused at that time.'

'Which was?'

'Between nones and vespers.'

'Before the light began to fade?'

The captain nodded. 'Look here.' He pushed open the first door and went across the chamber to open a casement window that gave onto the yard.

Chandler jostled at his elbow to have a look. 'It would be difficult to wield a bow in such a confined space,' he murmured as he looked down into the yard.

'But not a difficult shot once he had made sure he could pull back the bow. I reckon he'd have to be standing just about here to make sure.' The captain paced away from the window and made as if to take aim through the aperture.

An imaginary figure standing out in the yard would be visible from the knees up, but even then it would have been difficult to place an arrow just so. He said as much and the captain's upper lip lifted. 'It's no distance for a trained man as I trust my bowmen are.'

'An ordinary militiaman, a pike-man for instance, could not pull off such a shot, could he?'

'No chance.'

'He would have to be quick in case somebody came in,' Chandler suggested. 'What were the chances of that?'

'High. He's clearly a man willing to take risks.'

'What about the other windows overlooking the yard?'

'Only two others might be possible although neither is as likely as this one. Come.'

He led back onto the corridor and moved along until he came to another door. This time there was the sound of someone inside and when he banged on it, the door whisked open and a clerk peered out. 'Ah, they said you might want to have a look round.'

'Were you here yesterday?'

The clerk nodded.

'Where were you when he was shot?' the captain asked.

'Out in the yard. There were three of us. Ask them. They're in the chamber opposite.' He frowned. 'I didn't know we were going to be questioned. I, for one, didn't see anything unusual . . . Before it happened, that is. It was an ordinary day. Quite uneventful.'

'That seems to be when he likes to strike.' The captain turned to Chandler. 'Not much help, is it?'

'We're getting a picture. Thank you, magister,' he addressed the clerk and made to leave but then turned back. 'No visitors then?'

The clerk shook his head. 'Not with the king in residence, not from outside. Only the usual in-and-out of clerks and their servants and a few scriveners going about their usual business before we all left. Certainly nobody carrying a bow!'

The captain led him to the third vantage point as he saw it although to Chandler it seemed even more difficult to pull off a killing-shot from such a position.

The narrow slit window was in an alcove, wide enough, certainly, for a man to work a bow, but at such an angle he would have had to put a curve on his arrow in order to hit his mark. It was not a question he was going to pose to the captain just yet. One man had already demonstrated that he could achieve such a thing, back at St Alban's, and Chandler decided it was not going to be him to draw attention to the fact until he had had a word or two in the right quarters.

As they went back down the wide steps into the Great Hall with King Richard's startling hammer-beam roof and its consort of wooden angels floating in glory above their heads he asked as an afterthought, 'Nothing found anywhere about when your men had a first look round?'

'A piece of parchment with his name on?'

'That sort of thing,' Chandler replied pleasantly.

The captain sniffed. 'Come and have a drink and we'll tell each other what we really think.'

4

When they were settled in one of the small back rooms in the Mitre the captain gave a swift glance round as if to make sure they were not being overheard, then leaned forward. 'So, what do you think? Anybody in your line of sight?'

'Not a one.' Chandler's reply was oblique. 'It's a mystery.'

'Aye, well that apart, brother, I'll tell you something. It's like this,' he began with lowered voice. 'It has come to my ears that a certain fellow has been trying to hand over a little silver badge belonging to somebody high up. And the story is, this high-up fellow is trying to undermine—' He lowered his voice still further and Chandler had to lip-read the name he mentioned. High up indeed.

'For which,' the captain continued, 'the accusation will be treason and the penalty for that we all know.'

'And you believe this first high-up fellow might get away with it?'

The captain nodded with the slightest movement of his head. 'But that would only be so if the high-up fellow had managed to draw enough support from among those who matter. Hence his little silver gift.' He leaned back. 'If a fellow can make himself invincible he can pull the strings of even the most powerful of . . .' He waved a hand, not wanting to mention a status so far above themselves again.

'And so what you're saying is that in some quarters strings are being pulled?' Chandler could be as enigmatic as the captain.

'When a high-up fellow is made even more high up, get me, he needs to have more to him than the mere knack of knocking some knight off his horse in the tourney. That might look good. It might impress the rabble who frequent these shows, but in reality it means nothing.' He tapped the side of his head. 'This is where it counts.'

'And this badge?'

'They're beginning to appear in certain quarters. Where do they come from? I think we know the answer to that. The recipients know it very well.'

Chandler dug his hand into his scrip and found the badge. 'Copper alloy,' he said as he produced it. 'Not silver.'

'Ever a mind to profit, our man,' murmured the captain. He took it between his thick fingers and turned it about before handing it back with a raised eyebrow.

'Some old fellow I've never seen before thought I'd be interested,' Chandler explained. 'He told me he found it at a certain place in St Alban's.'

The captain sat back. 'So there you are. Dropped by accident as he lined up his victim? That confirms what they're saying.'

'What are you going to do?'

'What I usually do. Obey orders.'

'And when the showdown comes, if it does?'

'All he has to do is appear in his full jousting gear and swagger onto the field and they'll be eating out of his hand again. You just watch.'

'Bread and circuses,' Chandler murmured but the captain failed to get the reference.

Before they parted Chandler explained his difficulty with Swynford and how it might turn out if he failed to produce a reliable suspect and the captain was sympathetic. He suggested that the line they might take was that an outsider had somehow inveigled his way into the hall and waited with the cunning of a fox for his prey to make himself available. He suggested that he tell Swynford that the captain – that is, himself – wanted permission to interrogate every clerk, lawman, beagle and bailiff who had entered the hall that day and that without a full account of their movements no finger could point reliably at any one man.

'I'll tell him that. And the badge of this high-up, how explain that?'

'He doesn't need to know about it yet. Wait for him to tell us about it. We watch. We wait. Then we'll see about serpents.'

Parting amicably but with little resolved, Chandler understood that the captain's main strength was conscious ignorance and a fine appreciation of which way the wind was blowing. He also understood that they were moving onto the more dangerous ground of counter-rebellion.

As he left the Mitre to cross the yard in search of Swynford's steward in order to fix up his temporary accommodation within the enclave, he noticed two people coming out of the poet's house. They did not see him but walked on towards the water stairs.

He followed and was in time to see them climbing down into one of the boats shortly before it slipped its mooring and began to head downstream. On an ebbing tide it was soon whisked into mid-river where the current was strongest and was then swiftly carried away.

He called down to one of the ferrymen standing by his craft waiting for trade. 'It seems I've just missed that boat. Where's it going?'

'Only down to the City. There'll be another one along in a while.'

Chandler raised a hand in thanks.

Mattie and Adam Pinkhurst. An ambiguous conjunction: a scrivener, drinking with the military and a pretty woman to whom a man might confess any secret?

As they walked along the fellow had reached out to take the basket Mattie had been carrying. She had resisted at first then handed it over with a look of concern. Pinkhurst had laughed and patted it as if to say it was safe with him.

5

Swynford was pacing back and forth in the chamber allotted him for the duration of his duties at Westminster and when Chandler entered he gave him a considering glare. To Chandler he looked like an unhappy man. He could almost hear him demand: where is your allegiance, to me or my stepbrother? And, Chandler felt like asking, where lies your allegiance, with your useless step-brother king or to the self-selected Archbishop who pulls his strings?

Much time could have been saved and mutual safety assured if they had been able to be so frank with each other. Their relative status of course made it impossible.

Swynford spoke. 'Got a roof over your head, brother?'

'I have, my lord.'

'Good. Any developments?'

Chandler outlined the ground plan the captain had mooted. It met with Swynford's approval.

'No doubt you will attend these interrogations?'

'That is my usual task.'

It may have been imagination but he thought he saw Swynford

shudder. Even the mention of the Tower could make anybody feel unsafe in these days of shifting power – especially so soon after it had housed the true king when they audaciously forced the crown from his head.

'I understand the heretics are being efficiently tracked down and encouraged to rethink their positions?' Swynford continued.

'That is so. The lord Archbishop is in enthusiastic pursuit of heresy in all its forms wherever it might be found.'

'One or two of the more prominent Lollards will no doubt soon find themselves set up as examples to deter anyone of like mind, hence Archbishop Arundel's new burning law he's rushing through the Commons.'

'No doubt St Paul's Cross will be busy.' Chandler referred to the open-air pulpit set up on the north side of St Paul's where heretics were forced to appear if they decided to recant.

'In Richard of Bordeaux's day you could more or less think what you wanted, correct or not, and say it out loud wherever you pleased, at court or in the lowest tavern, and you could write what you thought for anybody to read in those damned news shops.' He added, 'What folly! Why would Richard ever have allowed such freedom? What in heaven's name possessed him to allow it?'

'Scholarship, the search for truth in open debate? Some are driven to pursue ideas which only later prove to be mistaken – with scant regard for consequences,' he added when he noticed Swynford frown.

'We know the consequences. We suffered all that when the bonded men rebelled against their lords in the Great Revolt. Strange they favoured Richard when king at the time. Odd, that. Tresillian soon showed them the folly of their ways. They say Richard was in tears when he witnessed the mass hangings at St Albans. Nineteen on one gibbet! Of course, he was a soft lad of fourteen at the time, not made of the same metal as his father when he was knighted at Crecy at the same age. Do you know what the old King Edward is supposed to have said when they told him his son was surrounded by French knights? "Let them get on with it. They'll either kill him or make his name." A hard man. It's what we need in a king. The principal virtue, wouldn't you say?'

'Indeed, my lord.'

Swynford gave him a suspicious glance. 'I can't work you out, Chandler.' He paused as if to say something and then apparently changed his mind merely adding, 'Continue to bring me the goods and we'll both be safe, get it?'

Chandler bowed his head. He wondered what Swynford would ask of him next in order to appease the new monarch. He must have been expecting a substantial reward for his own recent activity to safeguard Henry's throne. Kin or not he must surely imagine he was in line for some accolade for his services?

Chandler wondered if he pitied the man. He decided on balance that he did not.

TWENTY-FOUR

The City.

I breathe a sigh of a relief as soon as I leave the mansion near Bread Lane. Once out in the streets again I'm able to merge in with everybody else, my hood up, the empty basket swinging by my side.

Adam had to leave me as soon as we arrived on the wharf, to avoid drawing attention. He said he happened to have business at the bookbinders in Paternoster Row.

The bulge of parchment he put inside his shirt under his surcoat, itself concealed under his cloak, is, I guess, the secret copying work he does on behalf of the Master. He told me he would be staying in the City overnight but to walk by a certain stationer's before I leave to let him know my task is done.

With this in mind I head along to St Paul's but before I reach the row of booksellers and the bookbinders' workshops I see a crowd gathered round a speaker on the north side. As it's on my way I walk over to see what's what, telling myself that I'm adding to my general air of being just another maid on an errand with time on her hands.

A fellow in ragged brown robes is standing on the wooden platform they use to make their proclamations, spouting some stuff that has the crowd gathered round him, some heckling while others cheer him on.

As I approach I happen to glance across the crowded yard and notice four or five bailiff's men issuing out of a side street. They halt within hearing distance of the speaker on the platform. All of them are carrying batons of course and I know at once by the way they look they mean no good to anyone.

The fellow in the brown robes of a Wyclif follower is talking about Speaker Cheyne, a known supporter of the Lollards, who has recently been asked to stand down by lord Arundel – as if it's anything to do with him, as surely it's the prerogative of the Commons to choose their own Speaker, as the orator on the hustings is now saying.

'. . . and I say, brothers and sisters, is it not the right of our representatives in the Commons to choose a man to speak on our behalf? And is it their right never to bend the knee to anybody unelected by them? And is that elected Speaker Sir John Cheyne?'

At the name of Cheyne there are loud cheers from absolutely everybody.

It's enough for the bailiff.

With a nod he unleashes his men and sends them in like a pack of hounds and they howl towards the platform, making a grab for the fellow in rags. He is too quick for them and jumps off into the crowd causing a great confusion with everyone scattering in all directions, obstructing the bailiff's men, shouting and tripping them and making as if they are trying to lay hold of the orator while all the while providing as many obstacles as they can.

Meanwhile the prey disappears up a nearby alley. Missiles are starting to be thrown at the bailiff's men and I guess some of the lads, mostly apprentices, have brought their own, and even as I watch, open-mouthed, they scatter, leading the bailiff's men away from where, clear as day from where I'm standing, the orator escaped.

It turns into a melee of men brawling with each other. The apprentice lads like nothing better than to fight and the bailiff's men are chosen for that same reason. As the latter happen to be outnumbered they begin to shout for reinforcements. Expecting armed militia, the crowd begins to disperse.

Meanwhile a few women with shopping baskets like me shelter near the alley and one of them points the bailiff off to somewhere on the other side saying in a country accent, 'That way, master-sir, look 'ee, the filthy losel can't have gone far, begod.'

Confused, the bailiff herds his men back among the remaining bystanders to where the woman pointed and when he's out of hearing she bursts into cackles of laughter and in clear Thames-side voices her friends set to mocking him and his men who, persisting in their search and following contradictory instructions from the onlookers, are now making a vain sweep on the far side of the yard before disappearing round the corner of St Paul's towards Ludgate. They eventually vanish from sight, merging with the pious folk flocking at the west doors for the next Office.

TWENTY-FIVE

Westminster Water Stairs. Same day.

He was sitting on a bollard by the waterside when the boat arrived. She was alone. He wondered where Pinkhurst was. He couldn't have come back already. It would have been impossible for him to return without being noticed. That hair, for a start. His height. And anyway, Chandler had been sitting here more or less the whole time waiting for them to show their faces.

It had not been a wasted few hours.

The king had appeared at the great doors of Westminster Palace and from where he sat he could make out in the distance the close formation of the bodyguard packed round the royal personage.

He could see the by-standers. He could also see any movement should anyone appear at one of the windows overlooking Palace Yard. The king, however, had progressed without incident towards the water-side where the royal barge was moored.

At a certain distance Swynford and his men were taking up the rear and only came near the king as he paused before climbing onboard.

Swynford approached. Chandler saw him kneel then rise swiftly to his feet. Henry gave a disdainful glance and was about to lift the royal foot to step onboard when Swynford put out a hand to restrain him.

Henry drew back. Words passed between them.

Swynford's jaw seemed to sag but he pulled himself to attention. As Henry swept onboard Swynford gazed after him with a face that looked as if somebody had slapped it.

Recovering his composure he barked a command to his captain and his men drew away. They were returning to their guard duty outside the hall as Henry was ushered to a comfortable cushioned seat in the stern of the barge beneath the scarlet and gold canopy.

The lines were quickly thrown off and the oarsmen applied their strength to the sweeps as the barge swung away from the quay, cutting across river in the direction of Lambeth Palace.

All this had fallen to Chandler's gaze without hearing a word but its message was as clear as if written in ten-foot flames across the sky.

He watched the barge for as long as it took it to reach the other side and allowed a handful of passengers to alight at the palace steps. Gold glinted on somebody's mail, on a sword, on the gold thread of a banner as the group of armed men hurried inside the walls with royal Harry in their midst.

Chandler rose to his feet. He wondered what it was that had brought that odd expression to Swynford's face. He thought of the serpent badge and its donor and he wondered whether Swynford himself already had one in his possession.

Turning away he strolled about for a while, making sure he was still able to see everyone who came ashore.

Maybe it was as well that Swynford was not invited to accompany Henry inside the archbishop's palace at Lambeth just now. He imagined the stilted conversation, the double meanings, the innuendo, the sidelong glances and he felt glad that he himself was well out of any additional treachery.

Soon the boat from the City wharf came up and he watched the passengers alight, noticing Matilda by herself.

As she climbed to the top of the stairs he stepped up alongside her. 'Fortune blesses the virtuous. How pleasant to see you, Matilda. Been on an errand to the City for your master?'

She gave him a flurried glance. 'I – yes. Obviously.'

'As long as you didn't have a wasted journey looking for me!' He tried to make it sound light but was ashamed at his poor effort. He kept pace with her as she began to cross the yard even though she increased her pace.

'You need have no worries about my wasting my time on fruitless boat trips,' she retorted. 'But I'm surprised to see you still here, brother. You seem to be spending a lot of time on Thorney Island. Are you setting up a chantry for St Serapion here as well?'

She was pert, he decided, and he grinned down at her despite everything. 'That's a good idea, Matilda. What say you become one of his followers?'

'I would not care to be handed over to the Saracens in exchange for a rich merchant,' she replied, 'otherwise I might consider the idea as, observing you, I would say he demands few duties.'

'Sloth may indeed be one my many sins,' he replied.

She stopped and they glared at each other, or, rather, she glared and he merely gave her that smile, infuriating her, and suggesting he found it amusing to bandy words with her.

'Mattie,' he began in a lower tone, 'I do know that your master is involved in dangerous work these days. I can't say it more plainly. It's one book in particular he must be careful not to publish under his own name. I cannot advise him not to translate it as from what you told me he has already done so but he must not associate himself with it. I asked you to tell him but I'm not sure you heeded me. Will you make sure he understands?'

'I'm going into the house now.' With that she turned and slipped through the gates of the precinct and he did not bother to follow.

It was Will he needed to sound out next. But first he sought the captain of the guard, finding him in his little privy chamber next to the guardroom after only a short delay while persuading the fellow at the entrance to the hall to let him in.

TWENTY-SIX

Chaucer's house. A few moments later.

The Master springs out of his writing chamber as soon as he hears me enter.

'Come inside, Mattie. Tell me what happened.' He ushers me inside and closes the door into the little hall. 'I saw you talking to Brother Chandler just now.'

'He was lying in wait for me when I got off the ferry,' I reply. 'Don't fret, Master, I did not breathe a word about where I've been.'

I notice a brief look of relief flit across his face but he is not fully reassured. 'What was he saying to make you look the way you did?'

'How did I look?'

'Never mind. What did he say to you?'

'It was another warning about the lion book. You are not to link yourself with it – even though he knows you've already translated it. I regret from the bottom of my heart that I ever mentioned it. Do please forgive me?'

'It can't be helped. Anyway, it's gone now. They can search all they want, they won't find it here. It'll be my word against his.'

'Was that the sheaf of parchment Adam took with him earlier for binding?'

He gives me a shining look, half-humorous and a little triumphant too but shakes his head. 'I have no idea what you're talking about!'

'Nor have I, Master.' I curtsey.

He adopts a grim expression. 'It's no light thing to be interrogated, Mattie. Whatever he says to beguile you, however sweetly he smiles on you, you must never forget who maintains him and by whom he is bought and sold. He means no good to you, whatever he might tell you.'

'They surely don't interrogate girls like me?' I can't help laughing at the thought but he gives me a stern glance.

'I would not want to bet on who they might throw into their

prisons to extract from them these newly invented heresies. We have heard no news about poor Aston. We all live in fear for him.'

I can't help feeling a snake crawling up my back. Adam's missing fingernails are horrible even though he makes no complaint.

'And the rest of your errand passed uneventfully?'

'It did. I handed your parcel to the steward at the big house. Adam left me as soon as we went ashore and took himself off to the bookbinders. He asked me to call by Paternoster Row to tell him I'd done as you asked.'

'Did you see Master Marburgh when you were there?'

'No, he was in his other shop and it was a brief visit because there was a disturbance outside on the hustings where the speakers hold forth and a fellow in russet had to flee for his life. He was objecting to Speaker Cheyne being asked to step down. I came away as quickly as I could after seeing Adam as I didn't want to get mixed up in it.'

'Quite right. And that's all that happened?'

'Quite all, Master. Nobody took any notice of me.'

'Tomorrow you may make a return trip if you will with another little bundle of pages.'

'Is this another group of stories?'

'There is nothing amiss about them, my elf. I simply want to make sure there are copies made. Adam will come back here with you after he's explained to them the marking up I've done.'

He was looking worried again.

'You may trust me to hold my tongue whatever happens, Master. I've learned my lesson . . . if that's why you're looking worried.'

'It's not that, Mattie. That orator you heard – I trust he got away . . .?'

I tell him about the group of cackling women sending the bailiff off in the wrong direction to allow the orator to escape. 'The crowd was definitely on the side of Sir John Cheyne. They cheered every time his name was mentioned.'

He goes to his desk and begins to search through a pile of parchment pieces, sighing all the while, shaking his head and suddenly looking quite old and tired.

I ask, 'Would you like me to fetch you a drink now and maybe something of Cook's to nibble?'

'That's a kind thought.'

'If I may say, it looks to me as if these new restrictions won't be accepted by the Londoners. They're used to the freedom to say and think what they will. I can't see them ever accepting laws that encroach on their liberty.'

'You're too young to remember the uprising, Mattie. I was living above the gatehouse at Aldgate and saw the Essex men pouring into London that first day of the Rising. Even with so many of one heart and accord they were defeated by the greater power of the King's Council and the armies of the barons. A violent and barbaric blood-letting was inflicted on those who yearned for no more than freedom from the chains of bonded labour.'

'I was too young but I heard about it. How they were brought down and suffered in consequence. Maybe it makes the survivors more determined to fight on?'

'Dear child, let us believe so. There is no argument to support the idea that one man – or woman – should be held in bondage to another.'

'One day, Master, one day . . . surely it will come to an end and everyone will be born free?'

2

It puzzles me how Chandler can choose to further the aims of men like Archbishop Arundel and that Lancastrian usurper.

Those two, like their captains who owe them fealty, care for nothing but power for its own sake. They are determined to keep things as they are and care nothing for the suffering they cause innocent folk.

Try as I might, I can't understand what makes it worthwhile to cause such sadness in a world that is already sad. Do they not see that everything will end, and us with it? Isn't that sad enough? Isn't it enough to make us want to help each other through our fragile lives?

They must see that our hopes and dreams will one day disappear like mist and come to mean nothing to anyone and that will be that? The end of things.

I do not believe in a life everlasting. I cannot believe in heaven. Where is it? Has anyone seen it and come back to tell us about it? No. Not that I know of and nor does anyone else. It follows that we should do our best here and now in the only world we have.

If they get this new law through I could burn for thinking this. But I trust God will understand my reasons and forgive me. I shall never utter such thoughts to anyone, not even to Adam or the Master, although I'm sure they will agree with me. No interrogator will ever get me to admit what I know in my truest heart. Let them try.

But Chandler – Rodric – how does he come to shut his eyes to the truth of our existence? Does he truly believe everything will go on forever and forever through all eternity, life everlasting? I'm filled with horror at the thought of time without end.

TWENTY-SEVEN

Westminster.

He found one of the lads playing in the yard waiting to run errands, and gave him instructions where to find Master Will the bowman over at Five Fields and the message he wanted conveyed. 'Come back to me with his answer and I'll make it worth your while.'

The lad ran off.

Then he went into the great cathedral of King Henry III within the precinct of Westminster Abbey, the church of St Peter. Inside, the soaring pillars and coloured glass made his spirits rise at sight of their beauty. Then he walked past the empty tomb of King Richard and felt cast down again. *Sic gloria transit.*

Finding a quiet corner he sat for some time contemplating his many sins of omission and commission and how long he could maintain his balance between the two.

Later when he judged the lad should be back with his answer he went out into Palace Yard again and found a place to wait. He was in time to see him running up from the bridge by the horse ferry and glancing round, his face dropping with disappointment, until his glance alighted on Chandler emerging from the niche where he was waiting.

Smiling he ran over. 'Brother! Here I am!'

'You've been quick, young feller. What did he say?'

'He said he would do as you ask.'

'Good lad.' He fished in his scrip for some coins and the lad looked at them in astonishment.

'Get something to eat, you little ruffian. Even the birds of the air need food.'

'I will, brother, right away. I'm right glad to do so. Blessings on you, brother.' Clutching the coins as if he thought someone might snatch them away he ran off on skinny legs towards the pie stall.

Chandler made his way into the Mitre where he intended to follow his own advice.

While he waited for his fish stew to be brought he had a good look at the other customers. There was always a constant floating population hanging around the court consisting of militia, obviously, especially now the king was in residence, but also petitioners and their entourages, merchants from out of town, lawmen, their clerks and assistants, as well as entertainers, jugglers, minstrels, and girls of course, of varying degrees of innocence and allure. At a glance it was difficult to pick out their protectors from any others involved in the continual traffic of buying and selling.

Everybody was selling something and hoping for profit. The military, selling their brawn, their power in arms, the bowmen, selling their skill for sixpence a day, and all the rest, even the poet, despite his recent complaint to his purse that had amused everybody so much, was himself selling the fruits of his mind and the acuity of his observations as well as a certain moral code that many found agreeable.

For some reason a picture of Matilda returned. She carried a basket over her shoulder as he had seen her that morning. Next to her was Pinkhurst. He took the basket from her with a somewhat intimate smile and patted it. He might have patted her in the same way if they had been in private. And then . . .?

He forced himself to take his mind elsewhere. Why, for instance, was she carrying the basket in the first place? It had looked empty when she left and it looked empty when she returned. Yes, he was almost sure that it had been empty when she returned. Clearly she hadn't been to market. So where had she been? That was one question that might be asked. Another was about Pinkhurst. Why would he, a scrivener, choose to drink with the military?

2

Will arrived shortly to put an end to his musings. He entered with some clamour, an imposing fellow among the serjeants-at-law and the merchants because of the force of his presence and his bowman's physique. He was greeted by several off-duty guards standing near the row of vats and when he noticed Chandler, he came straight over.

'Are we all right talking here?' He glanced at the busy to-ing and fro-ing of the customers with servants weaving in and out, full trays carried above their heads.

'It's nothing much.' Chandler called for a couple of ales for them. 'I thought you might want to know what Swynford's captain said to me this morning.'

'Does it concern me and the lads?'

'It concerns arrows.'

'Concerns us, then,' he grinned affably and sat down but Chandler noticed his right hand clench.

'That incident yesterday,' Chandler began. 'You know Swynford himself wants it clearing up. His captain has a mind to draw out his investigations for as long as he can. So do I. But there is something that needs sorting out.'

Their ale was placed in front of them and Chandler handed over some coins.

Will glanced furtively from side to side, 'Do we need to go elsewhere to talk?'

Once the servant left there was no one within listening distance as far as Chandler could see but to allay Will's anxiety he nodded towards a side chamber where only a couple of old fellows could be seen seated at a board game. He got up and Will followed carrying both their mugs.

They found a table in the window and Chandler sat with his back against the light. He took a drink.

Will hesitated. 'Arrows, you said?'

'Remember that war arrow from the first killing shortly after we left Pontefract? I believe you took possession of it – so we would know where to find it if necessary?'

'That's right.' Will looked wary.

'Do you still have it?'

'It'll be around. It's too powerful for what we're doing here. It's more a souvenir than anything. I'm not intending to go to war.'

'I think maybe you can help me. I'm no bowman as you know. Is it possible to put enough curve on a shaft to give it a certain flight path?'

'Obviously.'

'I thought so.'

They looked at each other in silence for a moment until Chandler said, 'I see you're not going to help me.'

'Look, I don't know anything I could say that could help. I don't know what you want to know.'

'So you didn't get rid of it?'

'Why would I?'

'I'd like to see it again.'

Will glanced away.

Chandler said, 'If you still have it.'

'I've told you—' Will began then stopped. He picked up his ale mug and drained it.

'Want another?' Chandler leaned to one side so he could catch the attention of a servant in the adjoining chamber and raised a thumb before Will could find an excuse.

He waited until the fellow came through with a loaded tray swilling with ale and after he left Chandler said, 'It's this. A difficulty. I don't know how much you know about yesterday's murder and as you know, I'm not a bowman – but the arrow was a war arrow like the one that finished off the first fellow after Pontefract. That to me means several things. The first arrow could have had a curve on it as well, like the second arrow. It could mean both arrows belonged to one and the same fellow, that it's his speciality if you like, making a distinctive arrow, like a scribe with a recognizable hand?'

Will frowned and nodded.

'Or it could mean it's one and the same arrow.'

Will gave the matter some serious thought.

'I'll have to look for it,' he said eventually. 'Either way, if you think it was made by the same fellow are you asking me if I happen to know him?'

'In short.'

'I see.'

'Well?'

'If you find out who he is you'll have his head in a noose before he can blink.'

'Will I?'

They looked at each other in silence for another long while. Chandler had time to notice the gradations of colour on Will's face, pale around the eyes and darker with weathering on the cheeks and forehead. Near his hairline it was pale again where his coif would protect him. He recalled the feeling of gladness he had felt once before to know he was not in Will's sights.

When he thought Will understood he said, 'Back to that little copper alloy badge I showed you. I'm not giving much away when I tell you the captain I spoke to has ideas about that and what it might come to mean if certain events occur.'

'You say so?' Will leaned forward. 'There's certainly talk in some quarters. A brief incident near the royal barge yesterday caused comment.' He sat back. 'Is that where you should be looking, you and this captain? Any man might be provoked into altering his allegiance if he felt unappreciated—'

'But then there is kinship – for what it's worth.'

Will stared down at his ale as if he was trying to work out how it had got there. Eventually he said, 'I've never met Thomas Arundel.'

'Do you want to?'

His head shot up and the fear in his eyes changed to sharp derision. 'Not if I can help it!' Then his smile wavered. 'Are you offering?'

'Not me. Never. Count on that.' He added, 'Try to make my life easier.'

Was anything settled between them? He couldn't blame Will for not trusting him. He hardly trusted himself. He wouldn't bring any of the three to notice whatever the evidence but they did need to tread carefully. Next time, if there was a next time, maybe they'd decide they were better using a cudgel instead.

3

His daily check-in with Swynford's captain happened sooner than expected. He had gone to the door with Will when he left, intending to leave too but while he was pausing on the threshold a young man-at-arms stepped into his path. 'I've been looking for you everywhere, brother. Message from my lord captain to go up to the guardroom.'

'Right away?'

'If you will.'

Chandler nodded and, after watching Will stride back across the yard towards Five Fields and his encampment, he went to the Great Hall and talked his way in and went up to see what it was the captain was hoping for and how he might oblige him.

TWENTY-EIGHT

Westminster. Same day.

I hardly dare go out across Palace Yard now for fear of being shot down. The Master reassures me when he catches me hovering in the doorway. He reminds me that so far it has only been men who are shot and, moreover, ones who were in Swynford's company so I have no need to worry.

'No one will ever mistake you for a palace guard, Mattie.'

'I should hope not!' I flare up then burst out laughing because he does not mean anything by it of course. It's just that every remark brushes me up the wrong way at present. What with the guard perpetually standing on duty watching the house from a distance as if he's doing nothing very much – now Chandler has brought him to my attention – and also this terrible killing out of the blue, it's enough to make anybody worried and nervous. It's one more thing to bring home to me the dangerous presence of the spy. How I hate him.

When I pluck up the courage to venture outside the precinct there is a small wreath of woven leaves and grasses with a few snowdrops twined among them lying in the yard. It is placed just so where that guard was shot yesterday. He was only doing his job. The king walked past later with his retinue and did not even turn to look at it.

I hurry into St Margaret's and kneel for a while and wonder if prayers ever do any good. The saint protects women especially and she is my hope that all will be well. Then I think about the poor dead man again, not even knowing his name, or whether he was married, or a father, or was loved or hated. Somebody must have cared because they left that sad little wreath. Even so he was just somebody who died and it seemed pointless for him to have ever lived as it is with most of us. It strikes me as scandalous that we know so little about him. In a few days people will be walking over the very spot where he breathed his last without even knowing it was where a human life ended.

Not much comforted, when I hurry back to the house darkness

is already falling. Torches are lighting up stretches of the precinct wall leaving gaps between the lights where shadows run up and down every time the wind makes the flames flicker in their cressets. The windows of the house are like blank eyes, watching me as I push open the door.

It seems strangely lonely now I know Adam is not here. At least he is someone, however irritating, a person alive. To my surprise I find I might be missing him, although not in the way I miss Rodric Chandler. That feeling is like a fever. It's like nothing else. It's an immense yearning, an absence, searing my skin and burning with a kind of heat and giving me no respite despite hating him so much and I wonder if St Margaret will ever cure me.

'Master,' I ask as I am taking off my cloak and he comes to the door of his chamber to see who it is. 'Are you sitting alone in the dark?'

'I haven't got around to lighting the candles yet, Mattie. I find darkness sometimes aids thought. You may light them now, if you will.'

I go round with a spill saying, 'May I ask if you remember that necromancer you invited to scry into the future?'

'That charlatan!' He beams. 'How could I forget him. Useless fellow. It seems like something from a pardoner's tale in this quiet lodging.' His voice changes. 'Do you mind not living in the City any longer, Mattie?'

'Only a little. I miss my friends in Cheap but they will never come back, not while there's unrest everywhere. I remember how the duke of Lancaster, before he took the crown, used to send his men into the market to scavenge for food. They say it was because he never paid them unless he was forced to. But it was the marketers like Izzie and Annie to foot the bill at the end of the day. They used to say that those who owed the duke knight's fee could not escape their obligations without becoming outlawed and I think Izzie felt they were caught in a similar web. If they protested their stalls would be tipped up by the men-at-arms as likely as not.'

'So then we are well out of it, would you say?'

I nod. I am not sure where this is leading. I would never wish to spend the rest of my life surrounded by monks.

'I have often wondered,' he continues, 'about Guelderland, where you and my wife came from, and what it would be like to live there. Do you remember much about it?'

'I was too young, only four or five when I was brought over in her father's retinue. I sometimes think I can remember things, the look of fruit in a bowl, the golden thread in a gown, a hand with a ring, clear pictures that make me wonder where they come from. I always suppose it must be from Mistress Philippa's household. And language,' I add, 'words I cannot make out, as mysterious as the speech of angels.'

'Perhaps one day you would not mind going back? What do you think?'

'I think it would be interesting.' I glance at him in alarm. 'You wouldn't think of sending me back there by myself, would you, Master? Have I not pleased you?'

'You do everything to my entire satisfaction, my little starling. But you would not mind returning to Guelderland if you were not alone? You might even think of it as an adventure?'

I burst out laughing and he nods as if something is settled.

TWENTY-NINE

Westminster. Later that night.

The captain was lounging in a wooden chair when he entered his burrow. His quilted jacket was unloosed revealing a sweat-stained undershirt. Both boots rested on a footstool. A couple of torches flickered over the chamber revealing his usual servant cleaning bits and pieces of plate armour scattered in the rushes.

A flagon of wine stood on a stool beside the captain and he called into an adjoining chamber for somebody to fetch a drinking cup and pour some out for his guest. It made Chandler feel sick to drink ale first and wine afterwards but he hoped the fish stew would absorb any ill effects.

Often he longed for the austerity of a Cistercian monastery and taunted himself with the steps he would need to take in order to be accepted into a cloister somewhere. St Alban's with its astronomers and well-stocked library would have suited him but Benedictines were generally too casual in their daily obligations to appeal.

'Ho, captain,' he said, pulling himself together. It had been a long day and still not yet Compline. 'You sent someone to fetch me?'

The captain glanced up from a piece of parchment he was scrutinizing. 'Latin any good?'

'Fair.'

'Then read this.'

He handed him the scrap and watched him while he had a look. When he finished and glanced up he was still watching.

'So, it's a somewhat heretical tract, the sort of thing the Lollards put out. I've seen plenty of these in my work at the Tower. How did you come by it?'

'It was fixed to the door of the Great Hall this morning but has only just now been handed to me.'

'And whoever handed it on wants you to find out who put it there?'

'This is not why I'm in Swynford's army. High-flown tracts are more suited to the court than to us. My men can hardly read English, let alone Latin. This is the last thing they would know anything about.'

'But someone thinks they might?'

'No, it's more like someone is getting desperate and put it up for general readership. I notice the word for bowman. Sagittarius, isn't it?'

'And it looks like a general warning that the vendetta is only just beginning. The *simultas* as he has it.'

'Swynford is taking it as a deliberate and personal affront. I won't tell you what he said. It would make even the devil's ears curl. Frankly, brother, I'm at a loss. I thought you were the most likely man to make sense of it.'

Chandler went to the narrow window slit and gazed out into the darkness. The captain's chamber was on the wrong side of the building to have a view onto the yard. Instead there was a probably unappreciated and now almost invisible vista of the river spreading its banks and at present brimming with a silvery sheen of flood water, its wide expanse marked on the opposite side by numerous small fires.

If Lambeth had not been so distant anyone with passable eyesight could have made out the swarms of peasants up from their manors sitting round the flames. They were optimistically near to the palace, the white walls of the Archbishop's enclave shining out of the night.

'I don't know any bowmen who write Latin. They must have got somebody to do it for them.' He peered at the letters again. It was a fair hand but hurriedly written.

The captain growled something and asked, 'If you've seen this sort of thing before do you recognize the hand?'

He shook his head. 'Not immediately. May I take it? I'll have a closer look and see if it reminds me of anyone who might have passed through our system at some time.' When he glanced up the captain was swallowing a mouthful of wine with his eyes closed. He remarked, 'This business with ex-Speaker Cheyne is causing contention in the City, I hear.'

'Damn him, damn them all.' He swung his feet from off the footstool and rose to his feet. 'You don't think it's anything to do with him, do you?'

He spread his arms. 'Who knows. There's enough discontent on so many issues. It's only weeks since the rebel earls were ignominiously beheaded. That will not easily be forgotten.'

'The prisons are full of malcontents. Help me, brother. This is not my territory. I would imagine the chances of finding the scribe about evens along with finding a needle in a haystack, wouldn't you?'

'Or as difficult as finding a bowman with the skill of a magician.'

He jerked his head up at this and Chandler had to explain that he only meant that the murderer was always uncannily in the right place to get his man. 'An unerring marksman? One never seen even though he strikes in daylight? The ability to disappear into thin air? Uncanny.'

'Oh, I see. I thought you meant it was the work of – well, leave it. I don't know what to think any more.'

'And the rumours don't help.'

'About—?'

He knew he must have heard about the snub Henry gave to Swynford with everybody looking on. He didn't know whether it had changed his mind about informing Swynford about the serpent badge or whether he was still weighing things up.

When he said as much he looked more worried than ever. 'I'm going to have to tell him and I might link it with that—' He gestured towards the piece of parchment Chandler was still holding. 'Latin. And a caduceus, is that the word?'

'Ah, the serpent coiling round a stave. Yes, that might give Swynford something to think about.'

As he stopped talking he realized that he might have unwittingly spoken the words of the plotters of this whole affair. It had the attributes of a cloister-game.

He could easily imagine the monks sitting round discussing how to get under the skin of their enemies and create dissension. Could it be a sign of an imminent monastic rebellion? He thought of the abbey monks in this very location but that would not account for the other murders on the way down from Pontefract. It would have to be someone under licence, maybe, a mendicant free to roam, or from one of the more obscure cults like his own.

His next thought was about the likely offer to a bowman to act for them, someone bought by silver or by a spiritual reward from a house of disgruntled churchmen. But no, it wasn't plausible.

'Maybe these two things are unconnected?' he suggested, beginning to take his leave. 'As I've said, there are enough contentious issues at present to give anyone pause for thought. Heaven forfend if these critics, rebels and heretics, ever join forces.'

The captain looked stricken. 'That's what Henry is mortally afraid of and he has not failed to remind lord Swynford that it's our God-given task to keep him safe.'

Or else . . . His unspoken fear rang in his ears as he descended the echoing stone steps to ground level. Chandler's over-riding thought was that if anyone knew how to keep Henry safe it was Henry himself.

Chandler's Chronicle

It has been some time since I added to my attempt at a true account of this unprecedented time: the murder of an anointed king and the establishment of a tyranny in a realm whose people, suffering the brutality of past invaders, have grown to have a strong pride in their rights and freedoms. It will be a daunting task to subdue them by any usurper, especially one with so little right to the throne as Henry Bolingbroke.

His now established lie of hereditary right of descent in a direct line from an ancient king of England will one day be seen for the chicanery it is.

The Mortimer boy by bloodline from Edward III's second son, Lionel, has more right to the throne than Henry as everyone knows, but there it is: those who shout loudest get the wolf's share. The modest are pushed to the wall. Thus it ever was.

The reason for my neglect of this poor record of events is down to two things: my own personal confusion over ancillary affairs and a lull in matters of state. I doubt not that much goes on in the secret chambers of our rulers while we common folk are holding our breath, as it were, collectively and in horror, at the new law about to be enacted.

Our parliament and more especially the tyrant king and his favourite advisor are, it appears, intent on bringing the ordinary folk, the rebellious folk as this king and his archbishop will no doubt see them, under the yoke of a new repression.

I list the many and unexpected, not to say, outrageous

encroachments on our freedom of thought, speech and assembly, enacted so far.

He made a note to do so later then continued.

I deplore the limitations placed on us that prevent us from arranging our own destiny as each man sees fit, on earth and in the life to come. With the interference of government in our very thoughts and utterances no man dare say even in private what he or she thinks of this king and his edicts for fear of betrayal by those acquaintances who think otherwise. Torture, demands to recant in public and crawl back into the fold of orthodoxy, are the threats hanging over anyone of independent ideas.

Do they not understand, this king and his string-pulling archbishop, that by repressing the natural freedom of the people a rebellion of even greater popular support than in the Hurling Time of the Great Revolt will burst forth with more violence than heretofore? It may not be this year nor the next but it will come, a true End Day in this, our known world.

In order to repress it they will have to turn the realm of England into the harshest prison, with the expedient of burning human beings at the stake as the ultimate penalty. When they have burned alive every free-thinking man and woman will they see their work well done? A charnel-house will be all that remains of this royal isle.

Chandler pushed aside his parchment, blotted as it was as his hand shook with ill-contained rage, and stretched his cramped muscles while frowning out of the window onto the small yard outside. It was surrounded on three sides by the high walls of adjacent buildings and he had the sense of standing at the bottom of a well.

It was time he reported to old Knollys again. He decided to do it in the morning to get it over.

He had nothing he was willing to tell him but at least he would put in an appearance for safety's sake. There was no need to mention the arrow he wanted to trace nor the Latin notice about bowmen that had been put up. Reluctant to feel the grasp of repression on his shoulders it was safer to catch the drift of smoke from the fires in a visit to Seething Lane than sit here haunting himself with suppositions.

It would at least get him out of this corrupted hole and into a different one. The old spider would be sitting in the middle of his web needing only to pull one single thread to send his information quivering along the line to the king himself.

THIRTY

Westminster. Chaucer's house.

The Master has arranged the Tales haphazardly into five booklets to make it easier to have them separately copied at a later date by anyone asking for them.

'It will be safer this way,' he tells me when I ask him why he is sending me back to the mansion off Bread Lane again. 'I may ask you several times more to do this errand for me if you will. You do not have to agree. I will never coerce you into doing something you do not want to do.'

'It is my pleasure, Master. I wish to help wherever I can,' I tell him.

Safety is on everyone's lips. But what is safe and what is not? You would imagine a few stories about pilgrims, showing them as they are, would have displeased no one – except possibly the ones held up to ridicule – but even I feel we are stepping into a world where it cannot be predicted who will take offence at the most innocent remark.

'Think no more about it, Mattie,' he answered after a long pause. 'Do as you have already done and you will be safe. Adam is having everything bound for me at Paternoster Row and from thence they will all be sent to a safer place until such time my stories are taken for what they are, innocent entertainment for the pleasure and amusement of my readers.'

'Why else would you want to write them?' I remark. 'Their pleasure must bring you the greatest joy.'

'Joy or its opposite, depending on who gets their hands on them.'

So it is, I go out again with my basket and its contents with a little cloth over them as instructed. I'm right glad to leave the precinct, to be honest. These days it's a place under a blanket of gloom that seems to prevail without any end in sight.

As I cross the yard to the water stairs even the jongleurs plying their trade seem to do so in a down-hearted manner as if they know their jollity will soon be forbidden by some law or other. Crowds, sullen and somewhat threatening, are as usual being beaten back by the guards on the other side of the bridge but they still pour down Whitehall and press up against the gate as if by keeping close to Westminster they can somehow stop the statute that is being drawn up. I refuse to think about it as there's nothing I can do about it.

A strong breeze is blowing the water into little white caps when I arrive and the boats bounce up and down, banging wood against wood and swirling spray onto the shore.

Fortunately the boatman knows me by now. 'Come and take a seat beside me, little doll, it's choppy today and you'll stay dry if you sit next to me.'

His men on the sweeps have something to say about this and he jokes back saying that even his own good wife knows she can trust him while they, a bunch of lying, ignorant losels, are such that no woman would linger with them for more than a moment except on payment of a very large sum, which none of them could afford anyway.

His remarks are met with derision which he scorns as being founded on jealousy at his God-given way with the girls.

'Isn't that so, my poppet?' He gives me a secret wink under the brim of his cap.

This is the only lightness for weeks, although it might not have been quite that long. It simply seems so because of the general darkness. By now we're already into late spring and the long rains of the early months are beginning to let up. Even so it's freezing cold on the water and I have to hold my hood tight round my face to keep the chill away. The further we are conveyed from Westminster the quicker my spirits rise. These dark times will soon be over. I know it. I feel it.

It is not until I alight at Wood Quay that I have a horrible shock.

Waiting my turn to climb ashore I notice who has travelled down in the same boat. It cannot be! He must have come onboard after I arrived and taken a seat at the back. Has he been watching me all this time?

I'm suddenly shivering as if he has stolen something from me.

As soon as I set foot on the quay I hurry off with my head down and my hood concealing my face so that he will not guess I've seen him nor go through a pretence of having suddenly noticed me.

I am already halfway up the street before I risk a glance behind me. As I cross over I see him standing on the quay talking to someone, a fellow I do not recognize, and after a brief glance up the street when he must have seen me he strides off towards the Vintry.

If he wonders where I am going then I wonder the same about him.

2

The big house in its quiet lane off Bread Street is familiar to me now as is the kindly steward. It is rare that he does not offer me some sweetmeat or little piece of fruit although we hardly exchange a word as I hand over the contents of my basket. I have no idea whose house this is beyond the fact that it is the town house of some lord who prefers to remain a mystery or maybe feels he is too grand to spare time himself to receive a few little books.

Of course I know the Master is trying to outwit the censor but it is nothing to do with me as I am only a messenger and anyway, who could complain about a few tales of ordinary people going on pilgrimage? I think he's worrying for nothing. I still take extra care as I've been instructed.

3

It is only as I'm leaving the house and have already reached the end of the lane and am about to join the crowds on the main thoroughfare that I give a wary glance round to make sure it's safe when I catch a glimpse of him again.

He is too far off in the thick of the crowd to be recognized for certain. I scold myself somewhat – how could it be him when I saw him hurrying off in the opposite direction? Am I such a dolt as to imagine he then turned round and followed me and spent the last while waiting out in the street until I reappeared?

Unease grips me even so. Could he have followed me and watched me turn off onto the lane of the mansion, even to the very steps of the house?

I try to lose myself in the maze of streets with my head down as if that will make me invisible and when I reach Cheap I wander among the stalls but it only reminds me of the time I first became aware of him and how we would accidentally come face to face in the market, not quite meeting, always appearing and disappearing, like two people shyly courting – a thought that now makes me blush at my absurdity, dolt that I am, and when I reach the end of the line of stalls, much depleted since the start of the repression, I linger as if only interested in the goods laid out for sale, selling I know not what, until I feel sure he is no longer in sight – but even as I start back again intending to get the ferry up to Westminster without delay, I clap eyes on him standing no more than a few yards away!

He is fingering through some goods on offer at a leather stall, holding up a belt while he inspects it with the air of a man biding his time.

Go away, I mutter, drawn towards him in the same breath and longing and fearing for him to notice me, but he is saying something to the vendor and they appear to be in discussion about the relative merits of one belt against another and I grasp the opportunity to slip away before he sees me.

It was him, I tell myself as I hurry towards Garlick Hill. I am so confused by his sudden appearance I'm even beginning to question the evidence of my own eyes. It was him, of course it was, but I can't believe he followed me. Why would he? It must have been by chance that we fetched up in the same place. He showed no intention of speaking to me even though there was the opportunity to do so and I'm sure he did notice me but only pretended not to.

It must mean that at last he has accepted that I don't wish to have anything to do with him. All thought of getting even with him disappeared some time ago. He is best avoided. I shall tell Adam when I get back. He was right to warn me off.

THIRTY-ONE

The City. Cheapside.

He followed her. After lying in wait near the ferry boat since prime and wondering whether she would appear with the basket and what the devil was in it, he managed to find a place in the stern of the ferry boat just before the lines were thrown off. He was forced to endure the banter that flowed round him, glad she did not turn her head.

No amount of speculation brought answers to his question about the errand Chaucer had sent her on. He imagined he could guess. His writings. Seditious as they no doubt were. But if so, why did she not go on up to Paternoster Row and do business there?

Later, hurrying onto Cheap, she seemed to have no wish to buy anything and her presence in the market was another mystery. She met no one. Her usual gossips from the old times were no longer there. She even avoided the fish merchant and seemed to be roaming randomly from stall to stall, picking things up then putting them down and moving on.

The important question was where did she go after leaving the wharf and later reappearing in the market? What happened in that gap of time? He lost her and it was his own fault for allowing a fellow from Aldgate to delay him.

A regular at St Serapion's, he was concerned that he had not seen Chandler about for some time and was missing the canonical hours at the chantry, and then he went on to tell him in more detail than was necessary about his wife's recent illness and how she had miraculously recovered only the other day. He couldn't believe it, he said.

'It was after I'd been in your chantry to pray to St Serapion, save his soul, and she began to pick up straight afterwards. Now she's right as rain.'

He replied how delighted he was but not at all surprised and then felt compelled to explain that he was staying over in Westminster at his lord's pleasure and by the time he glanced along the street she was nowhere to be seen.

Reproving himself for negligence he saw it as an opportunity to call on old Knollys but was told by his porter that he was still abed and to come back later. At first he suspected it was a ploy to put him in his place and it brought back his anxiety and the fear that something was afoot.

2

After watching her heading towards the quay to take the ferry back to Westminster he returned to Seething Lane. The door was swiftly opened and he found the old fellow sitting as usual in his solar with a roaring fire and his usual ruby-red carafe of wine beside him.

He may indeed have been abed when he first called because his wife appeared fleetingly in an embroidered wrap covering her night-gown with night slippers on her feet. It amazed him that she was still voluptuous at sixty but it also amazed him that at ninety Knollys still liked his bed and the pleasures therein. Maybe, like a spider, he fed off the choicest morsels of information that fell into his web and was thereby given the energy of eternal youth.

He had to admit that he was greeted with a show of great friendliness, and was told that he missed their 'jousts' as Knollys called their verbal thrusting and how his day was now improved by his return.

'I trust,' he added slyly, 'that your excuse for keeping an eye on the poet is proving pleasurable?'

He contrived to look abashed and told him that he was at a loss as, so far, the maid had proved impervious to his powers of attraction and he feared that women in general had become hard of heart in these present times. Knollys concluded the discussion by rubbing one thumb over his palm and saying, 'This is all they want these days, the hussies,' and so they reached the crux of their meeting.

'We are of a mind,' he began, 'to see *de haeretico comburendo* take effect before the summer's out. It will only need to be law for it to have an immediate effect on these trouble-makers. Our lord Archbishop is right to be so determined to push it through.'

'You suggest it will never be enacted, my lord?'

'I think the threat of it will be enough.' He gave a comfortable chuckle. 'These Lollards will scurry to leave the sinking ship like the rats they are as soon as they know what's in wait for them.'

'At present they are hoping to bell the Cat to give themselves fair warning,' Chandler pointed out.

'You have something definite for me on that score?'

'Only what I hear rumoured in the vicinity of Westminster Hall. A clerk there let slip a remark that Henry was reluctant to give his agreement to one of their drafts and had sent it back to be amended.' He added, 'There is in existence, I understand, also a mouse unafraid of cats.'

'He?'

Chandler nodded.

'He has a rival.' Knollys smiled. 'It's another literate fellow putting his work out for anyone to read. A strict fellow wasted in Malvern.'

'You must mean Master Langland? I heard he had given up his plough and was living in a hovel in the City?'

'I heard he'd gone back to tramping the hills.'

He bowed his head. 'Ever the first to hear the latest, my lord.'

'But you have the advantage of hearing in Westminster what only reaches my ears as a faint echo,' he consoled. His eyes became pinpricks of light when he was extracting some new thread from the tangled skein of intrigue. Aware of this he veiled them now, asking, 'And your lord Thomas? Faring well?'

'Not as well as he would desire. He feels his services have been taken for granted as he is himself taken for granted. He feels it keenly. Lack of funds to pay his men is one complaint. Lack of his own advancement is another. Dismay at having put his immortal soul at risk for, it seems, no reward, is yet a third.'

'And he thinks to shift his position somewhat?'

'His loyalty is not questioned by anyone.'

'But for how long will it remain so? That's what Henry has to ask himself. I would not like to make enemies for the mere price of a manor or two. He has enough to spare.'

'The king keeps his lands and men ever tight in his grasp and will regard his success as founded on—' he was about to say avarice but thought it unwise and merely added, 'on dynastic strength.'

'Let your lord Swynford know that he has friends here but one above all who believes loyalty should be properly rewarded.'

He took this straight invitation as a warning of things to come. With a command couched as a request to return within a few days with something about that other business – which he understood was to do with the poet – he was shown out with reassuring ceremony.

Back in the street he stood for a moment to take a deep and astonished breath.

THIRTY-TWO

Westminster. Chaucer's house.

Adam appears straightaway when he hears the door. He is covered in ink. 'You took your time. I was beginning to think we'd have to send out a search party.'

'Good day to you too, Master Pinkhurst. I consider that I was quick enough, given the circumstances.' I go into the kitchen and he follows.

Cook gives us both a searching glance. 'Do I need to hear this?'

'You may, dear Cook. It's just Adam.'

'I've said nothing.'

'You implied I'd been playing about in town.'

'You could have caught the first boat back. It doesn't take long to go there and back, does it?'

'I didn't dare come straight back. I was followed and you can guess who by.'

'"By whom,"' he corrects. 'Did he see where you went?'

I shake my head. 'He vanished almost as soon as getting off the boat. I gave him the slip straight off. But then I thought it best to go up to East Cheap to hear what's new but I saw nobody I knew until he put in an appearance. I gave him the slip again and came straight back.'

Adam goes to the window and looks outside into the Close. When he turns back he holds Cook's glance.

After a moment Cook says, 'Who was it claimed the serpent was scotched?' He turns to me. 'While you were away, Mattie, even though you were only absent for a little while, a crowd broke through the cordon of guards near Whitehall and tried to get into the council chamber.'

'And did they?'

'Not a chance. A few broken heads and a group of them carted away under armed escort no doubt to finish up in Newgate, that's all.'

'It felt violent out there. I could hear the shouting in the distance as the boat reached the wharf. It scared me a bit.'

Adam returns to the Master's writing chamber and I can hear them discussing something in grave undertones.

'Oh, Cook, what are we to do?' I ask feeling suddenly overwhelmed.

He puts a fatherly arm round me. 'Worry not, sweeting, the Master is too well-known to be in danger. We are safe here.'

He goes to the Master's door and knocks. I hear him say, 'I'll have a casual look round. To set our minds at rest.' He goes out, shrugging on his cloak as he steps outside.

THIRTY-THREE

Westminster Hall. Same day.

With so much going on behind closed doors he feared his chronicle could give only half the story so he took it upon himself to ascertain the exact nature of the mooted law Knollys had referred to. Returning from the City as soon as he could he went up to Westminster Hall under a barrage of objections from those detained outside to find out if he could lay hands on the latest draft to see for himself what was being discussed.

From an acquaintance working in the clerks' office he managed to have a draft in his hands long enough to ascertain that it was as extreme as everyone feared.

Such was the cautious language in which it was phrased he had to read it through to the end to discover how unobtrusively the threat was made. The sting was in the tail.

After the usual references to false and perverse people and their divers new doctrines encompassing wicked, heretical and erroneous opinions, the serjeants-at-law had cobbled together the main drift to include a full set of forbidden activities.

Unsurprisingly these were aimed at the schools of theology, Oxford in particular, and also against the general writing of books and the spreading of information designed to incite and stir people to sedition – with what they called 'hurts, slanders and perils'. Well, we could all do without those, he thought as he read on. It then pleaded for God to prohibit them 'unless the king himself would speedily act on His behalf', thus absolving his royal majesty from any blame as he was only taking action in God's stead.

Further on came the more relevant lines and he recorded them here as noted in this rough draft.

It went: '. . . after arrest and while under safe custody in prison and unless he, that is, the prisoner, purge himself and abjure such wicked and erroneous doctrines as the laws of the Church demand, he shall be handed to his diocesan and then left to the secular court to appear before the people in an high place and be burnt, that such punishment may strike fear into the minds of others.'

So there it was.

After handing it back to somebody in the clerk's office he went for a walk in the freezing air of Palace Yard. A mist was rolling up from the river and the far bank was like a distant country spun from ice. He had never known a spring so cold and seemingly without end or hope.

THIRTY-FOUR

Westminster Abbey. Later.

Before the light fails we are going out together like a family to pray in the abbey. I'm puzzled and ask if it's a saint's day, not that I know of one, and the Master mutters, 'There are no saints. Only dead folk whose names have come down to us for one reason or another. Usually because they met a spectacular and ignominious end.' I put my arm in his as a warning to hold his tongue.

He seems glad to be away from his writing for a while. Since more convivial times in the City he hardly sets foot outside and sees no one. As we walk along he starts to reminisce about Abbot Lyttlington whom he liked and who was abbot here before Abbot Copthorne, telling us a scandalous rumour about him being an illegitimate son of old King Edward.

'How he used to exult in that story! He claimed his mother was a washerwoman from Southwark but she died when he was only two years old and the monks brought him up.'

'Are we permitted to listen to this, Geoffrey, or are we breaking the law?' Cook asks with a sardonic smile.

'If there isn't a law against it yet, doubtless there soon will be, so make the most of your freedom.'

'They're taking their time about bringing in the burning law,' I remark. 'Maybe they'll think better of it.'

Nobody says anything.

The abbey church is full of music as the quire monks let their voices soar into the vault as into a woodland full of trees and as the notes dance above our heads, angelic descants weave patterns of sound with the returning harmonies.

I feel transported and clasp my hands over my stomach. How beautiful it is, how wondrous the skill of the masons to create this soaring mass of worked stone in the shapes of leaves and flowers and coronets, and the glass-painters, how capture such living colours inside the molten liquid before it turns to brittle glass and now, in sound, the monks of flesh and blood how beautifully they craft their harmonies in such music. This is what will last, I believe, when our chains have long fallen away and we live in perfect harmony one with another . . .

Adam nudges me. 'Wake up, Mattie.'

Dazed, I open my eyes. 'I'm not asleep.'

He gives me a sweet and genuine smile and his eyes soften. I'm glad he's no longer angry with me. I push my elbow against his to try to convey my gratitude. He clamps his lips and looks down. It's so easy to embarrass him.

At the west end of the nave where it is still under construction a group of sanctuarymen are huddled, some praying, some looking straight ahead. Perhaps they are begging forgiveness for the crimes which have brought them to seek safety here. Their eyes follow us as we leave. I feel they might be envying us for being free and for looking prosperous and content in what they might imagine is a little family group.

At the porch door we linger while the Master greets some acquaintances. Night has fallen while we've been inside. I feel uneasy and want to hurry back to the safety of the house. The guards are on duty round the Great Hall as always but of the spy there is no sign.

The uneasiness I felt earlier in the day at his sudden appearance is probably what makes me feel ill at ease now. A dark angel seems to be hovering over us no matter what we do. The Master's acquaintances move apart. We leave the warm candlelight for the ice-cold glitter of Palace Yard under a million stars.

'That's strange,' says Cook as we approach the house. 'Did somebody leave the door open?'

The Master asks, 'Who was last to leave?'

'It was me,' Adam admits. 'But I'm sure I closed it.'

'You did. I saw you.' I grip him by the arm.

'I'll go first.' Cook strides ahead.

'Is he armed?' Adam asks. He goes after him and may not have heard the Master murmur, 'He usually is,' as he too follows.

By the time I reach them Cook is standing on the threshold saying to Adam, 'Back me up. I'm going in.'

2

The Master stands to one side of the door and waves me behind him, mouthing, 'Safer here, Mattie.'

I show him the little knife I always carry. 'They won't get past me without causing trouble for themselves,' I whisper.

Our eyes are trained on the open door. Inside a light appears as either Cook or Adam lights a candle and we can hear both of them tramping about, first in the writing chamber, then on up the stairs until the upper windows flame with brief light as they bang about from chamber to chamber. We can hear no sounds of fighting. In a few moments they reappear in the doorway.

'You don't want to come inside just yet,' says Cook with a grim look.

The Master, ignoring Cook, pushes past him to enter the house. 'Give me a light!'

I hear him exclaim in dismay as light blooms in the window of his writing chamber making shadows leap like phantoms against the walls.

When I try to follow Adam bars my way. 'Don't. Not yet.'

'What is it? I can help, let me in.' He comes after me as I duck under his outstretched arm and run into the hall.

The Master is standing in the doorway of his chamber gazing round with a dazed expression. Everything is destroyed. Even from the doorway and with only a couple of candles for light I can see sheets of parchment scattered over the floor. Ink wells are unstoppered and their contents spilled out. Chairs are overturned, some easily righted, some smashed to matchwood, and a chest that usually contains all the copies of his stories gapes open and empty.

Cook enters. 'It's the same upstairs. Only my copper pans seem undamaged but tomorrow's soup is all over the floor.'

I go into the kitchen to have a look. It's a thousand times worse than that time I knocked a milk jug off the ledge and foolishly burst into tears.

The Master, with all his work stolen, must want to howl at the moon.

Adam comes up behind me. 'Don't go upstairs yet. They've even slashed the hay bag on your bed.' He tries to joke. 'You'll have to sleep with me tonight, Mattie.'

'The Master would have something to say about that – on top of everything else.' I feel desolate. 'What is he going to do?'

Adam makes no reply. How can he?

Later, after Cook has filled a bucket of water and scraped what looks like excrement off the walls he leans on his broom and says, 'It'll not be so bad in the morning when we can see what we're doing. There are feathers everywhere in your chamber, Mattie. Let me clear it up then you can at least lie down on your bed.'

'I've told her she can come in with me,' Adam repeats, making me think he means it.

After a longish period when we all work as one to put things back to normal in the flickering half-light he asks the Master, 'Did they get anything?'

'Everything has gone from the chest but they were only copies. Available to anybody. Nothing new there. Let them clutter their own cupboards with them.'

'And the rest . . .?'

'Safe. As we hope and pray.'

'They won't have gone down there to search, will they?'

'I can't see why they should. I trust Mattie to have been careful.' He turns to include me. 'You've always been like a little wraith on your excursions into the City, haven't you, Mattie?'

'More than ever after that first mistake.'

He turns back to Adam. 'He'll be away out of town as soon as he hears about this. Maybe he's already left. They'll only be trying to frighten us. I wonder which devils did it?' He speaks in a dull, flat, stunned tone like a dead man if dead men could speak. 'So it looks as if it's to be me next, does it? . . . I will not have them threaten my household.' He makes an attempt at a chuckle but it sounds desperate to me and adds, 'I'd better get that panegyric written – though Lord knows, it'll be even more difficult to come up with any flattering lies after this.'

Cook brings a jug of hot valerian from the kitchen and pours it into beakers while we stand about with our usual routine disrupted.

The contrast between the former time and what will now be the after-time spins on the pinhead of a moment. It is ever impossible to grasp because it runs before us even as we perceive it. It feels like a vortex sucking us into the dark heart of the future. What would have happened if we had been here inside the house when they arrived?

The Master looks at us one by one. With an effort, obviously aware of the threat for which this is a foretaste, he says, 'We're unharmed. That's the main thing. I think we know what we have to do next.'

Adam follows me up the stairs. Before I can open my chamber door he reaches out to detain me then lets his hand drop.

'It was clumsy of me to put it like that, Mattie. You must know I mean no disrespect. I've waited a long time for you to get over your romantic illusions about Brother Chandler. It's what girls do. Fall for some unsuitable fellow and only later recognize their folly and – well . . . Mattie?' He moves closer and then in a rush says, 'You must realize who is at the back of this?'

'Don't say it—'

'It's a warning. They'll get the burning law onto the books and then it's going to be ten times worse. We are in danger just as much as the known Lollards and the rest of King Richard's supporters. Remember Cirencester—' He comes close enough to grip me by both arms and hold me so he can look down into my face, his tone urgent when he says, 'Do you understand our danger?'

I stare at him, fumbling for words to express how I feel. 'I don't know what to say.' I put out a hand to ward him off. 'I suppose you must be right—'

'Do you doubt it?' He shakes me by the arm but sorrowfully and asks, 'Who else watches the house?'

'He said there were others—'

'He would, wouldn't he?'

'Even so—'

'They're only guards,' he points out. 'They don't have the same connections—'

To prevent him seeing my face as I feel it break into a hundred pieces, I escape into my chamber and shut the door.

Sitting in a cloud of feathers I rock back and forth in the most misery I have ever felt. To have Adam confirm who had done this and not even having to mention his name makes it a thousand times worse. *Rodric*. Always Rodric to make me weep.

3

The next day is so busy with all the work we have to do to bring the place back to something like habitable that I find it easy to avoid Adam and what I must tell him. I have to tell someone. I also fear that, after the way he looked at me last night, he will say something he will later regret. I must say something if only to save his face.

When we have a little pause I get the chance to go and walk about inside the enclave to get a breath of fresh air and somehow desperate to stave off what I have to do, I decide to walk down to the wharf to clear my head – and then I'll do it.

When I reach the river it has flooded onto the quay and the stairs are under water. It might be possible to climb down when the tide recedes but nobody will get away by ferry yet. The boatmen will have been forewarned with their knowledge of the tides and the height of the flood and are presumably off downriver in a safer mooring.

A clear, sharp breeze sweeps downriver bringing with it scudding puffs of clouds with grey underbellies.

There is nothing to be done. Nothing to be done about anything. The year unfolds. Nothing to be done.

In the distance I can hear the captain of the guards shouting at his men followed by the clash of arms. I don't believe in what it's all for. I don't even know what it's for anyway. It seems the best thing is to join a nunnery, after, and dedicate my life to something – but what? How is it they are so certain of everything?

I feel there is a good chance of catching a glimpse of him in Palace Yard. I fear to see him but then I find myself walking slowly to where he might be walking himself. It looks as usual. The usual people going about their business as if it is as important as they seem to think. The usual sameness. The same. The usual.

I wonder how it can be so after the wreck they made of the Master's little leasehold? I want to see his face to see what guilt looks like. He must surely feel guilty? How could he instruct them to do such a thing?

The yard is as busy as usual, continuing as normal. Like the time the guard was shot by an arrow the other day. Everything continued.

Why is nobody running around bewailing such violence? I feel it will be much the same if someone had been killed last night. It looks the same, even now when the real king is killed.

I begin to cross the yard.

He is nowhere. He is nowhere to be seen. He is everywhere.

I make my way back towards the house. Only when I reach the gate into the abbey precinct do I turn to glance over my shoulder for one last look.

Summoned by the strength of my longing, unbelievably he is crossing the yard towards me.

He has been summoned. I am fixed to the ground. It is as inevitable as death. Fortune is spinning her wheel and all I can do is stand and wait.

THIRTY-FIVE

Westminster Yard.

It was she, over by the path leading down to the quay. He watched in puzzlement. She could surely not expect to make her usual trip downriver today? Besides, she didn't have her basket with her. She carried nothing but stood with her hands inside her sleeves staring at the flood waters as if she might make them draw back so she could walk across.

Somewhat to his relief she turned away and began to wend her way across the yard towards the precinct. If he hurried he could catch up with her. He even considered calling her name but feared she might take it as a signal to hurry into the house.

Then she turned. Saw him. This time did not pretend he was invisible but took a step towards him.

He lifted one hand.

They gazed across the intervening space. He felt it was not the barrier he expected but a space filled with dancing atoms just as the ancient philosophers taught, each atom linked and sporting forever with the others in angelic and luminous harmony – drawing them together.

THIRTY-SIX

Westminster Yard.

Somehow we are only a stride or two apart, held by an invisible power. His silence makes me tremble.

I speak as into a void. 'Why did you do it?'

My voice comes out in a croak so I repeat my question more loudly and he stares at me as if I'm speaking in tongues.

Standing so close although I don't remember either of us taking a step towards each other – his scent of musk, of incense, no more than a wisp in the air – I ask again, almost too desolate to speak, knowing there is no answer, 'Why did you do it?'

Something in my tone wipes away any pretence at friendliness and he frowns. But still he doesn't say anything.

'Why, Rodric? Why?' My voice is rising and I can't control it.

Is it disdain in his eyes, triumph, when he asks, 'Do what?'

'You know what!'

When he looks blank and fails even to admit it I lose control in a flash and start to shriek, to scream, accusing him of everything I fear he's done and beating him with my fists, crying, clawing at him, giving no thought to the spectacle I must make of myself. How could he?

I am unable to stop myself. 'How could you?'

How could he destroy the Master's work?

'You've destroyed his life! You've defiled his sanctuary! You've ruined the place where he makes his stories. How could you?'

I can see nothing. Everything is red like blood. Like flames. Blinded by it, by fury, I claw his face again and he steps back, one arm shielding his eyes, the other reaching out to pull me towards him, pinning himself to me to prevent my flailing, his lips against the side of my head saying, 'I haven't done anything. What's happened? What are you saying? Tell me what's happened—'

I wrench away in fury. 'Liar!' I scream. 'Double times liar! Burn in hell!'

It must have been Adam who heard me and came out of the

house to take me back inside. I don't remember. All I remember is his lying lips against my skin as he denies it, lying even now to the uttermost end.

Are we dead and finished, condemned under these new laws to a terrible punishment because of him, I wonder, all of us, the Master, Cook, Adam, me myself for my little crime of smuggling books to the house in the City? Are we to burn because of him? I don't care. I will do it again. I will defy him. Lie as much as he likes I will never – never what?

2

'Come now, Mattie, my elf, no need for tears. We will find somewhere safe. Trust me.'

They stand round me in the little front chamber looking stern and I feel like a fool. I wipe my eyes.

'I shouldn't have said anything.'

'It's done now. Of course you're angry. He would expect it.'

'He kept on denying it.' I feel shame-faced. Somehow it all seems to be my fault. In a bid to make amends I say, 'I'm calm now, Master. I lost control. It's over. I'm calm now. He kept pretending he didn't know what I meant. I'm calm now. Am I to take anything else downriver for you or will he try to follow?'

Adam attempts to make a joke saying, 'For sure he'll keep his distance from you now, Mattie. You had me scared and I was behind the wall!'

Cook goes back into the kitchen without a word. When he returns he says, 'Eat these.' He hands round some griddle cakes hot from the hob.

3

'Are you sure about this, Mattie, my little viper?'

'I'm more sure than ever before.'

'Then let me tell you something you need to know. When you took my books down to the house near Bread Street, I believe you had no idea to whom you were handing them?'

I nod. 'Some lord of wealth and power, a patron?'

'It was a great and unexpected misfortune that our patron as you call him died at about the same time as King Richard. Either it was a sad coincidence or it was timed to occur, a crime committed when nobody was looking his way. His brother was one of the greatest and most loyal followers of the king and died, or was killed as some believe, in exile. You know who I mean? No need to say his name.'

I nod. He must mean Robert de Vere. I'm too shocked to speak.

'Now the new earl, his nephew, no more than a child, is here. He is waiting at a different safe address on the river and this is where I want you to take the rest of my papers, if you will. Then we are finished with them.'

'Are these the papers hidden in the secret chest?' He has mentioned them before and, as I believed, only did so to console us after the break-in but now I realize it is true.

He is stroking his beard and looking anxious and apologetic. 'I would not ask it of you, Mattie, but I think it unlikely that he will follow you now after—' he waves his arms to indicate my public show, 'but the others are marked men, Cook because of his past allegiance in the army and Adam, well, you know about him. They have Arundel's godless hounds following them every time they set foot outside the precinct. And as for me—' He looks helpless and without thinking runs his fingers across his neck.

I must look astonished and he gives me a quizzical glance. 'Did you really not know? I fear it is only a question of time before they come for me.'

'I'm ten times a dolt. I didn't imagine they could mean it . . .'

He – the spy – had told me himself about the guards, that time in his chantry. Guards, he said, watching the house.

Now I recalled all the many times I had seen men-at-arms hanging about the entrance to the precinct and had mistakenly connected them with the sanctuarymen – even though the sanctuary was behind walls on the opposite side of the enclave. How self-deluding I had been.

All I can say now is, 'I didn't know they were Arundel's men.'

'The quicker you learn the truth the better.' The Master holds out a small parcel, book-size, wrapped in a cloth. 'The last of my work to date.' A light comes into his eyes. 'But there will be more. Trust on that. Maybe not under my own name – under a different one for others to discover when this turbulent time is over. Who knows how this story will proceed? Take it,' he urges. 'Go now before the spy can report back and receive his instructions. If he follows you – we'll follow him!'

4

I could have reminded him that the river was in spate, a high tide meeting the floodwaters surging down towards the City. He could even have worked it out by using his astrolabe. Although an hour or so had gone by since lady mass the tide would not yet be at the turn. Even better than the astrolabe and his astronomical calculations he could have discovered it for himself, merely by going down and having a look at the waters with his own eyes as I had done earlier.

I took the package he handed to me and went into the hall to take down my cloak. I would go and wait on the quay out of sight until the first boat came along.

Adam followed me to the door and put his hand against it to keep it shut. 'Listen, Mattie, hide your bag inside your cloak so no one will see it.'

'I was going to—'

'Then walk as if you're simply going to have a look at the water. The old fellow's forgotten about the tide. Wait somewhere out of sight. It shouldn't be long before the boats can get out again. Take the first one.'

'I know all that.'

'I'm just reminding you.'

He hesitates then opens the door for me. 'I'd come with you – except that it would draw attention to us—'

'I'm all right, Adam. I understand everything now. I see it all clearly. He's one of Arundel's men. I'll do the right thing.'

He still hesitates.

'Open the door, please.'

'That row earlier . . . There is something more between you two, isn't there?'

I bite my lip. This is not how I would choose to tell him. Yet he deserves the truth. I decide to take the plunge.

'The thing is, I'm with child. His child.'

His hand lifts off the latch in astonishment and I take the opportunity to hurry outside. I do not look back. He does not follow.

5

One or two people are loitering about on the quay, a merchant and his servant, one or two others, all presumably like me, waiting for the first boat down to the City.

Meanwhile the river waters are immobile doing that invisible shift of power from one direction to another. I've often stared and stared to see if I can make out that exact moment when the tide changes but conclude that change occurs in some deep place long before we become aware of it, as it does in life itself.

THIRTY-SEVEN

Palace Yard.

He had no idea why she would fly at him in such a rage. It was an astonishment and for some time to come seemed without reason. When it did – well . . . there it was.

As he was going back to his lodging the hungry little lad with the spindly shanks came running up. 'By, she gave you what for! What have you been up to, brother?'

'Mind your own business if you want me to buy you something to eat,' he retorted.

'I'm on your side, brother. There's no reckoning how women will carry on, is there!'

He stopped in his tracks and gazed at the young scamp. 'And what would you know about that? You're scarcely out of swaddling clothes.'

'You should meet my mam!'

'If she's anything like that one over there I'll run a mile,' he replied. 'Thanks for the warning. Now get lost.'

'No errands this morning, brother?'

'You know when you're on to a good thing, don't you? Here,' he gave him a small coin. 'Now scarper.'

'I'll be waiting in my usual pitch. Just call!' He ran off.

As Chandler continued across the yard he longed to regain such youthful impudence. Long may he flourish, he murmured to himself. Now to drench his smarting wounds with some antidote to her clawings. He was pondering what misdemeanour she thought he had committed but was soon left in no doubt because when he approached the entrance to his quarters near the guardroom Swynford himself came hurtling out in another of his rages.

'Did you know about this?' he demanded, skidding to a momentary halt.

'About what, my lord?'

'This outrage!'

He waited.

'The lord Archbishop Arundel,' Swynford snarled.

'Is his statute—?'

'Not that! This! Last night! He had the audacity to set his men onto a house I was having watched.'

He stood still, somewhat agape as his imagination began to piece things together.

'That cursed poet causing Henry so much trouble with his jibes! He was our prize! We would have burned his books in Palace Yard if that interfering losel—' He broke off and hurriedly crossed himself.

'Was anyone hurt?'

Swynford blinked in surprise. 'What?' Shook his head. 'Not yet. They were all out. He had his men wait until they were at vespers. Curse them all! He was our prize!' He made off again with a flotilla of servants and personal guards hurrying in his wake.

So that's what she was so enraged about. He couldn't blame her for being angry. But why did she imagine he had anything to do with it? The answer to that was not far to find.

He went up to his chamber but after he'd sorted out his wounds, not so bad as it turned out, he could not rest so he went down again intending to find out a little more about last night's goings-on.

He was crossing the yard when Pinkhurst appeared. He caught sight of Chandler, swiftly changed direction and came over to him. Planting himself squarely in his path he gave him a hard stare and then taking him by surprise lifted a fist and drove it straight into his face.

His reactions were quick but not quick enough and the blow landed on his jaw making him stagger. Naturally he bunched his own fists and landed a good thump squarely under his chin in exchange. They both staggered back and glowered at each other, on edge to strike again.

Guards had already begun to run towards them as he noticed out of the corners of his eyes and a crowd, ever quick to heckle two fighting men, began to gather round. Chandler dropped his hands to his sides. 'What the hell was that for, Pinkhurst?'

The scrivener glowered and rubbed his jaw where a bruise was already building.

He muttered, 'Did you know she was with child?'

Aware of who Chandler was the guards left him alone and dived instead for Pinkhurst but before they could tackle him to the ground Chandler called them off. 'It's a personal matter. Leave him.'

With great reluctance, after they'd roughed him up a bit, they let him go. He gave Chandler a black look and strode off to wherever he was going before their paths crossed.

2

What a web we weave, he was thinking as the disappointed crowd and the guards dispersed, leaving him to recover his wits.

Seeking some mode of escape he found himself heading towards the river. How long had she known? Why had she not told me? He did not doubt that it was his. Pinkhurst's reaction told him that plain enough. He recalled her unexpected visit. She must have told Pinkhurst everything. Why tell him and not me?

The first ferry boat of the morning was just about to leave. It was full and sat low in the water. She was there like an apparition, sitting amidships in that cloak she wore. As he gaped somewhat her head turned and for a moment their glances, at least in his imagination, locked and held for as long as the boat turned in the cross-current and the lines tightened.

The nameless little lad ran up at that moment. 'You're in for it from all sides today, brother!'

'And it's not yet midday you doubtless want to remind me?'

He grinned. 'I'm still ready to run errands for you.'

'Then you can do this for me.'

He stiffened as if expecting a blow and said quickly, 'I can run to Five Fields again if you wish—'

'Not this time. I need somebody to watch a boat for me.'

'I can do that.' Then he looked worried. 'Will we be going near the water?'

'On it, not in it. What's the problem?'

'My dad drowned himself. He was a boatman and couldn't get work on account of sickness. I've since been a bit nervous of water.'

'I'm sorry about that but it means you'll be an expert on boats with all the knowledge he imparted?'

'Where is this boat?'

'Follow me.'

He led him briskly to the waterfront where her boat was surging away and as expected, boats, large and small, were already plying for hire now the ebb was flowing.

He hailed a fellow he knew and rummaged in his pouch. 'You needn't come with us. It's just me and the lad.'

'Will you bring her back?'

'Of course I will. If I don't you know where I live.' He thrust the coins into his hand before he could object and jumped aboard. The lad followed. When Chandler grasped the oars he grimaced.

'I thought I was going to do that for you?'

'I can manage. I'm not helpless.'

'I didn't know friars learned to row.'

'You'd be surprised what we learn.'

There was hardly any need to pull on the oars with the tide whisking them on. He said, 'See that ferry boat ahead of us?'

'That far one?' He squinted his eyes. 'I see it.'

'Then warn me when it next turns in.'

3

It wasn't far. The ferry was steered towards a private landing that served one of the mansions lining the riverbank and, before they were near, it was out again and heading off downriver. This time she was not on board.

'Here we are,' he told the lad as he rowed towards the inlet. Turning his head he was just in time to see her walk up some steps and go inside a house. She did not look back. Two passengers who had alighted at the same time and walked up the alley towards the street reappeared. They went to stand outside the house. He noticed they were drawing broadswords and pulled on the oars more vigorously to get out of the current and bring them to the landing stage.

Ever eager the lad was about to jump ashore but he told him to secure the lines then get back in the boat as he did not want any City lads making off with it and causing inconvenience.

'What's your name?' he asked as an afterthought before stepping ashore.

'Aethelstan. But you can call me Stan.'

'Stan the man. So wait here. You're in charge.' Then he went ashore himself and was about to walk across the jetty towards the steps of the house when all hell broke loose.

THIRTY-EIGHT

The house on the river.

After a short while the steersman manages to bring us into the sheltered waters of a narrow channel belonging to one of the private houses along the strand. A watergate lies ahead. It is open but the ferry boat only stays long enough for me to spring ashore before reversing down the channel to continue its onward journey. To my surprise two passengers also alight. They ignore me and march off up the lane beside the house.

The ferry, swept back into mid-river, leaves the landing stage eerily empty. I'm not sure what to do.

Visible through the open watergate inside the harbourage is a carrack with an old man holding a line. But for the gurgling sound of river water running past the wooden piles of the jetty the whole place lies in death-like silence.

I look up at the house. Three or four storeys of shuttered windows show no sign of life. Shallow steps made of white marble curve up to nail-studded double doors and I'm considering whether to bang on them to announce my arrival or whether to try to find another door at the front near the street when they begin to open and a servant peers out. Seeing me he beckons and not without some trepidation I ascend the steps.

The servant opens the door wider. 'You are right welcome, mistress. We are waiting for you. My lord hopes to catch the tide as soon as this business is done. He has a difficult voyage ahead. Pray enter.'

A high echoing chamber greets my gaze as I step inside. It is more like entering a church than a house in which people live. Everything is white marble and black tiles, with a glint of gold as the light strikes some ornament throwing everything else into shadow.

From out of the darkness steps a figure. It is a youth of no more than fourteen or fifteen. The child. *The serpent is scotched. The child awaits.*

He is strikingly handsome, his confidence, despite his youth, somehow accentuated by the austere black velvet he wears. I notice he carries a sword in an impressively beautiful scabbard. He stands before me now with his hand resting on the hilt.

'I am Oxford. I believe you have something for me?'

'Here it is, my lord.' I pull the parcel containing the Master's books from inside my cloak.

He holds out his hand for it and I have to walk up to the step where he is standing and hand it over. He opens it briskly, peers at a page or two, then smiles. 'I am honoured, mistress. Convey my sentiments to the Master. This will be safe with us. My father, as you no doubt know, died last month but I am pledged to honour his wishes. This will be secretly conveyed to a safe place and kept until such time as it may be brought forth to be read and enjoyed by all those who appreciate the Master's work—'

An eruption of shouting and a clash of arms from the street side of the house makes him glance in alarm towards an inner door and call, 'Ho! Guards! Ho!'

Five or six armed men crash immediately from out of an inner chamber just as another group forces its way in from the street, pushing aside the servant in the doorway, and storming towards the young earl.

As they draw swords their captain roars, 'Oxford? Hold! In the name of King Henry!'

A skirmish ensues as some of Oxford's men surround him and he is hustled out through the doors by which I entered while his remaining men engage the intruders in hand-to-hand fighting to halt their advance. In the confusion one of the Master's booklets falls to the floor and finishes up close to where I'm standing. I make a grab for it before anyone sees it.

While the young earl is being scrambled onto the quay I try to find an escape for myself as the two sides engage. Through the open doors I see the carrack burst out from the watergate and skim alongside the quay. Still trying to snatch Oxford from the protection of his men the intruders swarm after him but he has drawn his own sword with a shout of rage ready to defend himself and both sides fight with great ferocity, neither giving ground. Oxford's men are passionate in their desire to get him away to safety and they back towards the carrack.

I can find no way to escape unless I manage to find a way onto the street and for sure there will be guards waiting outside.

Before I can decide what to do the carrack, its crew trundling the sail rapidly up the mast, nears enough to allow Oxford and his men to leap on board. The wind fills the sail and the ship gains her freedom. It leaves the king's men shouting impotently on the quayside.

I'm still holding the book in my hand when one of the men runs back up the steps, shouting and cursing, notices me, sees the book, and storms over, yelling, 'Is that it?'

I back away unable to speak.

He reaches out and makes a grab for it but I hang on for dear life. He turns to the doors, bellowing for his captain.

To my astonishment, shouldering his way towards us, comes Chandler.

I can only gape as at the approach of death.

THIRTY-NINE

The river house. A moment earlier.

As a score or so of armed men came tumbling and cursing down the steps onto the quay to skirmish with each other a carrack flew out of the channel to allow some of them to leap on board. A mob of thwarted swords-men were left on the bank while their unlucky captain fumed and shook his mailed fist to no avail.

There was no sign of Matilda.

He hurried past and sprinted up the steps into the house.

She was standing irresolutely in a shaft of light, hair tumbling about her shoulders, looking quite glorious in her rage.

'You!' she shouted. 'I should have known you were behind this!' Her blazing glance fell on Chandler without any warmth.

Against howls from outside he replied somewhat incoherently, 'Nothing is me. What do you mean?'

They stared at each other and the shouts outside seemed to fade to a miraculous silence. He gathered his wits.

'So what are Arundel's men outside bothered about?'

When she didn't reply he reached out. 'Is it because of this?'

'It's nothing.' She drew back.

'Evidently it is something. I can distinctly see it. Seeing is believing. It looks like a book to me.' He grasped hold of it and they wrestled to gain possession until she suddenly gave up and backed away from him, looking frightened. 'Is this what your trips downriver have been about? Smuggling the master's books to de Vere?'

'Who—?' she stammered.

'The earl of Oxford on whose property we now stand?' Surely she knew that?

He glanced down at the cover page of the book and read out loud, 'The Book of the Lion.'

He sighed and was about to say something along the lines of, 'not again,' when a shout behind him made him turn.

A guard was storming up the steps and in ringing tones demanding, 'Arrest this woman!'

He pushed past Chandler and waved a mailed fist in front of Matilda's face. When she flinched away he raised it as if to strike her.

'I wouldn't touch her if I were you.'

As Chandler grabbed him by the arm, he grunted, 'Who the hell are you?' Chandler forced the mailed fist behind the man's back without answering.

Already the other guards were swarming up the steps with a spokesman yelling, 'That's her! That's the woman!'

Stepping in front of Mattie as the only female present Chandler addressed the fellow eager with his fists, 'What's happening, captain?'

If he didn't recognize him at least he noticed Lancaster's gold lion stitched to his cloak. His manner changed.

'I have orders to take her into custody, brother. She is accused of passing prohibited books to a third party.'

'Into custody? On whose orders?'

'Those of my lord Arundel, Archbishop of—'

'Yes, I know who he is. What's the name of this forbidden book? Is it this one?'

He held it up.

The captain looked uncomfortable. 'I'm told it's called the Book of the Lion and—'

'What's it about?'

'I know not—'

'So what makes it forbidden?'

'It is a Lollard story, heretical, and undermining the regality of King Henry and the authority of Holy Mother Church, and is therefore banned—'

'Have you perchance read it yourself?'

'Not I, brother. I only have orders to convey any copies to my lord so it may be burned—'

'Waste of good parchment,' Chandler remarked.

Going towards the door with the book in his hand he added, 'Think how many calves were killed in order to provide the vellum on which to copy out this story, think of the goose grieving for its purloined feather, of the painstaking work of the scrivener, of the skill of the illustrator, think of the bookbinder—' By this time he was at the top of the steps leading onto the quay, the military following in a cluster, swords sheathed uncertainly halfway back in their scabbards as, despite his air of authority and his insignia he was obviously a species of madman, even though they outnumbered him half-a-dozen to one and, moreover, they themselves wore the insignia of the lord Archbishop of Canterbury which permitted them to do anything they liked this side of hell. Despite their confusion they were wary about what would happen next as they followed him down the steps.

He turned when he reached the water's edge. 'What did you say it was called?'

The captain was at the door. 'I believe it to be The Book of the Lion, brother—' He looked mystified.

'Never heard of it,' Chandler replied.

Then, drawing back his arm as if to throw a missile, which indeed he was, he hurled the book as far out as he could into the fast-flowing waters of the Thames.

When he turned the captain was looking aghast. 'But . . . was that evidence?'

'How would I know, captain? It's gone now, unless one of your men wants to dive into the river to retrieve it.'

He walked back up the steps to where Mattie was standing. She, too, wore a dumb-struck expression and when he was close enough she whispered, 'Did you throw it into the river?'

'Didn't you see me?'

'Yes . . . but unlike you . . . I'm not sure seeing is believing.'

He looked down at her and crinkled his eyes. Even in these dire circumstances she managed to arouse in him a sweetness of feeling that must, he realized too late, be a sign of love.

The captain understood that he now had permission to express his official and righteous rage at having his orders flouted. Striding to where Chandler stood with an arm round Mattie as she gazed into his eyes, he made the mistake of trying to arrest her but Chandler instantly fumbled under his cloak and produced a sword. He had it against the captain's throat before he could move.

The rasp of several other swords simultaneously drawn from their scabbards did not deter him. He said, 'Move another inch towards her and I'll kill you. Instead, take your hands off her.'

'But she has a prohibited book—' the captain protested as he followed Chandler's orders.

'She has no book. She is innocent. Further, she is with child. Would you harm a woman bearing the innocent soul of an unborn baby? It's me you can take. I'll come with you in her place.'

He reached inside the neck of his undershirt to pull forth the little silver image of St Serapion, not that the captain would know what it was. But it had its effect.

He gibbered, 'But you're – you're a—'

He explained who St Serapion was and what he required from his followers. 'I'm on king's business if you like. But which king? You might well ask. Move away.' More firmly he demanded, 'Call your men off.'

He gave Mattie a little push towards the doors to the quay. 'Go, Mattie, there's a boat waiting with a lad in it called Aethelstan. He'll take you safely back to Westminster. Tell him I say so.'

With a kindling expression of bewilderment and something else she began to back towards the doors. Her glance never left his face.

Chandler put his sword away and when she hesitated he urged her to hurry. In an attempt to say what he should have said before now he simply placed one hand over his heart and could not stop himself from smiling.

The men-at-arms, unsure what to do, looked to their captain for guidance. He signed for them to arrest Chandler and in a trice his wrists were lashed behind his back and a blade of sharpened steel was at his throat. He did not flinch nor resist. He was certain they would not wish to curtail their fun too soon.

Further than that he dare not imagine.

The captain said, 'Take him away.'

His last sight of Mattie was as she fled down the steps onto the quay.

2

He was right about fun. They had great expectations which were unstintingly fulfilled. He wearied of wiping away his own blood. Happily they broke no bones.

And Arundel did not disappoint.

Although his bill *de haeretico comburendo* was not yet on the statute books he was eager to demonstrate how it might work in practice.

Held overnight in a cell somewhere at Westminster, Chandler knew Swynford would be fulminating over the snatching of another victim, rightly his, by whom he might have reinstated himself in Henry's esteem. He did not expect him to visit. Instead he was entertained by the guard who described in detail the fire they were building in Palace Yard on which they intended to burn him and all his heresies in flames hotter than hell.

Once the guard fell asleep he had the rest of the night to think over what he had done. He knew it had only been a matter of time before they discovered that he was unfaithful to their cause, that he had colluded with the proponents of free speech, with Lollards even, and he knew he would eventually pay the penalty his saint exacted. He had got away with handing a knife to King Richard before the mayhem against the assassins ensued – but he would not get away with openly throwing away a vital piece of evidence against Master Chaucer.

His thoughts turned to Matilda and her astonishment when he revealed his true colours as he threw the book into the river – at least, he hoped she saw him truly, freed from lies and double-dealing at last – and he wondered a little about the Master and whether he would manage to escape to freedom when he finally understood how close he was to a final reckoning.

He had never been in any doubt about the dangers he was running when Bolingbroke's treachery forced him to question his allegiance but it was a relief to find that now he had acted he would not change anything even if he could. Matilda would have a chance to live her life with their child despite what they might do to him. He knew they would not be kind, as a serpent is not kind to its victim. So be it.

After resolving things in his mind he spent the rest of the night in a glory of gold with his saint, murmuring, *Matilda, consummatum est. Amen.*

FORTY

Palace Yard.

Next morning as first light smeared the edges of the night Chandler was escorted under heavy guard into a yard already seething with onlookers. What was about to be enacted had never before been seen in England. To his surprise he felt indifferent. He did not struggle when they tied him to the stake that had been erected in the middle of a mound of brushwood. He merely looked round as at something interesting that did not concern him. The onlookers pushed and shoved to get a better view.

Men were building up the kindling and throwing on bigger branches, dried hazelwood mostly, reaching to the height of his waist. He scarcely noticed them. Instead he was in a dream, in communion with his saint who even now must be rushing to welcome him.

The crowd pressed forward. The ones at the front were the most eager to see what a burning man looked like.

Speculation was rife. They had seen an ox carcase on the spit and maybe it was like that when a man burned? Some discussed whether it might be quicker than to roast an ox because human flesh is more tender. Others hoped it might be so. Yet others shuddered, probably glad it was not themselves waiting for immolation. There were mutters against the spectacle. Some were saying it's not right. They repeated as if to reassure themselves, '*We are not barbarians, are we?*'

A chant organized by the military drowned out any murmurs of opposition. 'Heretic! Heretic! Burn the heretic!' But it soon petered out for want of support.

As Chandler waited out his last moments he remembered all the things he hadn't done. He hadn't been out to see Brother Daniel to tell him how sorry he was he hadn't done better, he hadn't had time to say goodbye to Martin and wish him safe days, and he had told no one about the terrible last weeks of the king at Pontefract.

He might have demanded the basic right of a condemned man to a last wish, or called for a confessor to listen to his sorry list of sins, but there was no one he wanted to tell anything to except maybe dear old Arnold Archer – *Do you remember that time when we were lads and scrumped apples from the provost's garden* – he might say – *and he came at us with a stick, eighty if he was a day?* – and he thought he could have been sitting in the Fleece with him now if he hadn't been such a devoted fool to abstractions, and he would have given much for five minutes with the old crowd and their tall stories. He wondered how many of them would survive the purge if Arundel persisted in trying to rid the realm of free-thinkers and how dull life would be if he succeeded.

He hadn't done enough himself to make a difference. Time always seemed too short. Right now a drink in the Fleece would be something. Small things taken for granted. In the rush of daily life they had a precious lustre now they were almost gone. But it was too late. The saddest words in any language. Too late for so much. For instance, he hadn't heard the rest of John Underwood's confession to ease his soul, poor fellow, and it was because he made the mistake of believing there was always enough time, and it was the same for everybody because secretly nobody believed time was finite. The Church itself made it an article of orthodoxy to believe in life everlasting. As if anything could last forever.

Then he began to wonder if brave John Aston was still alive and suffering for his Lollard thinking in the dungeons at Saltwood, and he wondered who would remember the name Aston and what he stood for, and whether they would honour his honesty and his courage, and he wondered if the big lie of Henry Bolingbroke's regime would eventually be seen for what it was, and how, if ever, the truth would come out.

He dwelt somewhat on the fact that he hadn't done anything to ask Adam to care for her, and above all he hadn't said what he should have said long ago, and he prayed that Serapion would forgive him for breaking his vows, but she would fare well with Adam by her side if both of them could keep their ideas to themselves, and the Master would thrive, alive or dead. He would outlive them all – Henry Bolingbroke, Thomas Arundel, the whole crowd of liars and evil-doers, his work outliving them and if he really intended to escape to Guelderland as she had almost hinted, he could be sitting there in Nijmegen or somewhere else like that, where he was welcome and among friends, scolding his scrivener, finishing his tales about those pilgrims, translating stories and even making up others in English for everybody's delight.

Holding up a mirror.

Revealing the truth.

He lifted his head. The fire was almost ready and a man was standing close by trying to get a flame from a tinder box, over and over sparking it and failing, until, taking him by surprise and causing him to step back, it ignited with a violent spurt. At the sight of it a sigh rose up from the crowd. Now they would see some action.

He had forgotten the onlookers. An air of something undefinable reached towards him. It might have been a feeling of grace – a benediction – and he remembered the feather he found in the king's prison afterwards and how before that he had told him he would fly free from the tower like an eagle on wings of gold and once more embrace his beloved Anne and be with all his friends again.

The companionship of the dead is a strange bedfellow, he felt now, but it enfolded him, bidding him enter its embrace, and he was unresisting and at peace.

2

Flames began to smoulder at his feet. The brushwood was alight. It puffed out clouds of black smoke just as rain began to fall in heavy, single drops, hissing on the flames and putting them out. The wood spurted and smoked and now and then a small jet of flame leaped forth to ignite a larger branch or two then itself sputtered out. New flames sprang more strongly to life. The fire caught hold. The resin in the bigger branches began to hiss in the heat.

Overhead came another sound.

It wasn't rain even though it was now falling heavily. It sounded more like a swarm of bees, or a murmuration of birds, alighting and settling, and it hummed overhead again almost at once and he heard a sudden shout, some screams, yells of pain from behind the smoke.

The man tending the fire pitched forward into the flames just as another fell to his knees in the embers and tried to scramble away, batting at the fires that had suddenly set his tunic alight – from all sides in a relentless hail came not birds but arrows, swarming over the heads of the onlookers in a dark cloud, war arrows penetrating the steel mail of the guards, fire arrows burning brighter than the pyre itself, arrows setting men and horses screaming and scrambling for shelter. Men rolled on the ground to extinguish their burning garments or ran about in panic, flaming like human torches.

Behind his back Chandler felt something sharp against his bound wrists and a voice urging him, 'Quick, brother. Follow me!'

With his arms released and able to kick the nearest flames aside he stepped away from the stake and jerked round to see who had released him. It was young Aethelstan. Grabbing Chandler by the arm he again urged him to hurry. 'Wake up! Get a move on! Follow!'

He began to drag Chandler along, shouting in his urgency, trying to rouse him from his stupor, urging haste as a horse appeared through the pall of smoke. Chandler stared. The horse was led by Adam Pinkhurst. Black smoke was billowing over the yard making it difficult to see anything. It had the quality of a dream. He felt somebody press something into his hands.

'Hurry, Chandler!' It really was Adam. He had a bag in his other hand and pushed that at Chandler as well. 'Keep it safe. The Master thanks you with all his heart.'

Jerked now fully awake Chandler stared at the bag then gripped Adam by the arm. 'What about Mattie? Where is she?'

'Safe. We're leaving. The four of us. We leave straight after this – a boat is taking us to safety—'

'Will you look after her? Tell her—'

'She knows. Trust me. We will not forget. Now hurry.'

Uproar caused by the storm of arrows continued and even increased amid the wails and curses of the wounded guards but the flight that had blotted out the sky had stopped. In the chaos Chandler managed to drag himself forward as a man, bow slung across his back, loomed out of the smoke. It was Will. He was grinning and pulling at the horse's bridle and with a curt, 'Follow us!' lent a hand to hoist Chandler into the saddle.

Aethelstan looked up at Chandler as the horse began to move off. He ran alongside and put out a hand. 'Brother? . . . Brother? . . . Aren't you taking me with you?'

Chandler looked down. 'We're outlawed.'

'I don't care!'

'What about your mother?'

'I told her I've sworn allegiance to the heretic friar—'

Bending, he swiftly scooped the skinny lad under one arm until he could claw himself into the saddle as the horse surged forward. Already Fulke and Underwood, mounted and leading another horse for Will, were visible through the clouds of smoke and soon the four horses were trampling people to left and right in their haste to escape.

Chandler turned at the last as Adam hurried through the billows to see a figure with streaming red gold hair standing stock-still on the other side of the fire staring after him.

3

Of course they were followed. Armed cavalry erupted from everywhere and converged in a yelling pack to pursue them across the yard. A guard at the gates onto the bridge put out his arms to stop them then saw they were driving straight towards him and stepped aside. One or two by-standers gawped as they fled.

The cavalry-steeds muscled on, accompanied by their riders' shouts to halt in the name of the king, but the bowmen had plans, as Chandler discovered.

Riding hard over the bridge to the horse ferry they hailed a man already appointed to row them across to the other side.

Scrambling onboard with the horses as the boat was pushed off they watched the pursuers in Lancaster's red and gold jostle impotently on the riverbank as the gap between them widened. Curses floated across the water but soon faded to harmless noise as the men could only gesticulate their dismay at being bested. It reminded Chandler of Oxford's escape from Arundel's men and he briefly hoped the child had reached his secret location with the rest of the poet's seditious books.

4

Once landed on the opposite bank and with the ferrymen's blessings ringing after them, they struck out for the road to the west.

They were bothered only once but it was by a small posse of local militia who picked up their trail from a distance and stuck to them for mile after mile. When they were no more than a small cloud on the horizon they finally managed to shake them off altogether and after clearing the settlements along the riverbank they left the road and began to ride through thick woodland. Late in the day they approached Radcot Bridge of ill fame and made the river crossing there and were at last on the open road.

'We've lost them,' observed Will, riding alongside Chandler and the lad as darkness descended. 'Are you coming on with us, brother? We're going to join Glyn Dŵr.'

'The Welsh magician?' piped Aethelstan, in awe.

'The very one. Notice how he brought rain to damp down your fire, Chandler?'

'I put that down to St Serapion, some deadly bowmen, and a south-westerly that happened to blow in.'

'A group effort on your behalf.' He gave Chandler a quizzical glance. 'You're yourself again?'

'I thought, this is what it's like at the end. No pain. Some regrets. A hope to be forgiven. But mostly kindness – and a warm welcome from those gone before.'

'You reckon?'

'Who knows?'

5

When night descended and they were convinced they had really thrown off their pursuers they searched for a suitable place to rest for a few hours.

The waters of a stream could be heard chuckling over stones at the bottom of a narrow dale, so they made their way down there and, finding it suitably secluded, set up camp. After watering the horses they made a small fire among some rocks for warmth and Chandler's saviours produced crusts of bread and some grubby lumps of cheese which they shared round.

Underwood was uneasy and got up to force a path through the wood and when he came back he said, 'If need be we can get out through yon dale end but I think we've lost them.' He sat down, careful to keep his bow and a quiver full of arrows by his side.

'What's yon lad doing?' asked Fulke, indicating Aethelstan standing motionless in the shallows. Water glinted in the pale light of the night sky, purling round a scattering of boulders like a ribbon of grey silk where the horses stood placidly up to their hocks. The men watched as he crept upstream and crouched as still as a bush, all the while staring into the water.

Talk returned to a discussion of the best route to take, to avoid any settlements and especially the towns that lay between here and the Marcher lands, and they had almost forgotten Aethelstan until he climbed up to them, grinning, with something silver in his hands.

'It ain't much, men,' he said proudly, 'and it almost seems wrong to catch them while they sleep, but that's life I reckon.'

He held out both hands and slowly opened them to reveal a few small fish. Without comment he laid them carefully on the grass while he broke off a stick then proceeded to toast them over the fire.

'I guess he's earned his place,' teased Fulke. 'An apprentice outlaw. Shall we accept him into the brotherhood, men?'

'I'll vote him in,' said Will.

The others agreed and made a great deal of the morsels of burned fish they were offered.

'Don't think I'm giving you this victualling for nothing,' Aethelstan stated after he finished chewing and wiped his hands on the grass.

Fulke chuckled. 'What are you after, young 'un?'

'I'll tell you. I expect to be taught to be a bowman like you three.'

'What? You don't aim to be a friar?'

'No disrespect, brother—' He shrugged.

'None taken,' Chandler replied.

'You'll have to work at it every day if you want to be a bowman worth the name,' Fulke warned.

'I'll do that.'

After a pause Underwood got to his feet. 'Come on then. I'll give you your first lesson now.'

'But it's pitch dark!'

'Do you want to be a bowman or are you all talk?'

Aethelstan scrambled to his feet. 'But what about the dark—?'

'Can't you see in the dark?'

'A bit.'

'Then search out a nice piece of flexy willow down by that

waterside about as thick as my thumb and as high as you in your boots and bring it to me.'

They watched the boy move off. Underwood unslung his bow and followed.

6

Chandler remembered that all this time he had been carrying the bag Adam had thrust at him before they made their escape and now he picked it up and opened it. As he expected there were pages of parchment inside, some bound, others loose. Holding one of them close to the fire to catch the light he peered at what was written.

'Here byginneth the cook's tale—' But someone, Adam presumably, had scribbled in the margin that it was unfinished, 'here he leaves off . . .'

Keep it safe, Adam had instructed. He would do that. He was not sure how but there must be a monastery, a castle, or some lord with a collection of books who would not mind adding another one to his store without making a proclamation about it.

Asking generally, he said, 'Where is Glyn Dŵr then? Does anybody know?'

'We'll hear the latest once we get closer to Marcher country,' Will replied.

Chandler remembered a Welshman he had interrogated in the Tower in what seemed another life and wondered if they would maybe meet and recognize each other and if so what would be the likely outcome.

He recalled how he had managed to get the fellow out of the Tower in all the confusion of the deposition. It was the time when Bolingbroke with Arundel at his shoulder had persuaded Chief Justiciar Thirning and Archbishop Scrope to force submission from the king and Richard, a prisoner in the Tower, had defended himself with a show of courage fuelled by a royal rage at what they were trying to do to him, but to no avail.

It had all seemed unbelievable then that Bolingbroke would triumph over his cousin and grab the crown itself. The Welshman in custody was thought to be spying out the situation in London for Glyn Dŵr, if he wasn't the Welsh magician in person, and an uprising by the Welsh under his leadership was expected. Henry Bolingbroke was rumoured to be making plans already to hammer the Welsh the way King Edward had hammered the Scots.

Whoever the prisoner was, with his long beard and bardic manner, he had been brought in for harsh questioning by Chandler who had merely sparred with the man as best he could in his dreadful Welsh, no more than a smattering of words, to be honest, and had then persuaded the guard on duty to turn the other way for the price of an ale or two.

The last he had seen of the Welshman, wizard or not, was when he crossed the Thames as they themselves had done, and set off on the road to the west.

He put the pages of the poet's work safely back inside the bag and tied it up. His own unfinished chronicle had been left behind when he followed Matilda to the house by the river. He knew that what he had written was enough to have him condemned to the flames when *de haeretico comburendo* came into law, without them even taking into account his destruction of The little Book of the Lion that Matilda had been carrying before he threw it to oblivion.

He wondered if anybody would ever read his chronicle or whether the guards had merely tossed it into the rubbish or onto the nearest fire? It was a shame if it had been destroyed because it was as truthful a record as he could manage about the events of these last few terrible months.

Someone, somewhere, might have had the same idea and written everything down. For the sake of truth he could only hope they had written an accurate version and kept it where it would later, in more forgiving times, be discovered.

When he glanced round now he saw that the others were beginning to bed down under their cloaks for what remained of the night. Underwood and the lad were sitting by the fire while the bow was being bent into some sort of shape.

He heard Underwood say, 'I'll lend you a string and we'll string it up in the morning then I'll lend you an arrow or two to start with to show you how to fletch your own. We'll have to be quick though. We don't want to find them armed men catching up with us. Go and grab some sleep now, while you can.'

Chandler had taken a sheepskin from under the saddle of his stolen horse and threw it to Aethelstan with the words, 'Bundle up inside that, young Stan.'

Then he went to have a closer look at the arrows Underwood

kept by him all the time. After that, somewhat thoughtfully, he went to sit by the fire himself.

7

Underwood continued to stare into the flames for some time until eventually he turned to Chandler. 'Not sleeping either, brother?'

He noticed that Underwood's cheeks were wet.

'Too many bad dreams.' He didn't explain. 'What about you, John?'

'I never did finish that confession, did I?'

'Do you want to?'

There was a pause while Underwood's shoulders seemed to tighten and shudder under the stress of some emotion. When he spoke he was scarcely audible. 'It's my lad,' he muttered. 'Same age as yon.' He indicated the motionless bundle of sheepskin on the far side of the fire. 'I was restringing his bow for him when Bolingbroke's army struck . . . I'll never forget nor forgive what they did to him. One man in particular.'

'Did he live?'

'My boy did – if you can call it living . . . Not the other one. I got him. There was a group of 'em. I never forget a face.' He stared into the flames. 'Never. But job done, as you might say.'

'Have you been back home?'

'Aye, after much travail. My lad hadn't forgiven me for being unable to stop them nor for leaving with the army. But it suited my plans. Hold your enemies close, they tell us. I had good reason for joining up. Before that I'd only ever hunted animals.' He paused. 'They run quicker . . . but men, they always believe they're safe. After Flint,' Underwood explained, 'when they took Dickon prisoner to London – we went back north. It was worrisome, not knowing what lay in wait. I had a mate from a nearby manor with me. A good fellow. Hod he's called. His family were wiped out during the first days of being conscripted when they were burning us into agreement and he found revenge was easy to come to. When he discovered I was of the same mind he helped me track down the . . . let's say, he aided my revenge. We found the leader of the gang all right. As Hod said, that losel will never again do that to anybody, man, woman nor child . . . nor will the rest of them – now.'

'So you caught up with them all . . .?'

In a scarcely audible voice Underwood added, 'Not until recently.'

A long pause followed. A branch shifted sending up a glitter of sparks.

Turning to Chandler he added, 'Maybe it's my own evil I need to confess? What do you think, brother . . .? I should have turned the other cheek?' He glanced at him with some defiance. 'I expect no absolution. I do not seek it. I would do to them again what I did when we caught up with them . . . if only it could blot out that vile desecration of my son and make all well again . . . So there it is, now you know me. No absolution. I'm not worth it.'

The flames of the fire began to die down when neither of them threw on more wood. The small circle of light it created became smaller still, drawing the shadows of the trees closer. The others were sleeping while they could. The flames danced and flickered over their still forms.

'If I may say so,' Chandler spoke into the dying glow, aware of the momentous thing Underwood had confessed, 'it's maybe somewhat vain on your part to claim you're not worth saving. Have you godlike knowledge of who is and who is not, in this sorry world? . . . Jack—' he used his everyday name without thought, 'believe me, you are no worse than any of us – different to most, sadly, because you were so severely tested . . . but I believe you'll be saved from hell if you honestly crave forgiveness. Whatever you've done that breaks God's laws it will not be beyond the power of his redemption.'

'The heretical friar, the lad called you.' Underwood gave a slight smile when he turned to look Chandler in the eye. 'I try not to see the images floating past. It's not in my nature to kill men - their ghosts keep me awake at night. I fear sleep.'

'Want me to sit with you a bit longer?'

'Aye . . . two wrecks together?'

8

As the misty pallor of dawn eventually broke over the woods it was Will, waking early and noticing the two of them still sitting beside the smouldering embers who, saddling the horses later, told Chandler more about what was torturing Underwood.

'We found him trying to set light to himself by the side of the road,' he began. 'He was raving. He had to be restrained by half a dozen of us. It was a big fellow called Hod who told us what they'd done. He was easy with the punishment they meted out, thought it right and just, but it gnaws at Jack and we can only watch.' He added, 'Best bowman I know. I don't want to lose him.'

'I understand.' He felt he understood a lot more than Underwood had admitted.

Will put his head on one side and gave Chandler a strong look. 'You know the story about King Edward – the second one – not the old war lord that came after? King Richard's great-grandfather? And how he was murdered in Berkeley Castle when his French wife went after the crown for herself and Mortimer?'

'Everybody knows that story.'

'Then you'll recall how they got rid of him. Jack and this other fellow took revenge along the same lines – know what I mean? . . . Now he just stares for hours at the burning brands in the fire and hears the fellow's shrieks of agony.'

'No wonder he can't sleep. The rest of the killings were clean enough.'

There was a moment of shared knowledge then Will confirmed it by saying, 'You reckon the good Lord will forgive him and his fellow justiciars?'

'Asking for my heretical opinion?' Chandler half-smiled. 'My guess is that He'll think it a justified revenge, a rebalancing of the scales of right and wrong, and a harsh warning for any who would transgress in like manner. He'll welcome—' he was about to say 'you all' thought better of it and instead said, 'he'll welcome them with open arms.' He added for good measure, 'That is if He exists . . . and if He has arms.' Despite his words he crossed himself for safety.

9

When they were near enough to Marcher country where loyalties might be divided in ways they could not predict, they decided it would be a good idea to risk trying to sell on their horses for less conspicuous ones.

Approaching a small vill of no more than a dozen houses on the road that ran along the ridge above where they were travelling they hailed a fellow pulling cabbages outside his croft and when he greeted them with some friendliness they broached the question of horse-trading.

Without many questions being asked they were eventually directed down another track through woods that finished up in the yard of a small farmstead. Hens flapped from post to post, a pig rootled in the garbage and the consoling buzz of bees in and out of a hive gave the place a settled air but they could see no horses.

A tough-looking, grizzled ancient with the bowed legs of a rider did his best to look unimpressed when he saw the quality of their mounts.

'We need a pony for the lad,' Chandler told him.

Without a word he led them round the back of the farm and through a gate into a meadow sheltered on four sides by overgrown hawthorns, well-buried from the gaze of passers-by should there ever be any. Horses of different sizes, colours and breeds were grazing peacefully in the long grass. Maintaining the fiction that he was unimpressed by three well-bred war-horses fit for a monarch and no doubt stolen from royal stables somewhere the horse master stated a price which in normal times would have made them walk away laughing in derision. Now necessity encouraged them to consider matters with less emotion.

Some bartering ensued and it was left to Chandler to make the final offer.

The upshot was possession of three average, dun-coloured animals and a lively skewbald for the boy, all of them fit for hill country but none with any likelihood of impressing anybody whatsoever.

The man gave a half-hearted apology before they left. 'It's not that I scorn your horses but more that few round here will have a need for such fine animals and I'll be stuck with them, feeding and what-not till summer. Worse, I'll have to think of a good story to tell about how I found them coming innocently into my own hands – you understand my difficulty?'

They did, and said so. And as they left he called after them, 'Oswestry is the place for horses. Them four have good stamina and they'll take you there where you can exchange them. You'll be properly in Wales then as well.'

10

'I didn't know you spoke Welsh, Chandler?' Will raised his eyebrows as they sat round the fire that night.

'I didn't know you knew Latin, Will.'

'What?!'

'Somebody put a warning of a vendetta from some bowmen written in Latin on the door at Westminster Palace. It sent Swynford into a frenzy. I couldn't help thinking of you and the lads.'

Will finished pouring the ale they bought at the last little town. When he finished he looked up. 'There is somebody you might have thought of,' he mused with a sidelong glance. 'What about Pinkhurst?'

'What about him?'

'He knows Latin. I doubt not he can write it as well.'

'He's no bowman. He's a scrivener.'

'His father was a bowman in the royal guard in the old days. One of Dickon's men.'

Chandler raised his eyebrows.

'And his grandfather was a master bowman for King Edward. You don't imagine Pinkhurst can't use a bow? He would doubtless be down at the butts every day with other lads before he took up book-learning.'

Chandler thought it over for a while, remembering when he had glimpsed Adam with a convivial group in the tavern yard where the military were drinking and how he had wondered about their acceptance of a scrivener, and now he said, 'I'm glad I didn't know at the time . . .' He shrugged. 'He redeemed himself in so many respects it would have been a shame if I'd mistakenly breathed his name to Swynford.'

Aethelstan was listening in while he practised the knots Jack had taught him for attaching feathers to his arrows to make them fly the way he wanted. Now he chipped in with a grin. 'I know what you mean, Brother Rod.' He turned to Will. 'When he says "many respects" he means taking that maid of the poet's under his wing.'

Will cuffed him on the shoulder. 'Stick to your fletching, young feller, and keep out of grown-up talk. And what's this Brother Rod business?'

'He's one of us, ain't he, Will?'

Aethelstan chortled at Will's expression and Chandler rolled his eyes to hide the grief his words caused.

11

The boy had touched a nerve – under his wing indeed, curse and bless him – and Chandler continued to grieve. His thoughts would not rest. He rode the maze of lanes and woodlands in an endless dream of supposition.

When they stopped to water the horses and fortify themselves with morsels of a rabbit Fulke had brought down the previous day, Aethelstan eventually came to stand beside him.

He was clutching his own small bow with a few arrows, somewhat clumsily made, as by a beginner in the art of fletching, saying, 'Brother. I am remiss. Will you forgive me? I fear I have done wrong.'

'What is it, Spindleshanks?' Expecting some misdemeanour concerning an extra portion taken from the communal pot, he patted the tussock of grass beside him where he was sitting. 'Sit and tell me about it and I'll give you a homily on the dangers of greed, starting with those who hanker for a crown not theirs down to a bad lad who eats too much while others go hungry.'

Aethelstan grinned and sat down. 'It's something more personal, brother. I fear I forgot in the hurry of escape and then learning to make this—' he proudly lifted his bow, 'and the strangeness of finding myself as a wolf's head running with an outlaw gang and a heretic.'

'So you're good at making excuses for your sins, I see.'

'It was that day when Swynford's guards dragged you into their keeping.'

'What about it?'

'I was sitting in the boat as you told me to, waiting for you to come out of the house. Then those two fellows who alighted at the same time as Matilda came back and stood outside the doors and I thought they were up to no good. As it proved.'

'Then what?'

'When Matilda came flying out of the house after all the commotion, I, not knowing they had arrested you, did as she told me you wanted and rowed her back to Westminster as fast as I could.'

'I guessed all that, Stan. There's nothing to forgive in that.'

'I might have tried to rescue you.'

'I doubt whether you would have stood much chance against a score of full-grown guards in fighting harness.'

'No. It would have been a bad idea. But that's not what I want to beg your forgiveness for – it's to do with what Matilda said.'

Chandler felt himself go still.

'She was in a daze when she flew down to the boat and demanded to be rowed back. A daze but also in a rage. She was cursing you, I have to admit—' he gave Chandler a quick glance, 'I've never heard such language except from my mother when the young ones misbehave – and all the while she was urging me to row faster and then cursing me for being too slow. We made it though not without her telling me with some tears and rage what you had done and how she had been mistaken and how she could not believe that she had made such an error of judgement and that she would never ever forgive herself and that—' he bit his lips, 'well, she's just a girl after all even if she is a few years older than me and you know what they're like when they start to rant.'

'Just tell me, in as few words as you can manage, what else she said to you?'

He blushed. 'Her exact words? You want those?'

'If you can remember them.'

Still blushing he mumbled, 'She said she loved you above all men and above life itself and always had done and would do so until the end of time.'

'I see.'

A long silence followed. Aethelstan gave Chandler a wary glance. 'She said something about a name she was going to choose, saying a boy would be called Rodric but as for a girl she had no ideas. Margaret after the women's saint maybe. I didn't get it. It puzzled me for a while—'

'And does it puzzle you now?'

Aethelstan slowly shook his head. 'I can make a guess – but it's too—' He frowned. 'You, a friar? I didn't know girls would . . .' Then he shrugged the idea away. 'That's all I wanted to tell you, brother. I didn't know whether it was important. And then I forgot. I'm sorry.'

12

He was still heart-sore and Aethelstan had driven a knife deeper into his soul than he would have thought possible. Having escaped death, his outlook had changed. There was only one thing to assuage his grief. He would have to get a message to her.

He would ask after Adam and the Master of course. But it would be a message meant for her. Somehow he would do it. He prayed they were all safe but he would never rest until he knew how she fared.

He was forced to a decision he had always known he would have to make. Waiting until everybody was sitting down together spooning broth into their mouths he said, 'This is it, fellows. You're planning to join Glyn Dŵr and I would come with you if I thought he had any need of my services. But I doubt not he has his necromancers and bards to whom I might play apprentice if he'd allow it. But there is something else I must do.'

They all listened with spoons halfway to their mouths.

'I've come to a decision. I've decided I'll be peeling off from you soon. Young Stan is right. I have unfinished business back at Westminster.'

Fulke was astonished. 'You're surely never going back there, are you?'

Chandler shook his head. 'Not yet. Not while Arundel is scorching and burning his way through the realm. I intend to stay this side of the Marches for as long as I can. But I must find out what has happened to the others after they helped rescue me from the fire. I owe them that at least.' He glanced round. They were friends and allies and he saddened at the thought of the parting of the ways. 'I owe you all,' he continued. 'You acted quickly when Matilda and this young 'un here told you what had happened at de Vere's safe-house.'

'All Westminster and beyond was in uproar when they dragged you back in chains then started building the fire. That Cook used to be a military man and talked things over with us. It was easy after that. Everybody played their part.'

Aethelstan leaned against Chandler and whispered, 'And mayhap there's somebody special you want to see? . . . Our secret, eh, Rod?'

Chandler looked down at the grinning, grubby face. 'One day,' he predicted, 'you will go too far.'

13

Will and the others were understanding about his need to leave but also warned of the dangers of lingering around the Marches where anybody could be playing both sides in the growing contention between the Welsh, the English, and the ones with connections to both sides. Fulke urged him to stay with them.

'We're still some way from the Berwyn Mountains where Glyn Dŵr is said to be massing his forces. Why not ride with us and send a courier from there?'

'It might be weeks before we can do that and a courier from this side of the border is more likely to be waylaid if he's suspected of carrying messages to Westminster.'

'You mean you are going back over the border?' He looked askance.

Underwood muttered something about a death wish and suggested riding with him if that was his aim.

'I thought I might head up towards Shrewsbury,' Chandler told them. 'I can find a courier there. Plenty of traffic to London through Oxford.'

Will nodded. 'And you'll expect a response from this message, will you? Where will that go?'

'I thought that after Shrewsbury I'll have some time in hand, enough to ride up to the abbey at Dieulacres. It's Cistercian and off the beaten track. They'll no doubt give me refuge. I can wait out for any communication there.'

'And the other end? You expect a courier to find them safe and happy in the house at Westminster?'

Chandler shook his head. 'I've got friends.' He didn't name Martin or Brother Daniel at the Hackney herb gardens. 'They'll be able to find out what's happened and see to whatever needs doing to get a message to me.'

'I can see you've thought it out.' Will looked unhappy, even so, and added, 'We'll get you a better horse before you go. Give us fair warning.'

14

They travelled north along the border of the Marcher country for another week. After many circuitous paths round towns and vills judged best left unvisited, and after forcing new routes through previously unwalked woodland to avoid groups of patrolling militia, after the hilltops from where they surveyed the dangerous country to the east, and after untold nights spent under cloaks with rain falling, they finally reached a place where they hoped to find friends.

The contrast with the place where they had come from was stark.

Open skies, a network of softly rounded hills and meandering, wooded valleys, with few people around and those they met unarmed and speaking a different, lilting language, the change after the hustle and push of Westminster bursting with armed fighting men could not have been more welcome.

Yet there was no ignoring the fact that some appalling news had filtered through as they were meandering along the border.

The news was so grim nobody mentioned it as they rode on until they happened to stop to rest the horses near the drove road between Shrewsbury and the Berwyns.

Standing in stunned silence with beakers of ale in the yard of a farmhouse where some fellow in a field had directed them, nobody wanted to be the first to speak.

The farmer, saying they were to tell his woman he would be along soon but to make sure the travellers got something to eat first, had pointed them to a picturesque holding where the wife, a thin, dark-haired, somewhat pale young woman, smiled and looked shy and appeared to understand what they were saying when they clattered into the yard. She offered no words in exchange beyond greeting them in Welsh but after ladling out thick scoops of pottage into wooden bowls she disappeared into a dairy across the yard where they could see her at a butter churn singing softly to herself.

They finished eating, rinsed out the bowls at the pump and were having a final drink in the same heavy silence when, to offer what solace he could, Chandler adopted a light tone, and said, 'You fellows caused me a lot of grief with Swynford, did you know that?'

There was no disguising the fact that it wasn't just Underwood whose mood was dark. Nobody said much until Will, mockingly askance, asked, '*We* caused *you* trouble?' He pretended to hoot with mirth.

'You know you did,' Chandler replied, keeping up the pretence. 'Swynford was determined to find the invisible bowman shooting at his troops. He was convinced it must be one of you and intended to string you up the way they did with that unlucky prisoner from the town jail at St Albans.'

'At least you didn't let on about us. We were a bit wary. We didn't know which side you were playing.'

'Luckily you left no clues – apart from that badge of Arundel's which meant nothing.'

'That was to put you off the trail a bit. Give you something to think about.'

'I guessed you were having a laugh at my expense. I assumed the old fellow who handed it to me had been nowhere near St Albans and doubtless had your silver in his pouch even as he sought me out.'

The men chuckled briefly despite their dark mood.

'What's more,' continued Chandler finishing his ale, 'whenever anybody was shot there was always a different one of you missing. Everybody was looking for one man. You tried to make me feel clever to put it down to the three of you working together. In fact,' he added, 'you've given me the runaround since that first meeting at Pontefract, to be honest. Then there was you, Fulke, with your poor showing at the archery contest in St Alban's mead. You stretched even my credulity.'

'It was best you didn't know for sure.'

'It nearly got me a boot in the face from Swynford, the devil take him.'

'How can he live with himself with what he did to the king?' Will asked with a bewildered grimace. 'We guessed what was going on at Pontefract. Nobody said anything. They were his men after all. But we guessed. And we could do nothing about it.'

'I trust Swynford will get his just deserts in the pit of hell where he belongs.' Chandler furrowed his brow. 'What puzzles me is Henry. How can he so consistently keep himself looking purer than snow in front of everybody?'

'The truth will catch up with him. Give it time,' Fulke growled.

'You're a Londoner, Chandler, don't the aldermen see what he's like?' Will was mystified.

Still nobody mentioned what was really on their minds.

'They might applaud his ambition to grab the crown – in the belief that he's the same as them – everything for God and Profit as their slogan goes – but there must be limits to what anyone will do for money.'

'I don't understand how he persuades men to risk the fires of hell to fight for him.'

'No choice. Knights' fee,' Underwood muttered.

Will agreed. 'And the fear of retribution makes them follow. He has no boundaries to what he'll do if they won't. Look how they burned Jack and his family out of their manor.' He paused. 'Look at this latest.'

He had mentioned it at last. The black mood returned. Even to hardened fighting men what had been done in London according to the latest news subdued them all.

The story reached them after they risked entering a small border town on the English side. It concerned a Master Serle, one of King Richard's loyal clerks in the Signet Office from the old days. What Henry had his men do to him was barbaric in the extreme.

It was Serle's fate to believe that King Richard was still alive and had escaped to Scotland to seek sanctuary with the Lord of the Isles, an old ally. Master Serle said he was alive. And so did others.

When Henry heard about this he despatched his men to fetch him.

There, at the gallows near Smithfield, he had Richard's loyal young clerk strung up without trial.

That was not the worst of it. Before he was properly hanged by the neck he was cut down and, still conscious, was dragged on a hurdle to the next gallows where he was put through the same punishment.

Three times more he had been hanged until nearly dead then cut down and hauled half-conscious through the streets to be strung up again.

Finally, his broken body, lacerated by being dragged over the stones of the London streets, flesh raw and bleeding, his neck nearly but not quite broken, he was hanged a final time and his body, mutilated with burning knives, was thrown into the town ditch.

It didn't halt the rumours about King Richard being alive. Henry's vindictiveness even inflamed the hope that Richard was still free and the rumours were true as good folk hoped and prayed.

Will's tone was unbelieving. 'Imagine if you can, hating a man so much you would do that to him.'

'What deep madness.' Chandler's flesh crawled.

'We're living through dark times,' growled Fulke. 'It's the End

Days as they foretold. The Prophecy of the Six Kings has come to pass. The Mold-Warp rules now.'

Chandler added, 'It's Henry's choice to nourish such malice. He could forgive, but he hates everybody to madness if they speak out on behalf of Richard. He has always been jealous of him ever since he witnessed the golden-haired child in Westminster Abbey with the Crown of England on his head and saw that everyone loved him. The only way Henry can get the better of him is to annihilate him. It must be hell itself living inside that man's head. He needs our pity.'

Underwood listened without adding anything. He walked to the field gate and stared towards the hills for some time without moving.

15

Shaken by the continual stories of the repression that now gripped England under the new regime the men were even more determined to join Glyn Dŵr. They intended to strike off deeper into Wales towards Sycarth, where they expected Prince Owain to be mustering his troops.

Meanwhile Chandler would ride north to either Shrewsbury or Chester, he had not decided yet, and from either of those border towns he would be able to send a message back to Brother Daniel at Hackney.

He decided to write it in the guise of a request for herbs to treat a patient. The old fellow would understand and show it to Martin who might be able to find out what had happened to the inhabitants of the house in the Westminster precinct. It would take time but he hoped he could sit it out at the Abbey of Dieulacres until word came through.

They came to a halt in a sunlit clearing full of bird song. It was the place where their paths would separate.

Chandler had been found another inconspicuous but sturdy Welsh horse and was making sure the leather bag, with the Master's pages of carefully copied tales inside, was securely strapped to the saddle.

Aethelstan came to stand uncertainly beside him with the reins of his pony looped in his hands. Chandler retied the laces of the leather bag. When he was ready Aethelstan gripped him by the sleeve. 'Am I coming with you, brother?'

Chandler looked him up and down. 'What do you think, Stan?'

Aethelstan looked stricken. 'Won't you need a lad to run errands?' His eyes were welling.

Chandler gazed down at him. 'You? In a little white surplice with your bows and arrows thrown into a corner?'

When the boy continued to stand there with tears trickling down his cheeks Chandler murmured, 'Go on, Stan, old fellow, you know they're waiting for you. They need an extra bowman. We'll meet when you come into England with the army. I promise.'

Not taking his eyes off Chandler he slowly dragged himself over to join the others. Chandler crossed the grove to say farewell.

'Keep an eye on old Spindleshanks here. Don't let his courage outrun his skill.'

'We will,' promised Underwood. 'We'll keep him in order.'

'And make sure you keep the rest of this bunch under control, Will. Make them learn Welsh.'

They thumped each other on the back. He turned to Fulke. 'Go well, feller. I hope nobody sees you missing targets like you did at St Alban's. You'll never live it down twice.'

To Underwood he said, 'Your mate Hod will find you one day to let you know all's well with your family. He'll have settled things. They'll be running a dairy, selling cheese and milk in the town market, and your son will be turning into a little merchant handling the business side of things, waiting for you to come home.'

'You been scrying again, heretic?' Underwood thumped him on the back and wished him well.

Chandler turned swiftly towards his horse.

They were rogues but they had been good companions and they had saved his life. He would miss them more than he could say but with promises to meet again when Glyn Dŵr's army began its push back against England it was time to part.

Will stood in his stirrups for a moment to call over his shoulder, 'If we don't hear from you we'll come up to Dieulacres to find you. Warn them monks. And remember, keep away from fires!'

With that the green leaves of the spring woodland closed between them and Chandler turned towards the north.

16

As he rode away his thoughts returned to Matilda and the Master and his little household. In fact, he scarcely ever thought of anything else. He wondered if they had made good their escape overseas or whether they were now incarcerated in one of Arundel's notorious prisons. Prayer seemed an inadequate way of keeping faith with the truth.

Two other things still troubled him. The first was about the killings on the journey down from Pontefract and whether it was Underwood working by himself, taking revenge four times, or whether the others covered for him as Will had led him to believe. Two of the arrows, the first and the fourth – if they were not the same arrow – were similar to the ones Jack made. He had passed on his method of fletching to the boy and they were unmistakable. Will had never produced the one he had taken at the first murder.

And the two middle killings? One by Will, one by Fulke? It seemed to Chandler that if Will and Fulke wanted to protect Jack it was up to them how they did it, given what had happened to him and his family. The least that could be said was that it settled things. Underwood admitted he had caught up with the men who had defiled his wife and son. Now the last of those brutes was dead, shot at Westminster, and could do no more harm and thus, anyone might argue, justice was restored.

The second thing to trouble him was whether it was true that King Richard had escaped from his prison cell in Pontefract Castle during or after his apparent assassination. He remembered someone hurtling down the stone steps inside the tower, knocking him aside in their frantic haste to get out. It could have been one of the guards hurrying to inform Swynford that their victim was fighting back and they needed reinforcements. It could have been anybody. No one would ever know unless the king returned. As Will remarked that night when they stood beside the coffin, nobody would be able to tell who was inside with only a small patch of face visible in the opening in the lead carapace.

Fervently hoping that poor, victimized Master Serle would be vindicated and that Richard would be discovered living in peace as a guest of the Lord of the Isles in distant Scotland as the rumour went, he considered the lines of another poet.

This time it was not Master Chaucer but the Cheshire poet, Langland, who had written about Meed, the lady of just deserts, and how she meted out reward as well as punishment as it was earned.

It led his thoughts back along the winding, everlasting road to Matilda and how she had saved his life and now carried it within her. He found himself praying that the serpent of repression coiling itself round the realm of England would soon be scotched and they would one day come together in honesty and love.